Shame th

Graeme Hampton was born in Paisley and grew up in Stirling. The Denning and Fisher crime thriller series is inspired by his time living in London in his twenties. He now lives in Hastings, East Sussex.

Also by Graeme Hampton

D.I Denning and D.S Fisher

Know No Evil
Blood Family
The Darkness Within
Run For Cover
Shame the Devil

GRAEME HAMPTON

SHAME THE DEVIL

hera

First published in the United Kingdom in 2022 by

Hera Books
Unit 9 (Canelo), 5th Floor
Cargo Works, 1–2 Hatfields
London, SE1 9PG
United Kingdom

A CIP catalogue record for this book is available from the British Library.

Print ISBN 978 1 80436 083 5
Ebook ISBN 978 1 80436 078 1

Look for more great books at www.herabooks.com

Printed and bound in Great Britain by Clays Ltd, Elcograf S.p.A.

I

For Rachel and Michael – one day you'll both be old enough to read this book.

Prologue

It's so high up she can glimpse the river in the distance, slipping its way through the city like a silver eel.

It's summer; she can feel the sun on her face and smell the pollen in the air, and for the briefest of moments she smiles at the receding memory of happy times. But then her thoughts turn, as they always do, to that fateful day when the happy times ended.

She replays the events again and again, as fresh and jagged now as when it happened.

The image of a child's face is imprinted on her brain…

The guilt has rooted itself inside her. It's like a leaden weight tied around her stomach.

She looks down. There are people below pointing up at her. Pointing and shouting, but she can't hear what they're saying. She doesn't care anyway.

She hears a noise behind her and glances round, slightly startled.

A middle-aged man in a T-shirt is standing a few feet away, reaching out his hand and speaking to her. His mouth moves but the words sound like he's under water. There's a woman behind him, dark-haired and frowning; talking into her phone.

The man in the T-shirt is edging closer.

She looks down again. There are more people staring up at her. An excited crowd has gathered now; all eyes turn in her direction.

She can sense the man behind her is close now.

It's only when she hears someone scream that she realises she's falling.

Falling.

Heading straight for the ground below...

Chapter One

It was getting dark by the time Detective Inspector Matthew Denning turned into Porter Street. It was a typical suburban street in Stratford, east London. Cars lined either side, while identical rows of terraced houses stretched along the street. As he looked around, he glanced at the clock on the dashboard.

He looked around for a parking space. Predictably, he couldn't see any. At least the strobing blue lights of the two police cars blocking the middle of the street told him he was in the right location.

He should have been having dinner, but his MIT – East London Major Investigation Team – had drawn the short straw and was working late.

Beside the two squad cars, a thin line of blue police tape danced slightly in the evening breeze. A couple of uniformed officers were turning back motorists and pedestrians who were complaining about the closed road. He decided to abandon his silver-grey Ford Focus in the middle of the street. It wasn't like anyone would ask him to move it. It was already starting to drizzle when he stepped out the car and headed over to nod his acknowledgement at the two uniformed officers manning the outer perimeter. One of them, a man, in his early twenties, recognised Denning and lifted the police tape allowing him to duck underneath.

The address he'd been given was for a ground-floor flat. The building was a typical terraced house, since divided into two flats. The outside of the building was painted a musty yellow colour, and looked like it would benefit from a bit of TLC.

CSIs were already busying themselves. He looked around for Sheila Gorton, the crime scene manager. Before Denning had a chance to speak, DS Deepak Neeraj appeared from inside the house.

'You're here, boss,' Neeraj said. He was dressed in his standard black leather jacket, with a checked shirt visible underneath. His hair, as always, had been gelled to perfection. 'I've only just got here myself. I've just been chatting to the uniforms. A bloke's been stabbed. Paramedics tried to save him but there wasn't a hope.'

'What are we talking about here, Deep? Robbery? Attempted burglary?'

Neeraj shrugged. 'It's a right mess in there, boss. His partner called it in. She's not saying much though. She's with a neighbour now.' He jerked his head towards the house next door. 'The paramedics reckon she's in shock.' He paused for a second. 'They've got a baby too.'

Denning slipped on a pair of protective shoe covers and a white forensic suit. The entrance hallway was narrow, barely the width of the front door. A trail of blood led to the door to the flat. He squeezed along the narrow hallway and entered. Although the outside looked a little shabby, the interior was pleasantly decorated: light walls and modern furniture. Small but homely.

The body was lying in the living room. A male, aged in his mid-twenties, by the look of it. It was obvious he'd staggered from the front door where the attack took place into the flat's living room, where he'd died. Gorton raised a hand as soon as she spotted Denning enter the flat. She made her way over to join him. 'Not a lot of room in here to work,' she grumbled. She nodded at a grey-haired, bearded man in his fifties who was tending the body. Denning recognised him as Dr Baker, the pathologist. It must be serious for him to come out. These days police budget cuts meant pathologists were becoming an increasing rarity at crime scenes.

'Stabbed once,' Baker said, nodding a greeting at Denning. 'In the stomach, puncturing the abdominal aorta. Quick and very messy.' Denning looked at the trail of blood that had followed him into the living room of the tiny home. 'He was still breathing when the paramedics got here, but there wasn't much they could do. The wound was too deep and the blood loss too great. He didn't stand a chance.'

Denning turned to Gorton. 'I take it we've got a name?'

She nodded. 'Kieran Judd, aged twenty-eight. His partner's called Cassie Bane. She's been moved next door. Number forty-two.' She threw a sad look at Denning. 'They've got an eighteen-month-old baby. Luckily, he was in the kitchen having his dinner at the time. That's where Cassie was when it happened.'. 'She's still in shock, so I'm not sure how much she'll be able to tell us.'

'Right now,' Denning said, 'anything at all would be useful.'

'I wouldn't hold your breath.'

'She must have heard something?'

'Apparently not. She heard the doorbell go, but she had the radio on, so whatever passed in the way of conversation between them was unheard by her.'

Denning glanced out the window and saw the crime scene investigators' van pulling up. He knew that within minutes the whole area would be sealed and turned over to Forensics. He took one last look at the body. The flat looked so normal: neat, tidy; pictures on the wall and books on the shelves. Normal. Ordinary. These were the words that shouted at Denning. Why would someone want to kill Kieran Judd?

–

Number forty-two Porter Street was the mirror of its neighbour. A uniformed officer led Denning and Neeraj along a similar narrow corridor into the tiny flat. Cassie Bane was sitting on a sofa staring blankly at a mug of cold-looking tea. She was in her early twenties, straight hair, tied back in a pony tail. The neighbour introduced herself as Beth Marshall. She was slightly older than Cassie; Denning reckoned she was in her early thirties. She was short and slim with curly hair. She asked them if they wanted anything to drink, which they declined.

'Where's the child?' Denning asked.

'He's sleeping in our bedroom.' She nodded at Cassie. 'Poor love wasn't in any fit state to think, let alone look after a baby.'

Denning sat down next to Cassie, while Neeraj sat on a chair by the window. 'Cassie, I'm Detective Inspector Denning and this is Detective Sergeant Neeraj. We need to ask you a few questions about what happened.' She stared at her mug for a moment, then looked up at Denning, an empty look on her face.

'I've been over it all already. I told one of your officers…' She was referring to the uniformed PC Denning had spoken to earlier.

6

'I know. And I understand it's difficult to talk about it again, but we need to know what happened.'

Beth reached out and placed a hand on Cassie's shoulder. 'Do you want another cup of tea, love?'

Cassie shook her head. 'I was making dinner. Nothing special, just a pasta thing out of a jar. I'd just fed Arthur.'

'Arthur?'

'Her kid,' Beth said.

'OK.' Denning smiled at her. 'Go on. Take your time.'

'The doorbell went. Kieran was in the living room watching the news. He said he'd get it. The next thing I knew he was staggering back into the flat saying he'd been stabbed.' She shuddered slightly and rubbed a hand over her face. 'He was bleeding and clutching his stomach. There was just so much blood.'

She looked like she was going to cry. Denning didn't want to push her, but he needed to know exactly what had happened. Right now, everything was so vague.

'I'm sorry, Cassie. I know this isn't easy. I just need to ask some more questions, then I'll go.' He looked up at Beth, who was standing by the door looking concerned. 'Did Kieran say anything else when he came back into the flat?'

Cassie shook her head. 'He just said he'd been stabbed. I ran over to him, then he collapsed on the floor. I dialled 999 straight away. He was unconscious by the time the ambulance arrived. The paramedics tried to save him but there was nothing they could do. I begged them to take him to hospital, but he wasn't breathing.' She clasped a hand to her mouth. 'There was so much blood. Everywhere.'

'You didn't hear any voices when he answered the door?' Denning asked. 'The person who did it, did they say anything?'

She shook her head again. 'I was in the kitchen. I had the radio on. Capital. It was still Drivetime. A song had just started: George Michael, I think, 'Spinning the Wheel'. I didn't hear anything. Just a cry when he was stabbed.'

'Can you think of anyone who want to kill Kieran? Is there anyone he's fallen out with recently, or has anyone threatened him?'

'No. He had a silly argument with the bloke across the road about parking, but it was nothing.'

Denning looked at Beth. 'It was all something and nothing,' she said. 'It's a small street. He owns two cars and a van. He takes up way more space than he should. We've all complained but nothing ever happens.'

'We might need to speak to him. What's his name?'

She pulled a face, then said: 'Calum Nelson. But I'm pretty sure he's got nothing to do with this. I mean he's a selfish prat, but he isn't aggressive. Well, he shouts a bit, but that's all.'

'Which address is his?'

'Across the road. Number thirty-one. He's not in because his lights aren't on.'

Denning made a note. He glanced out the living room window: neighbours were twitching at windows, curtains pulled back just enough to try and make it too obvious they were rubbernecking. He spotted a couple of what looked suspiciously like journalists gathering on the street outside. They were trying to engage the uniformed officers in conversation, but from the looks on the journalists' faces they were getting very little to work with.

8

It always amazed him how these vultures managed to find things out so quickly. He wondered whether yet another London stabbing was really newsworthy, and the thought depressed him.

'Did you see or hear anything, Beth?' Denning asked.

'No. Like I told the uniformed officer… the first I knew was when I saw the ambulance outside. A few minutes later, an officer knocked on my door and told me there had been an incident next door. She had Cass with her and was holding little Arthur. She asked if I would mind looking after them as the flat was now a crime scene. It was then that Cass told me that Kieran was dead.'

'Does anyone else live here with you?' Denning asked.

'No. I'm divorced. I've lived here for about a year. Another woman lives upstairs, but she's a nurse. She's probably working tonight. She won't be back until late. Most of other neighbours keep themselves to themselves. Quite a few students live round here, so you get a lot of people passing though.'

'The doorbell. Is it a communal bell for both your flat and the one upstairs?'

Cassie looked confused for a moment, then came back into focus. 'No. We have a bell each. We're forty-four A. Upstairs flat is B.'

'The bells are clearly marked,' Beth said. Her voice was trembling. It was obvious from the smudged mascara that she'd been crying.

'Could whoever did it have pressed the wrong bell by mistake?'

'The flat upstairs is empty. The guy who lived there moved out a couple of weeks ago.'

Denning was thinking fast. 'What was his name?'

'I can't remember. Tony somebody. Hallam. Yes, that's his name. Tony Hallam. I don't know where he moved to. We didn't have much to do with him. We only moved in six months ago.'

'Tony Hallam?' Neeraj was suddenly animated.

'Recognise the name?' Denning asked.

He seemed to give the matter some thought. 'I'm sure I've heard that name before…' He shrugged. 'I can't place him though.'

'What about Kieran? What's he do for a living?'

Cassie looked at Denning. 'He worked in a gym. He was a personal trainer.'

'I'll need the address,' Denning said. 'I know it seems unlikely, but there's a chance he was targeted deliberately. If so, we need to find out why.'

'But why would someone want to kill Kieran? Everybody liked him. He was popular at work. He went out of his way to avoid fights.'

'At this stage, Cassie, we have to keep our options open. It's unlikely this was a random attack. Not if someone rang the doorbell.' He paused, reluctant to press her too much further, at least for now. 'Are you certain you didn't hear anyone say anything? Either Kieran or the person who stabbed him?'

She shook her head again. 'I've told you… I didn't hear anything after the doorbell rang.'

Beth reached out and touched her gently on the shoulder. 'You can see she's upset. Perhaps you should come back later.'

Denning agreed. It was obvious Cassie Bane was still in shock. She'd just lost her partner. She had a baby to look after. Her mind was probably doing somersaults right now. The biggest question would be why this had happened to her? She was in the middle of a horrendous nightmare. She was probably hoping she'd wake up and it would all never have happened. Except it had. And it was his job to find out by who.

Chapter Two

Denning started the briefing as soon as the room was quiet. Already there were photos pinned to the whiteboard at the top of the room: the tiny flat; the bloodstained body of Kieran Judd. The scene of violence in total contrast to the homeliness and warmth of the flat.

DS Molly Fisher had been with this particular MIT for just over a year. She'd joined the team only a few months after Denning, and still felt like a bit of a newbie. She'd previously served with CID and after helping to solve a murder, had bagged her promotion to the murder squad.

She watched as the team settled down. This had all the hallmarks of an open-and-shut case. Yet somehow, she had a feeling it was going to turn out to be anything but as straightforward as she thought. She admired Matt Denning as a competent and fair detective, but his designer clothes and expensive haircut made him appear like he belonged in an episode of *Miami Vice* rather than an east-London-based Major Investigation Team.

'Kieran Michael Judd, aged twenty-eight,' Denning said. 'Stabbed to death on his doorstep. Partner and young child in the property at the time. His partner claims not to have heard anything as she was in the kitchen at the time preparing breakfast and the radio was on. She recalls hearing the doorbell ring at just before eight-thirty. Her partner went to answer the door. She heard a shout, wasn't sure what it was. Kieran Judd staggered into the living room and it was clear he'd been attacked. Cassie phoned an ambulance straight away, but he died shortly after the paramedics got there.' He wrote the names Kieran Judd and Cassie Bane on the whiteboard. 'No witnesses to the actual stabbing, but it seems one of the neighbours spotted someone running along the street at about around that time. Description is vague.' He glanced at his notes. 'Hooded male. Didn't get a look at his face, but said he was average height and running fast, which suggests he was young. We'll look at whatever CCTV is available and continue with house-to-house enquiries, but what would help at this stage is having an obvious motive.'

'There are no obvious enemies,' Neeraj said. 'We've spoken to his employers. Seems he was the near-perfect employee. Always turned up for work on time, got on with the other members of staff and was popular with the clients. No one had a bad word to say about him.'

'Someone clearly didn't like him,' Kinsella said. 'They disliked him enough to stick a knife in his guts.'

Kinsella was a gruff DS who'd been around for years. The only original member of this particular team, he was never shy when it came to reminding the others that he liked to be shown a bit of respect.

'A motive would help,' Trudi Bell said. 'A jealous ex is a possibility, or maybe he owed money to someone?' At thirty-five, Trudi was two years older than Molly. Unlike Molly, who preferred to wear tailored trouser suits to work, Trudi generally opted for a slightly more casual approach: tight-fitting skirts and low-cut blouses.

Molly and Trudi went way back. They'd been friends before Molly had joined the team. Sometimes it was reassuring to have another woman to help distract from the raw machismo that accompanied these briefings.

'Both are possibilities we need to explore,' Denning said. 'And anything else that comes to light.'

'Are we ruling out a crime of passion?' Kinsella said. 'His missus didn't do him in after they argued about whose turn it was to peel the spuds?' He looked around the team for a reaction. It was sometimes difficult to tell when Kinsella was joking. 'I mean,' he added with a sardonic look on his face, 'have we checked her out for previous?'

'I don't think it was his partner,' Molly said, rolling her eyes. 'For a start, he was stabbed on the doorstep. She was in the kitchen at the time.'

'Only got her word for that,' Kinsella replied, then leaned back on his chair with his mouth shut and his arms folded.

'We'll wait for Forensics to confirm it, Dave,' Denning said with a patient look, 'but early indications would support what Cassie Bane says.'

If Denning was hoping for a reaction from Kinsella, he was going to be disappointed. He just sat there, arms folded looking like he'd already solved the murder and was just waiting for the others to catch up with him.

'Have we spoken to this neighbour yet?' Bell asked. 'The one who had the beef about parking?'

'We're going to speak to him later today,' Denning said. 'But at this stage it doesn't look like he was involved. We've confirmed with Tyler Nelson's employers, and he was working yesterday evening: driving between Portsmouth and London. However, it's still worth speaking to him.'

'A drugs debt?' Kinsella said. 'It's a possibility. Young lad, into fitness; a partner and a kid. Could be he likes a little something to help him keep the energy levels up.'

'Except from what his employers said, I get the impression he wasn't into drugs, at least not in any big way. And with a baby in the house...' Molly didn't finish the thought. She didn't want to come across as naïve: all sorts of people used drugs for a variety of reasons. Being a young father who liked to keep fit was no reason not to indulge in something illegal from time-to-time.

'All valid points,' Denning said. 'But there's something else we need to consider. It's just possible Kieran Judd wasn't the intended victim in the first place and was killed in a case of mistaken identity.' He looked over at Neeraj. 'Deep, care to fill us in?'

Neeraj looked around the room, making sure he had everyone's attention. 'The couple only moved into the flat a few months ago. Until recently the bloke living upstairs was a nasty piece of work called Tony Hallam. Hallam was released from prison a few months back. I recognised the name, I just couldn't place him.'

'Yeah,' Kinsella nodded. 'I remember Hallam. He and his brother-in-law, Declan Meech, used to work in tandem. Robbing, sometimes armed. Banks, betting shops. They weren't fussy. That was until they had a falling-out.' He folded his beefy arms across his ample chest. 'Hallam must have made a fair few enemies over the years.'

'Has anyone spoken to this Hallam bloke?' Molly asked. 'I mean if he was the intended target and the killer realises they've got the wrong man, then what?'

'We don't know for certain the killer did get the wrong man,' Bell said. 'Right now, we don't really know anything.'

'What else do we know about Tony Hallam?' Denning asked. 'What was this supposed falling-out down to?'

All eyes turned to Kinsella. 'Hallam thinks Declan Meech did the dirty on him last time he was sent down for something that Meech did, or so the rumours go. Hallam got sent down for five years.'

'That would give Hallam a motive for trying to kill Meech,' Bell said, 'but hardly the other way round.'

'There's more to it than that,' Kinsella added. 'Complicated history between the two. Apparently Meech hates Hallam because of what happened with his sister.'

'Care to elaborate, Dave?'

'Maria Hallam claimed Hallam was violent towards her. He denies it. Claims she had been having an affair and made the domestic violence story up to cover her tracks. I don't know much more than that. But I do know there's no love lost between the two men.'

'Could there be any truth in the domestic violence claim?' Denning asked.

'A typically male response,' Trudi said. She looked at Denning, Kinsella and Neeraj. 'I mean, no offence, guys, but when a woman makes an accusation of domestic violence, there's usually something in it.'

Kinsella pulled a face that said he wasn't bothered either way. 'Whatever the story, the details will be on the system if you want to check it out. Anyway, Hallam and Meech fell out, which is not necessarily a bad thing.'

Denning was curious about the relationship between the two men, specifically before it turned sour. 'Tell us about Meech, Dave. What kind of character is he?'

'He's got a record, naturally. And he's a ruthless individual: armed robbery with violence, and sometimes the violence was for no other reason than just because he felt like it. He and Hallam had known each other since school. Real birds of a feather.'

'Gives us a motive right there,' Neeraj said. 'If Meech hated Hallam that much.'

Denning looked at Kinsella. 'What do you think, Dave? Is Meech capable of murder?'

A shrug from Kinsella. 'A knifing's a bit neat for him. He's more likely to batter someone to death.' Another shrug. 'But who knows. I doubt he'd lose any sleep if he did kill someone.'

'But why wait until after Hallam had been out of prison for six months?' Trudi asked.

'Maybe it took him that long to track Hallam down?'

'He's definitely worth speaking to.' Molly watched as Denning wrote his name on the whiteboard.

'Right, Dave. Get on to your contact. Find out everything you can about Tony Hallam and Declan Meech. Especially the nature of this alleged feud between them. Now that Hallam's out, there's a possibility it could have escalated. If Meech does have it in for his brother-in-law, then that's a good enough motive. We'll need to speak to Hallam.'

'If you think he's going to tell us anything,' Kinsella growled, 'you can think again.'

'We have to warn him that his life may be in danger,' Denning said.

'Even if he is a scumbag,' Kinsella added.

'We're obviously assuming Meech paid someone to do this,' Molly said. 'Taking Dave's point, and assuming Meech had done this himself then we would expect him to recognise his own brother-in-law, even if it was dark.'

Kinsella nodded. 'Declan Meech may be no stranger to violence, but something messy like this, he'd get someone else to do the dirty. Probably some daft kid doing it for drugs money.'

'And if all they had was an address and a vague description,' Trudi said. Then she shrugged. 'But isn't there a worry that we're being a bit quick in assuming Kieran Judd definitely wasn't the intended target?'

Denning seemed to give the matter some thought. 'OK, let's do a bit more digging into Kieran Judd's background, see if there's anything that rings any alarm bells. At least establish him as our intended victim if nothing else.'

'Waste of time,' Kinsella muttered under his breath. 'My money's on Tony Hallam as the intended victim. Let's just cut straight to the chase.'

Molly could see Denning thinking this over. Kinsella talked a lot of crap a lot of the time, but sometimes he hit the nail on the head. He'd been a detective for a long time, and as such had developed a copper's sixth sense for knowing which way the wind was blowing. That didn't mean he was always right, however…

She was suddenly aware that the briefing was over. Denning was heading towards her desk.

'Molly, if you've got a moment…?' He perched on the edge of her desk. She could smell his aftershave: something expensive by Tom Ford probably. Everything about Denning was expensive, from his designer suits to his flash apartment in trendy Shoreditch.

'Sure,' she said, turning to face him.

'I'd like you to talk to Maria Hallam with me.'

She glanced over at Neeraj's desk.

'Yes, I know it's Deep's call, but I think I'd prefer a more sensitive touch.' Neeraj was good, but he didn't do subtlety. Sometimes that was a good thing, especially with a suspect who was unwilling to talk. However, there were times when his direct approach caused more problems than they solved.

'I was going to do a follow-up visit to Cassie Bane,' she said. 'But I suppose I could swing round via Maria Hallam first.'

'Good.' Denning rose from the desk. 'I'll drive. I'll drop you off at Cassie Bane's afterwards.'

Chapter Three

Maria Hallam lived in a second-floor flat in a red-brick block on an estate in Hackney, just off Homerton High Street. The flat was tidy and cared for, but it was clear that very little money had been spent on it for some time. Maria was dressed in a pair of jeans and a grey-and-black striped top. She had a slightly pinched look about her face, though that was more than likely down to the exasperation of seeing a couple of police officers standing on her doorstep.

'I haven't seen him since your lot got him sent down,' she said. She showed Denning and Molly into the flat's sitting room. Tidy, with glass ornaments scattered around the room on shelves and tables. Framed photos of children, but none of her husband, from whom she claimed she was estranged.

'According to his probationer, this was the address he was officially registered at,' Denning said.

'But he hasn't been here,' she insisted. 'He hasn't lived here since before he went to prison.'

'What about the children?' Denning asked.

'They're at school,' she replied, as though she was being accused of being a bad parent as well as the wife of a criminal.

'I mean, has Tony been in contact with them?'

Maria Hallam threw Denning a withering look. 'No. I took a court order out against Tony when he was banged up. He hasn't been near any of us.'

'Why is that?' Molly asked.

She stared at her glumly before answering. 'That's none of your business. Let's just say Tony was as rotten a father as he was a husband. They're better off having nothing to do with him. We all are.'

'We need to contact him, Mrs Hallam,' Denning said. 'He's no longer living at his last address.'

She shrugged. 'I can't help you. I haven't seen him for months and I don't want to see him again. How can I get that through to you lot?'

'What about your brother? Have you been in contact with him recently?'

She looked warily at Denning when he asked the question. 'Why?'

Denning sighed. 'We believe Tony's life may be in danger, and we need to find him and warn him.'

'What do you mean "in danger"?'

Denning didn't want to go into detail, so he kept it light. 'We have information that leads us to believe someone might be going to attempt to harm or possibly kill Tony. I can't tell you any more than that. But I stress we do need to find him.'

She looked at Denning and then Molly. 'I'm sorry, I can't help you. I don't know where he is, and I don't want to know.'

'Can you think of anywhere he might have gone? Any friends? Relatives?'

Another shake of the head. 'No. All of his friends are criminals, and he has no family.' She glanced over at the photos of the children. 'Well, apart from us and, like I've tried to tell you, we want nothing more to do with him.'

'What exactly was the nature of the relationship between your brother and your husband?' Molly asked.

She stared blankly at Molly before answering. 'They worked together.'

'Doing what?'

Maria Hallam's shoulders twitched. 'You'd have to ask them about that.' There was a pause. 'Tony worked as a painter and decorator until a few years ago. Dec's a bit of a Jack-of-all-trades, you might say. He can turn his hand to anything.'

Including crime, thought Denning. 'Both your husband and brother have extensive criminal records,' he said. 'Burglary, assault, threatening behaviour.' He looked at Maria hoping for a reaction, but she continued to stare blankly back at him. 'I understand that relations between the two men recently soured. Is it possible your brother bears a grudge against your husband?'

She snapped out of her trance-like state and looked sharply at Denning. 'Look, I don't know what went on between them and I don't care. Tony's no longer a part of my life and I haven't seen Dec for months. Not since before Tony was sent down.'

That made sense to Denning. It reinforced the feeling that there was a grudge between the two men.

'You made a claim that Tony assaulted you,' Molly said. 'Then you subsequently withdrew that claim. Why was that?'

She shook her head, making it clear she didn't want to talk about the matter. 'We had an argument. Tony shouted at me.' She looked at Molly. 'But he didn't hit me. I just said he did because...' Another shake of the head. 'I don't know why I told the police he hit me. I just wanted to punish him. I was angry. It was all ages ago. Why are you brining this up now?'

Denning realised they were getting nowhere. Either she genuinely didn't know where Tony Hallam was, or she wasn't going to tell them. Whichever it was, it was clear to Denning that they were wasting their time there.

'OK,' he said, getting to his feet. 'I'll leave you my card and if he does get in touch, or you hear where he is, let me know straight away.'

She took the card and looked at it. 'I wouldn't hold your breath.'

Chapter Four

Cassie Bane greeted Molly Fisher with an exasperated smile. She clearly looked like someone who was trying to process a lot of things in her mind.

'I'm sorry,' Molly said. 'I know this is not a good time, but I need to ask you some more questions.'

She was still staying with Beth Marshall. Beth had gone to work that morning. She'd offered to take the day off to sit with Cassie, who had insisted she would rather be on her own, to get her head together if nothing else.

'You'd better come in,' Cassie said. Molly had tried not to pay too much attention to what was happening next door. The forensic team was still going over the property, even though Kieran's body had now been taken to the mortuary awaiting the post-mortem. Uniformed officers would be going door-to-door again, hoping to speak to anyone they'd missed the previous evening, while a public appeal had been launched for any dashcam or doorbell CCTV footage. It was slow-going, but it was often this kind of relentless plodding that gave them their breakthrough: somebody seeing something they didn't realise was significant but that ultimately led them in the direction they needed to go.

The living room was compact, but clean. Cassie looked like she hadn't slept, or washed. Her eyes were bleary and voice was hoarse. 'Can I get you a tea or coffee?' she offered.

'Yes, but let me,' Molly said. 'I'll make us a pot of tea.'

She headed to the small kitchen at the back of the flat. It looked like it was a modern extension, probably added when the houses were converted into flats. She found a teapot and a glass jar of teabags in a cupboard. As she waited for the kettle to boil, she thought about what the future would hold for Cassie and her son now that they were alone. In a way, now that Molly was newly single, she felt like she was alone too. Though the circumstances were very different.

Once the tea was made, she returned to the living room, placing the tray on the table by the sofa. She waited for a minute, then poured out two mugs. 'Milk and sugar?' she asked.

'Just milk, thanks,' Cassie said, and Molly handed her a mug.

'I appreciate your forensic people have to do their job, but I'm really keen to get back home.' She looked almost embarrassed to be saying it. 'I know what you're thinking, but it's our home: mine and Arthur's. And despite what happened to Kieran...' She started to cry. Molly took a couple of tissues from her bag and handed them Cassie, who dabbed her eyes.

'I understand. It will probably be another couple of days, Cassie,' Molly explained. 'We'll arrange for a specialist cleaning firm to go in first. I know it's a small consolation, but it'll be one less thing to worry about.'

She nodded, drying her eyes with the tissues, then scrunching them and clutching them in her hand as though they offered her some sort of comfort.

Molly waited until Cassie had composed herself, then continued. 'I'm sorry to have to go over this again, Cassie. I know it's difficult for you.' She took a sip of the tea. 'Silly question, but how are you coping?'

She nodded. 'Beth's been great. I must admit, I never really knew her that well before all this. Just the odd chat anytime we bumped into each other in the street. But she's been so kind.'

'And what about Arthur? How's he getting on?' She had made sure to remember the baby's name before she left the office.

Cassie stared at her tea. 'I don't know. I'm sure he can sense something's different, but I don't know how much babies pick up on.' She gave a little shudder. 'What's it going to be like for him growing up without a father? I don't even know if I want that for him.'

'You've got family, though? People who can help out?'

She was still staring at the tea. 'There's my mum. She lives in France. She coming over today sometime, just as soon as she can get a flight. I haven't seen my dad in years, and my brother's worse than useless. I don't really know Kieran's family. We haven't been together very long. In fact, it was Arthur that brought us together. I haven't spoken to his parents yet. It'll look like I don't care.'

Molly could see that she was upset. 'Has anyone from Family Liaison been in contact with you?'

'A woman called this morning to say someone would come round later. I thought you might have been her when you knocked on the door.'

'Family Liaison will be a great help, Cassie. This is a difficult time. You shouldn't have to deal with everything on your own. The police will have contacted Kieran's parents, and I'm sure they'll be in touch with you, but you should have your own family around you at a time like this.'

Cassie nodded. 'What about funeral arrangements?' She clamped a hand round her mouth. 'God, I don't even know if Kieran wanted to be buried or cremated.'

Molly explained about the post-mortem, how there would be a delay before the body could be released. She felt sorry for Cassie, but she was there for a reason.

'Cassie, I need to ask you some questions about yesterday evening. I know you've been through it all with DI Denning and DS Neeraj, but I need to ask if you've remembered anything else. Try to think back. Take your time and talk me through the events of yesterday.'

'I don't know. It's all so crazy. It was just a normal evening. We'd both got back from work at the usual time. I'd collected Arthur from the childminder earlier in the afternoon. I work part time in the Tesco next to Bromley-by-Bow station. Kieran got back about six. He was in the living room watching the news. I was in the kitchen preparing dinner – it was my turn to cook. Arthur was in his high chair. I was listening to the radio, then I heard the doorbell go. Kieran shouted through that he would get it. I didn't think anything of it. A minute or so later, I heard a crash, I looked round and I saw Kieran standing in the doorway to the flat, clutching his stomach. I ran to him, helped him into the living room and saw that he was bleeding. He collapsed on the living room floor and passed out. I called an ambulance. I waited with him until it arrived. He kept drifting in and out of consciousness. I couldn't get much sense out of him.'

'Did he say anything else? Anything at all?'

She shook her head and rubbed a hand over her face. 'No. He just said he'd been stabbed. I couldn't understand it. Why would someone stab Kieran? We've only lived here for a few months. It's a safe street. Or as safe as anywhere.'

'We're going to find out who did this, Cassie. But we need more information first. You told my colleagues last night that Kieran didn't have any enemies, but if the two of you hadn't been together for very long, how can you be sure?'

'Kieran wasn't the kind of person who made enemies. Everybody liked him. He was just a big, daft lad. He'd never harm anyone. We never argued, well, not seriously. He was great with Arthur. There's no reason why someone would want to kill him.'

But Molly knew there must have been a reason. Yes, people did murder random strangers from time to time, but it was rare. And even then, there was usually a reason for it: a gang initiation, or someone suffering from mental health issues. But these cases were incredibly rare and invariably happened in the street. It was unheard of for someone to ring the doorbell of a complete stranger and randomly stab them to death. This had to be about something else. Unless Denning was right and Kieran Judd hadn't been the intended target all along.

'What about the man who used to live in the upstairs flat? Did anyone ever call round for him? Maybe press your doorbell by mistake?'

'No. Not that I remember anyway. The bells are clearly marked. And he kept himself to himself. In fact, we always used to jokingly refer to him as "the bloke upstairs" as we rarely saw him.'

'And he moved out a few weeks ago?'

She thought for a moment. 'About three weeks ago, I think. He never actually said he was leaving, he just wasn't around anymore. We never heard any movement coming from upstairs. Then I bumped into the landlord in the communal hallway one day and he said he was going to have the flat decorated and then look for another tenant. He still hasn't got round to decorating it.' Cassie looked at Molly. 'Why? Do you think he had something to do with what happened?'

Molly smiled, trying to reassure her. 'We don't know at this stage. But it's a possibility.'

There was a puzzled look on Cassie's face.

'What is it?'

'I'm sure I heard...' She shook her head. 'No, forget it...'

'What is it, Cassie? Anything you can think of will be useful.'

'I wasn't paying attention, but I remember I kept half an ear out. I was curious as to who might be at the door.'

Molly felt there was something more she wanted to say. 'Go on. It might be important.'

'I thought I heard him say something like "yes, that's me". I don't know though. I couldn't really hear over the sound of the radio.' She shook her head again. 'I mean I could have imagined it.'

'But you're sure you heard him say *something*?'

She looked confused for a moment. 'Like I say, I'm not sure.' Another shake of the head. 'But I'm certain I heard him speak.'

Molly was thinking hard. 'Can you remember how long between the doorbell ringing and Kieran appearing in the hallway?'

'A couple of minutes. Maybe.'

'Think carefully, Cassie. It might be important.'

'When the doorbell rang, the clock on the oven said 6:17. I remember thinking if it was someone coming to visit, then it wouldn't be long until dinner was ready. But I can't remember how long before Kieran appeared bleeding in the hallway. I mean, not long. A minute. Two minutes.'

Molly was thinking. Rather than a random attack, what if the killer had taken a moment to confirm that Kieran Judd was living there.

That then raised the question: what if Kieran Judd had been the intended target all along?

–

She left the flat and spoke briefly to one of the forensic officers who were still working next door. They were in the process of finishing off and Molly confirmed that Cassie would be allowed back in within a couple of days. She understood Cassie's concerns. Even though the flat was the scene of her partner's murder, it was her home. She was going to have to take the first steps at rebuilding her life, and that would be easier if she was living somewhere familiar. It was going to be a long process.

Molly crossed over the road and knocked on the door of number thirty-one. There was a dirty Transit van parked immediately outside and another smaller van parked further down the street.

The door was eventually answered by an overweight man in his forties, sweating slightly and looking dishevelled.

'What do you want?' he asked.

'Calum Nelson?'

'Yes?'

Molly showed him her ID and explained why she was there. He glanced across the street at Cassie's flat, then jerked his head back indicating for her to come in.

Nelson lived in a house rather than a flat, but the ground-floor layout was almost identical to Beth's. The living room was cluttered with magazines, and dirty crockery littered the floor. There was a faintly sour smell about the property.

There was no offer of a seat, so Molly remained standing. 'One of your neighbours was stabbed to death yesterday evening,' she said. 'I was wondering if you knew anything about it?'

Nelson sat on an armchair that faced an over-sized television. There was a black and white tattoo of an eagle on his neck, and another of a snake on his right arm. Despite the situation, Molly couldn't help appreciating their beauty. 'I heard about it on the news this morning,' he said. 'But I wasn't here last night so I can't tell you anything.'

'OK, well, maybe you could tell me about the feud you had with Mr Judd. It was about parking, wasn't it?'

He laughed. 'Who told you it was a feud?' Another laugh. 'He whinged at me a couple of times because he claimed I parked my van outside his flat. I pointed out there are no designated parking spaces in this street. It's first come, first served. He doesn't own the street. And I've been here a lot longer than him and his missus.'

'What exactly happened?'

He sighed. 'One Saturday morning, he had a go at me because I'd parked in front of his place and he wasn't happy. Said he'd had to park miles away and it meant carrying his baby and shopping and shit.'

'What did you say?'

'I told him to get lost.'

'So it was aggressive?'

He laughed again. 'It wasn't aggressive. I admit I deliberately parked in front of his gaff again a couple of days later to wind him up. Nothing came of it though. I'd made my point.'

'You can confirm where you were yesterday evening?'

'Of course I can. Look, we had a bit of verbal about parking. Him and just about half the fuckers in this street. Parking's hell round here, and I have a van and two cars. The van is for work and the car is for personal use. When I first moved here twenty years ago, you could park anywhere on this street. You were unlucky if there were more than a dozen cars the length of the entire road. Now, every sod's got at least one car, sometimes more. Parking spaces are like gold round here now, and I have to park somewhere.'

His tone suggested it was fine for him to have more than one vehicle but not OK for his neighbours. The 'me and mine' mentality, she thought.

'So you admit there was animosity between yourself and Mr Judd?'

He was silent for a moment, as though thinking over his answers, wary that Molly was trying to catch him out.

'Look, if I knifed everyone on this street who'd had a go at me over the years, half the street would be brown bread.' He sighed. 'I didn't dislike the guy. I just don't like people telling me what I can and can't do in my own home. But I didn't kill him, and I can prove I wasn't here yesterday evening. I had to make a load of deliveries between Portsmouth and London, and I didn't get home until almost midnight. I saw loads of Old Bill blocking the road, so I had to park my van in the next street. I'm sorry the bloke's dead. He might have been a bit of a twat, but he didn't deserve that.'

'What about the man who used to live in the flat above Kieran and Cassie? Tony Hallam? Did you ever have anything to do with him?'

He pulled a face. 'Do you think I spend my days chatting to my neighbours? I've got a job to do.'

'I'll take that as a no, then.'

Chapter Five

Tony Hallam looked at Denning and Neeraj with annoyance when they knocked on his door. He was now living in a flat on the tenth floor of a tower block that overlooked the Mile End Stadium in Tower Hamlets.

'What do you want?' he asked, eyes dancing from one to the other.

They showed their ID and asked if they could come in. For a moment it looked like he was going to refuse until he realised that would mean having his business discussed on his doorstep with all his neighbours listening in.

He reluctantly showed them into his living room. Denning had to appreciate the impressive view from the large living room window, but the room felt draughty and slightly damp. Denning chose to ignore the view and sat with his back to the window.

'So, what's this about? I've kept myself clean since I got out and you've got nothing on me.'

'Mr Hallam,' Denning said calmly, 'we're not here in connection with anything you've done. At least, not directly.'

Hallam seemed edgy; eyes flicking between Denning and Neeraj, never quite remaining focused on either of them for more than a couple of seconds. 'What are you talking about? I told you, I've kept my nose clean since my release.'

Denning explained about Kieran Judd's stabbing the night before. 'The bloke who used to live downstairs?' Hallam's eyes widened. 'Shit! I'm sorry to hear that. He seemed like a decent guy. I mean, I never really knew him, but any time we chatted he was friendly. He's got a kid too.' He looked at Denning. 'Look, I'm sorry to hear about what happened to him, but this has got nothing to do with me. I was in the pub last night. And anyway, I didn't have any beef with the bloke. OK, his kid used to cry sometimes and it got on my nerves a bit, but that doesn't give me a reason to want to stick a knife in his guts.'

'We're not suggesting you killed him,' Neeraj said abruptly. 'That's not why we're here.'

'What then?'

'Mr Hallam, we have reason to believe that you might have been the intended target. It's just possible Mr Judd was stabbed by mistake.'

Hallam looked incredulous. 'You're joking, aren't you? Why would someone want to stab me?'

'That's why we're here, Mr Hallam,' Denning said calmly. 'If you were the intended target, then there's a good chance whoever killed Mr Judd may come after you. Is there anyone you can think of who bears you a grudge or has recently threatened you?'

Hallam laughed. 'If you think it's someone who bears me a grudge, then look in your own ranks. You lot have been after me for years. I insisted I was fitted up for the last job I was sent down for, but none of you believed me. You've got me labelled as a criminal for ever more and that's that.'

Denning sighed, while Neeraj rolled his eyes. 'OK, Mr Hallam. Let's just rule out members of the Metropolitan

Police for now. Can you think of anyone who bears you a grudge? Someone you met in prison, maybe?'

Prisons were a melting point for grievances to fester and it wasn't uncommon for them to spill over into the outside. If a serious falling-out had occurred, and the individual responsible still felt aggrieved, there was a good chance whoever bore a grudge would come after Hallam.

Hallam shook his head. 'No. Nothing like that. I did my time. That prison was a shithole, but I survived.'

'But there were never any incidents you were involved in? No threats made against you?'

He looked at Denning like he was mad. 'You're off your heads if you think what happened to that poor sod has got anything to do with me. I moved out of that flat weeks ago. If someone wanted to come after me, why would they go to my old address?'

'How many people know your new address? Your ex-wife doesn't even know you've moved.'

'She doesn't have any reason to. Besides, she's made it clear where things stand. She wants me to have nothing more to do with her, or the kids.'

'Why did you move?' Neeraj asked.

He looked at Neeraj as though deciding whether or not to answer his question.

'I couldn't afford the rent. The landlord told me he wanted to sell the place. My probation officer found me one.'

'And that's the only reason you moved out of that flat?'

'Look, I've told you. There's no one after me. Nothing happened while I was in jail. You can check that out.'

'OK,' Denning said. 'What about before you were sent down? What was your relationship with Declan Meech like?'

'Declan? What the fuck's he got to do with anything?'

'Is it true the two of you had a big falling-out? If so, there's a chance he might bear a grudge against you.'

Hallam shook his head. 'That's crap. We used to be mates. He's got no reason to want to kill me. Why would he?'

'Maybe because of the way you treated his sister,' Neeraj said. 'There's an injunction out against you because you've been violent to her in the past.'

Hallam looked caught. 'That's got nothing to do with anything. Me and Maria went through a bad patch. We had no money coming in and two kids to feed. She was on at me all the time. All we did was argue.'

'So you hit her,' Denning said coldly. 'When things got bad, you took it out on your wife.'

'You can judge me all you like. I was in a bad place back then. I did stupid things because I was desperate.'

They needed to work out what all this had to do with what had happened to Kieran Judd. Denning took a punt. 'But it is possible Declan Meech could bear you a grudge?'

Hallam thought for a moment. 'I don't know. No. No, he wouldn't try to kill me. You're insane if you think that. As I said, I'm sorry about what happened to that bloke. But this has got nothing to do with me. There's no one after me and I can't think of anyone who would want to kill me.'

Once they were outside heading to the car, Denning looked back at the flat on the tenth floor. He didn't believe Hallam. He didn't believe him for one moment.

Chapter Six

Molly Fisher was at her desk reading over her notes, eating an apple and tapping away at her keyboard as she entered anything relevant on to the database. She wanted to speak to Denning, but he and Neeraj weren't back yet.

It had been a productive morning. After she'd spoken to Nelson, she'd swung round to the sports centre where Kieran had worked. They'd confirmed what they'd already been told: Kieran Judd was a model employee, popular with staff and customers. He'd worked for them for just under two years and had never been involved in any trouble. She was still chewing over what Cassie Bane had told her, letting her brain replay Cassie's words and hoping something significant would jump out at her. She glanced up to see Denning and Neeraj come in. She waited until Denning sat down, then headed over and perched half a buttock on the edge of his desk.

'Any luck with Tony Hallam?'

He was waking his computer by shaking the mouse. 'He claims there's no one after him. But obviously we're not going to take his word for that. What about Cassie Bane and the neighbour across the road?'

'I think we can rule out Calum Nelson. The guy's a prat, but he didn't do it. I ran the numberplate through the ANPR database, and his van is shown as being where he said he was yesterday evening. I need to confirm that he was the one driving it, but I'd be surprised if it wasn't.' She took another bite of her apple. 'Besides, I just don't think he's our man.'

'What about Cassie? How's she holding up?'

Molly tried to choose her words carefully. The truth was, in her opinion at least, Cassie wasn't holding up at all. She was putting on a brave face, pretending that by focusing on funerals and families she could hold it together. Whether it was delayed shock or she was doing it for Arthur's sake, Molly couldn't say. But this wasn't what Denning wanted to hear. He wanted to know how the case was progressing.

'She's coping,' Molly said blandly. 'However, she did say something interesting.' She paused. 'Well, maybe not exactly interesting, but it made me think. She seems to think there were words exchanged between Kieran and our killer. It doesn't mean anything, but it does suggest the possibility that our killer first established they had the right person.' She looked at him for a response. 'It would make sense. Assuming this was a targeted attack, our killer would want to ensure their target was correct.'

'It's possible. Unless they didn't wait for a response. Just assumed Kieran was Hallam, even if he denied it. If our killer was all fired up, running on adrenalin, then they could have knifed him without thinking too carefully. Perhaps we're being a bit quick in assuming Kieran Judd wasn't the intended victim. It could just be coincidence about Hallam.'

Denning thought about this. 'Hallam's clearly not telling us the truth. His reaction upon being told about Kieran was one of fear rather than shock. My gut tells me that Hallam was the intended target, but keep digging into

39

Kieran's background… see if you can find anything that might present itself as a credible motive.'

'It's going to be a hard slog. The guy seems like Mr Perfect.'

Denning smiled. 'We can't rule anything out at this stage. It's possible Cassie misheard or thought she heard something when in fact she hadn't. But we have to accept the possibility Kieran pissed someone off and that someone wanted revenge. I know, it's unlikely, but we have to explore all our options. Check phone records, see if anything comes up. And social media. But don't waste too much time on this. My money's still on Tony Hallam. There's something going on there.'

Chapter Seven

DCI Elizabeth McKenna originally hailed from Mother-well and at some point in her police career had been given the nickname Betty Taggart, which was only ever uttered out of her earshot. She had a reputation for not suffering fools gladly and Denning had to admit it had taken him some time to push through the barbed-wire defence she hid behind and discover that, when the occasion struck, she could actually be good fun.

'How's it looking, Matt?' She was sitting behind her over-sized desk, sipping coffee from a chipped mug, a stack of paperwork covering the desktop. She was dressed in her trademark black denims with a white blouse. 'I've got a press conference booked for later this afternoon and it would be nice to do more than stand there looking pretty.'

He smiled despite himself. He'd had to do a press conference a few months back when McKenna wasn't around. He would be lying if he said he'd enjoyed the experience. McKenna, while she didn't exactly relish them, at least took them in her stride.

He filled her in on what they had so far, reiterating his theory that their killer had got the wrong man.

'Hallam is acting strangely,' Denning said. 'The reason he moved out of that flat into the one he's in now doesn't seem entirely credible. He fed us some cock-and-bull story about the landlord wanting to sell the place, but my honest opinion is he was frightened someone was going to come looking for him there. He wanted out.'

'Hallam has previous?' McKenna said it as a question, but it sounded more like a statement.

'Yes. He's violent, and he's been no stranger to a prison cell over the years. Got out of the last one a few months ago after finishing a sentence for assault. We're going to speak to the governor there and see if anything happened while he was there. There's a chance Hallam might have made enemies while he was inside and, now he's out, someone's decided it's time for payback.'

McKenna nodded slowly. 'OK, sounds credible. Are we thinking this has the hallmarks of a professional hit?'

'Difficult to say until we get the post-mortem results. But a knife... And it was messy. My gut feeling is that this isn't a professional killer. It feels like this is something personal.'

'If we're going down that route, we might need to speak to Hallam's victims. Could be one of them has been waiting for him to get out of jail, tracked him down and decided prison wasn't enough of a punishment.'

'That's certainly worth looking into.' Denning paused. 'There's also the possibility this has got something to do with his bother-in-law, Declan Meech. We're still trying to get hold of him – he's a pretty elusive character – but he's someone worth speaking to. Meech is a person of interest. He's got a criminal record going back decades and rumour has it relations between the two men recently soured.'

'Rumour...?'

'A "reliable source", according to DS Kinsella.'

'Dave and his "reliable sources"…' McKenna sat back in her chair and observed Denning. 'You're pretty certain this is down to a case of mistaken identity? I mean, you're confident Hallam was the intended target and not our actual victim?'

Denning nodded, slightly taken aback by the directness of her question. It was still very early days in the murder investigation: he couldn't say for sure he was certain of anything at this stage.

'It seems the most obvious conclusion,' he said tentatively. 'Kieran Judd was a young father who seems to have been a decent bloke; popular, hard-working. Not the sort to make enemies. There's no obvious reason for someone to want him dead. Hallam, on the other hand, is a nasty piece of work.'

McKenna was thinking. 'On the other hand, it is all a bit convenient. Casting Hallam in the role of the intended victim. In the worst-case scenario, we can tell the press our killer is only after one person and what happened to Kieran Judd was unfortunate but unintended. It would put people's minds at rest thinking the target was a known criminal. There's going to be considerable media uproar around this case. A young family man stabbed to death on his own doorstep. Mix that in with the unending and depressing talk about knife crime in the capital… People are going to use this death to score political points and highlight the perceived inefficiency of the Met. We're going to be held under a microscope over this. Everyone and his granny will be waiting for us to fuck up.' She looked at him. 'You see our problem?'

Denning wasn't sure he did. 'I wouldn't describe what happened to Kieran Judd as "convenient".'

She offered Denning one of her withering stares. 'I'm not saying that at all, Matt. What I am saying is that we don't want to go down a specific route simply because it makes our job easier. However, I'm fully prepared to accept the possibility Tony Hallam was our intended victim all along. In which case, yes, there's a likelihood our killer will try again. She folded her arms and sat back on her chair. 'You've spoken to Hallam… What exactly did he have to say?'

'Very little,' Denning said. 'Though I expect that was mostly down to bravado. I think he's rattled, but he's never going to admit it.' He considered his next sentence very carefully, already second-guessing her response. 'I think we need to consider offering him police protection.'

McKenna gave a dry, throaty chuckle. 'Seriously? We barely have the resources to protect people who are in real harm. Can you honestly see us being granted permission to offer twenty-four-hour police protection to a known criminal on what is little more than a suspicion his life might be in danger? That's assuming Hallam would agree to it, which I would doubt.'

Denning could see where she was coming from. Public perception of the police was always skewed by what they read in the right-wing press. If it were to be discovered that the police were using the public purse to protect a criminal, it wouldn't make for good PR.

'I agree, it's going to be a difficult to sell to the powers-that-be. But if something were to happen to Tony Hallam after we've officially identified him as a potential victim… At the very least we have to cover our arses here.'

She looked at him, fixing him with one of her gimlet stares. 'If someone is after Hallam, then there's a strong chance it's down to something he's said or done to piss off another criminal. There really is no honour among thieves, Matt. If he's done that to the wrong people then – to be blunt – he's only got himself to blame. We certainly can't justify offering any kind of police protection to Hallam. How would it look?'

'Even if his life is in danger?'

'*Possibly* in danger. We're still not certain that Hallam *was* the intended target. We can't start talking about police protection until we're one hundred per cent certain of our facts.'

He wanted to argue, but sensed he was fighting a losing battle. Unless they could prove that Hallam was the intended victim, police protection was a luxury they couldn't afford.

'So, where do we go from here?'

She sighed. 'If you're convinced Hallam's in danger, speak to him again. Try to get him to take a few precautions; change his route into work, the places he drinks in… all the usual bollocks. At least he's changed his address. With a bit of luck our killer won't know where he's now living. Do we know what Hallam's been up to since he got out?'

'He's got a job in a warehouse, apparently. Claims he's going straight.'

'I suppose we have to believe him when he says it.' McKenna's face suggested otherwise. She offered him a wry grin. 'Keep an eye on him, but don't waste too many resources. If he comes to us shouting that he's in fear of his life, then we'll crank things up a gear. In the meantime, let's focus on Kieran Judd. Dig a bit deeper. Let's see if there's anything that rings alarm bells. If he's still coming up cleaner than a nun's conscience, then we'll focus our attention on Hallam. But let's not be too quick to discount Judd, just in case there's something we've overlooked.'

Denning knew she was being thorough, ensuring every avenue was explored before they faced up to the inevitability that someone wanted to kill Tony Hallam, and, once they realised they'd screwed up first time round, they would try again. He knew McKenna belonged to the old school of flog 'em and hang 'em. He believed in giving people a second chance, as long as they deserved it. Though the number of times he'd been proved wrong meant he did sometimes wonder if McKenna might have a point.

'Right,' he said, 'I'll get DS Fisher to look into Judd and I'll have another word with Hallam.'

'Good. In the meantime, I'll take the press conference. There's going to be the inevitable allegations about how the death of a professional white man is attracting greater police attention than that of a black male.'

'I'm not sure that's fair,' Denning countered, but he knew how it would inevitably be depicted in the media.

'I'm not sure fair comes into it,' McKenna replied. 'But you do see the problems we're facing?'

'Then we counter that argument by showing that it's not the case. Murder is murder. We don't discriminate when it comes to the victims of crime.'

'Tell that to the media,' McKenna countered. 'You know the reputation knife crime has in London, and the accusations the Met face on an almost daily basis. And I'm the one who has to go out there and convince them they're wrong.'

And Denning didn't envy her. He didn't envy her one little bit.

Chapter Eight

Molly knocked on the door with some trepidation. Beth opened the door and smiled at Molly. 'DS Fisher, come in. Cassie said you might be calling round.' She led Molly down the narrow hallway and into the flat.

Cassie was in the living room, sitting in front of the television. It was a programme about the Pyramids, but she didn't seem to be taking any of it in.

Beth offered to make them tea, but both declined. 'I'll be in the kitchen,' she said. 'I'll give you a chance to chat in private.'

Molly thanked her, and she closed the living room door behind her. Beth's flat wasn't big: just a living room, kitchen and one bedroom. It was kind of her to give her space up to accommodate Cassie and Arthur. But Molly had learned over the years that some people were capable of the most extraordinary acts of kindness when tragedy struck. Just as others were capable of the most appalling acts of cruelty.

Cassie had phoned Molly earlier to say that she had remembered something that might be useful. Molly thought it better to speak to Cassie face-to-face. She wanted to make sure if Cassie remembered anything, then there was a chance she could be prompted to remember more. But also, she wanted to see how she was coping. She knew she'd been allocated a Family Liaison Officer, but there was only so much they could do for the victims in their care. And Cassie would inevitably be part of a much bigger workload. It was always against both her better judgement and the advice they were given as police officers: don't get too involved. But there were times when she couldn't help herself. Sometimes an incident affected her more than she cared to admit. Somehow, Cassie had got to her: a young woman with a baby, now on her own in the world. Sometimes life really was unfair.

'How's Arthur?' Molly asked.

'He's sleeping at the moment. Beth's kindly let him sleep in her room. I think he can sense something's not right.' She picked at a fingernail for a moment. 'I might go and stay with my mum for a while. It just feels a bit creepy staying there after what happened.'

'That might be a good idea,' Molly said. 'Just until you've got your head together.'

'The only problem is, my mum and I don't have the easiest of relationships. The thought of the two of us living under the same roof – especially with Arthur – is asking for trouble. And besides, despite what happened, it's still my home. I mean, it's not much, and it was way too small for the three of us, but the rent's not bad. It's not like we could afford to buy anywhere round here.'

Molly nodded. She sympathised. She was 'between homes' herself and not looking forward to the prospect of finding somewhere new to live. 'I take it you've spoken to someone from Family Liaison?' she asked.

'Yes. Someone was in touch. They're going to come round tomorrow to speak to me. And I've spoken to Kieran's parents. What we all really want to know is when can we bury Kieran? I know there are processes to go through and things take time, but I just want a bit of closure for him.'

Molly smiled and tried to appear reassuring. 'As soon as the post-mortem is over, we should be able to speed things along slightly.' She didn't want to tell her the truth: that there might be some time, at least until they had a suspect in place and the Crime Prosecution Service was happy enough to progress the case. 'Your Family Liaison Officer will keep you posted. Or you can contact me any time.'

'Thanks. To be honest, I don't think any of this has truly sunk in yet. It all feels like a horrible nightmare. Except I know I'm never going to wake up from it.'

Molly didn't know what else she could say. She understood what Cassie was going through, having lost her best friend to murder when she was eighteen. She couldn't say she would get over it, because she never had herself. Somehow, you just learned to live with it.

'Cassie, you said on the phone that you'd remembered something that might be relevant to the case. Can you tell me what it is?'

Cassie stared at her fingernail before answering. 'It's probably nothing important and, to be honest, I'm not even sure why I called you.'

'Perhaps if you tell me what it is, we can take it from there.'

Cassie sighed. 'About a week ago the phone rang. The home phone, which is unusual as no one calls us on that, except my mum and that's only because she still thinks it's cheaper than phoning a mobile. I answered it and a woman asked for Kieran. When I called him in from the kitchen, the person had hung up. I thought it was strange

49

at the time, but Kieran just laughed it off, insisting it must have been a wrong number.'

'But they asked for Kieran? By name?'

'Yes. Well, they must have done otherwise I wouldn't have called him through.'

'They didn't say something like "your husband" or "the man of the house"?'

Cassie thought about it, twisting her face into a thoughtful grimace. 'No, I'm pretty certain they asked for Kieran.'

'And it was a woman's voice on the other end of the line?'

'Yes. It was definitely a woman.'

'And Kieran didn't speak to her?'

'Apart from saying who he was, no. He looked at me and said whoever it was had hung up.'

'But it didn't bother him? Someone asking for him by name and then not speaking?'

'Not really. He just laughed it off.'

'But it had never happened before? Or since?'

'No. Just that one time.'

Molly thought about this. If someone had asked for Kieran by name, then they obviously knew he lived there. There could be any number of logical and sensible reasons for this, but it made her suspicious. 'And you definitely didn't recognise the voice? Or have any idea who it might have been?'

'Well, I did think it might have been Scarlett.'

'Scarlett?'

She pulled a face. 'Scarlett Rennie. She was Kieran's ex. They split up ages ago, but she wouldn't let go. When we first got together, she was always hassling him. In fact, one of the reasons we moved here was to get away from her. He changed his mobile number so she'd stop phoning him. We kept the same landline number when we moved in here, mostly for my mum's benefit. I expect Scarlett knew the number. I mean, it had to be somebody who knew us as we're not listed anywhere.'

'It would be fairly easy for someone to find your number if they tried hard enough,' Molly said.

'I suppose.' Cassie shrugged. 'It sounds mad though. I thought she was over him. But then again, I don't know for sure that it was her on the phone.'

'So, it was an acrimonious split?' Molly asked. 'Scarlett and Kieran?'

'I don't know. They were together for a while, but it didn't work out.' She looked at Molly. 'You can't think she had anything to do with what happened to Kieran? I mean she's harmless.'

'It might be worth speaking to her,' Molly said. 'Just to rule her out.'

'I've got her address somewhere, but I expect you'd be wasting your time talking to her.'

Molly wasn't sure she would be able to persuade Denning to let her speak to Scarlett Rennie. Despite his claims to be open-minded over this, she was certain he was still adamant on pursuing the Tony Hallam option. But the more she thought about it, the more she began to think Kieran Judd could have been the intended target after all.

Chapter Nine

When Denning got home, his wife Sarah was in the study – a glorified box room off the large, airy living room. Sarah worked as a hedge fund manager with one of the major banks, and it was her income that mostly paid for the luxury apartment in Shoreditch. Even on a detective inspector's pay they would have struggled to afford somewhere half this size. Not that he minded. Money was mostly a means to an end as far as he was concerned, and it didn't bother him too much how the bills were paid, just as long as they were paid. But sometimes other people felt the need to reference his domestic set up. He remembered Kinsella making a barbed comment in the pub once about how lucky Denning was to be a kept man. The scathing look Denning threw him in return meant Kinsella never broached the subject again. However, it had reinforced Denning's conviction that it was sensible to draw a distinction between work and his private life.

He looked around the vast, double-height living area, with its impressive views over the City and towards east London, and found himself frequently contemplating moving somewhere more sensible. But Sarah argued the location was convenient and refused to move to the sticks. However, it was a move further afield that occupied their thoughts at the moment.

Sarah waved a hand to acknowledge his presence and continued with her phone call. To her boss, presumably, discussing the job she'd been offered in New York. Although they had discussed the matter, and were yet to reach a decision, he knew Sarah had been looking at properties in New York.

Sarah made her excuses to her caller and put the phone on mute. 'You're home early,' she said with a smile. 'Do you fancy eating out tonight?'

He stood in the doorway to the office. Sarah had had the room painted in a grey-blue that was subtle and yet effective. 'It's my turn to cook tonight, remember?'

She flashed another warm smile at him. 'I know. I thought, maybe, you might like a night off.' Usually, she suggested a meal out when it was her night to cook. If she was tired, or there was something on her mind, often it was easier just to head to one of their favourite restaurants and give her credit card another airing. As it was his night to cook, he supposed he should appreciate the generous offer.

'I don't mind cooking,' he said. 'In fact, it might even be the perfect distraction.'

'Bad day?'

They had a rule: never discuss work. He had little interest in how she made vast sums of money for people who were already very rich and equally he had no wish to share the more gruesome aspects of a murder investigation with his wife. 'Let's just say, not untypical.'

He headed upstairs to their bedroom on the mezzanine level and changed out of his suit. He had initially thought about going for a run, to clear his head and give him the opportunity to do some thinking, but he was tired and

53

the grumbling emanating from his stomach told him food was of a greater priority right now.

He hung the suit on a hanger and placed it in the wardrobe that took up one entire wall of the bedroom. Most of the space was taken up with Sarah's expensive work clothes: designer suits and jackets that all came with designer labels. He could hear Sarah downstairs, catching the occasional word. The move would have meant a substantial promotion for her and more money. But, he had argued, they already had a good income and a nice life where they were. There were days he would gladly walk away from his job in the Met, but for the most part he enjoyed it. It was challenging yet rewarding. He'd been promoted to detective inspector shortly after turning thirty. When McKenna finally decided to retire, he stood a good chance of making it to DCI.

And then there was Jake. His son was nearly ten and was just settling into his new school and seemed to be enjoying it there. Jake had ADHD and lived with his ex-wife, Claire. He didn't see as much of him as he liked at the moment. A move across the Atlantic would only make that harder. But then, it wasn't all about him... Sarah worked hard at her job. She deserved a break. And this job could be it.

He slipped on a pair of chinos and a T-shirt, and headed back down to the main living area just as Sarah was finishing her phone call.

'That was Johan,' she said. 'They're prepared to keep the job offer open until the end of the year. But it means we will need to discuss the situation and what we intend to do about it.'

Denning knew another heavy discussion would be coming up involving his and her jobs, and what would happen about Jake. It felt like they were going round in circles.

'Let's get something to eat first. It's been a long day.' He headed to the kitchen to make a start on dinner. He kept thinking about what McKenna had said about Tony Hallam. He could accept the fact Hallam's background made it difficult to justify offering him twenty-four-hour police protection, but they still had a duty of care towards him, irrespective of his background.

He was distracted from his thoughts by Sarah's arrival in the kitchen. She sidled up to him and gave him a peck on the cheek. 'What are we having?'

'Salmon and broccoli pasta.' It was quick and easy, and all the ingredients were lurking in either the fridge or various cupboards. 'It won't be long.'

Sarah opened the large, American-style fridge and took out a bottle of Evian. She removed two glasses from the cupboard and poured them, passing one to him. 'Sounds lovely.' She leaned against one of the worktops as he prepared the food. 'Look, I know this is difficult, and I know we keep putting off having the discussion, but we're going to have to make a decision.'

'It's only September. We've got ages before we need to decide anything.' He emptied some pasta into a pot of water and placed it on the hob, lighting the gas underneath it. 'This is a big decision for us.'

He heard her sigh. 'I know. Which is why we can't keep putting it off indefinitely.' She reached out and touched his arm affectionately. 'I am aware of the dozens of factors that need to be taken into account before we decide anything.' She took a sip of the mineral water. 'And how this is going to affect Jake. But they want me over there. I've already established a rapport with the team. They know I can do the job. They want results and they know I can deliver them.'

He was chopping up a fillet of salmon now, having first checked the sell-by date on the packaging. It was still fresh. 'We have a nice life here. We have good jobs and a decent place to live. That's more than a lot of people have.' He thought about Cassie Bane living in her tiny flat. The whole place barely bigger than their master bedroom. He and Sarah had it good; why try and fix something that wasn't broken?

'Since when was being ambitious a crime?'

He finished cutting up chunks of salmon, rinsed the broccoli and began slicing it. 'Can we talk about this later?'

She returned to the living room with her drink.

He loved Sarah and their marriage was worth fighting for. But he was struggling to see how there was room for a compromise here. They'd met through mutual friends when both were in a difficult place in their lives. She had just been dumped by a boyfriend and his marriage to Claire was moving towards its eventual demise. They'd quickly discovered they had a lot in common: a love of classical music and a determined work ethic. Sarah had ambitions and she supported his own. In so many ways they were compatible. Yes, she could be tactless, and there was a definite lack of self-awareness about her at times, but she was kind, supportive and generous. She was good with Jake. Children had never been high on Sarah's agenda, but she knew he and his son came as a package and she made an effort to get along with both Jake and Claire. But then perhaps that was part of the problem: it was obvious that she was making an effort.

After dinner, Sarah said she was going to do some more work then have a soak in the bath. Denning decided to find out more about Tony Hallam. He remotely logged on to the police national computer database and typed in Hallam's name. Hallam was a career criminal, with a string of convictions for crimes often involving violence. There were reported incidents about his behaviour towards Maria: she had reported a domestic violence incident but had subsequently withdrawn it. His brother-in-law, Declan Meech, was another career criminal. They used to work together in the past, but fell out just before Hallam was sent down a year ago.

Next, he typed in Meech's name, and a lengthy string of convictions came up. There was surprisingly little to connect Meech with Hallam though, and Denning wondered just how close they'd been.

Been… past tense.

The falling-out intrigued Denning. It might be significant, or it might be nothing at all. But whatever the story, he knew he wanted to speak to Meech. Was it enough to underpin the motive for murder? He played things over in his head. If Meech did want Hallam dead, then he must know by now that he'd failed. That meant it was only a matter of time before he tried again.

Chapter Ten

Molly was trying hard not to feel like she was getting in the way. She was staying with Trudi Bell and her partner Charys; sleeping on the uncomfortable bed in the cramped spare room at the back of their flat in Limehouse. But she didn't complain. She was just grateful she had a roof over her head.

It had been nearly three months since she'd left her partner, Jon, after their relationship had inexorably ground to a full stop. Trudi had insisted she stayed with them until she got herself sorted, even though she had no idea how long that would take.

While she got on with them, it wasn't the same as having her own place. However, she realised she would be unable to buy anywhere in London on her salary, but didn't want to rent.

Charys appeared from the kitchen. 'How's it going?'

'Good, thanks. Trudi's stopped off at the Tesco Metro to buy some more wine,' Molly said. 'She shouldn't be long.'

Charys smiled and returned to the kitchen.

Both women had a thing for house plants. They were in danger of taking over the flat: a massive spider plant occupied most of the space on the coffee table and the bathroom felt like something out of a botanical garden.

Molly checked her phone for messages. Jon hadn't been in touch for a while, which was something. For the first few weeks after they split, she'd lost track of the number of voicemail and text messages he'd left for her. Sometimes they just asked her to get in touch; other times there were lengthy messages pleading forgiveness for whatever he had done to piss her off. He kept promising he would change and wanted them to try again. At first, she worried he might do something stupid, but she'd made her decision. She couldn't go back.

She pondered the decision again, as she had done every day since she'd left him. They'd been together for over five years – hardly a lifetime but long enough to allow the feelings to develop into something tangible. They had never talked about marriage – and with four unsuccessful marriages to his name, Jon's reluctance to commit to a fifth was perhaps understandable – but she had always considered their relationship to be strong. There had always been issues; the twelve-year age gap for a start. And, of course, the previous marriages. It was only when a long-lost daughter had pitched up a few months ago, relegating Molly to little more than a bit-part-player in her boyfriend's life, that she realised she was deluding herself into believing their relationship was actually going some-where. Or more to the point, it had reinforced something she'd been feeling for some time – but had mostly been pushing it to the back of her mind – the knowledge that their relationship was over.

But it still hurt. Jon had been such a massive part of her life that she still found herself thinking of things she wanted to tell him, or jokes she knew he would laugh at. A gig she knew would be perfect for them…

She couldn't entirely walk away blame-free. Her job took over their lives too often. She knew Jon had tried his best to understand. But the truth was she had found it increasingly difficult to balance her professional and personal lives. In the end, it was Jon who had to go.

She could hear Charys pottering round in the kitchen. Charys was vegetarian and Trudi supported her by not eating meat at home as much as possible, but she enjoyed the occasional Big Mac and was partial to a bacon sandwich.

She thought about Cassie Bane, now bringing up a small child on her own. And then there was the possible significance of a clingy ex… So far, their only witness had described the person seen loitering on the street before the stabbing as being of 'slim build'. Taking that into account, alongside what Cassie had said about Kieran's ex phoning, suggested their killer could be a woman. However, the witness statement clearly said the person running away was male.

Then there was Anna Klein, a CID officer based in Islington. They'd worked together on a case back in June, when Molly had discovered Klein had lied about her involvement with a suspect. After wrestling with her conscience, she'd reported Klein to Professional Standards. Despite knowing she'd done the right thing, it still niggled away at her. There was still no word on the investigation into Klein's conduct and the last Molly had heard was that she had been suspended on full pay until the investigation had been concluded. She knew Klein and Denning had been friendly, though he had backed her decision. But reporting a fellow officer for misconduct was unlikely to win her any friends in the long run. Even Trudi had been slightly shocked when she'd found out what Molly had done.

Molly was suddenly aware of Trudi coming back to the flat. 'OK, Moll?' Trudi was carrying a bag stuffed full of wine bottles, crisps and cakes into the kitchen. 'I thought we could make a night of it. Find some rubbish on Netflix or Amazon Prime, crack open a couple of bottles of white and stuff ourselves with comfort food.'

'Cool,' Charys said. 'It'll be good to let our hair down.' She looked over at Molly who tried her best to smile a response, but she knew it didn't convince either of them. Trudi and Charys were good friends, and this wasn't the first time she'd stayed with them. Just over a year previously she'd moved in for a short while after she suspected Jon might have been seeing someone behind her back. It had turned out she was mistaken but, as both Trudi and Charys had pointed out, the fact she even suspected he was having an affair should have been enough to ring warning bells. She'd chosen to ignore their advice and had regretted it ever since.

Chapter Eleven

Denning called a briefing for eight-thirty the next morning. There was depressingly little to report and even less to discuss. But only by bumping heads and throwing ideas around would the team have any chance of moving forward with this case. Sometimes it felt like trying to make water flow uphill.

The team were sitting around their desks in the large, air-conditioned room that served as their office. Ordinarily, the building contained several conference rooms that were better suited for briefings, but Denning had learned that his team preferred the intimacy and familiarity of the main office.

'The knife used to stab Kieran Judd still hasn't been found,' he said, addressing his team. 'Forensics have discovered some DNA traces we believe belong to our killer, but unhelpfully they don't match anyone on file, and there is still nothing useful from CCTV. The PM results will be sent over later this morning, but I've got the edited highlights here.' He held up a grey folder. 'Apparently the angle of penetration confirms that our assailant was of average height and right-handed. The only saving grace is that it would have been quick.'

'Our victim probably didn't know what was happening until the blade was stuck in his guts,' Kinsella said, shaking his head.

'The PM report also confirms that Kieran Judd was stabbed in the abdominal aorta,' Denning continued, ignoring Kinsella, 'resulting in considerable blood loss.'

'So, our killer was either very lucky, or he knew what he was doing,' Kinsella said. He was eating his breakfast at his desk: a McDonald's sausage and egg McMuffin and a milkshake. Some of the McMuffin's contents had made their way onto the front of his shirt. 'That kind of stabbing is almost always fatal.'

'It's possible to find that kind of information on the internet,' Trudi said. She had a mug of steaming coffee on her desk. Denning had heard from the rumour mill that Molly had recently split from her boyfriend and was now staying in Trudi Bell's spare room. He wondered if that was going to put a strain on their friendship and, more importantly, their working relationship.

'Or from watching a good crime drama on the telly,' Neeraj added.

'Which are we going with, then?' Kinsella asked. 'Lucky or well informed?'

'Right now, we need to establish a motive,' Denning said. 'And we still need to confirm who the intended target was. I've arranged another round of door-to-door enquires in case there's someone who hasn't been spoken to and who might have seen something.'

'Well, here's hoping for a more productive result this time,' Kinsella said, 'because the first lot of witness statements threw up naff all.'

'OK, we keep looking and we keep asking around,' Denning said. 'Molly, you reckon we can rule out the neighbour behind the parking dispute?'

'He's an arsehole, but I don't think he's a killer,' she said. 'Besides, his alibi checks out. It looks like that was all something and nothing.'

'Personally, I still think we should be looking into Meech and Hallam having a falling-out,' Kinsella said. 'If Hallam has betrayed Meech, he'll want blood.'

'Why would Hallam have betrayed Meech?' Trudi asked. 'I thought they were friends.'

Kinsella gave a snort. 'Rumour has it Hallam blamed Meech for him being sent down last time. Apparently, he wanted to get his own back and was going to sell Meech down the Swanee. There was plenty he could tell if he was in a particularly talkative mood. Meech got word to Hallam to keep his lips sealed, or else. Must have done the trick because next thing Hallam's saying he knows nothing about his brother-in-law's dodgy dealings.'

'So Meech threatened Hallam?' Denning asked.

'Impossible to prove,' Kinsella said, 'but whatever he said, it did the trick. Hallam backed down.'

'So why would Meech go after Hallam now?' Neeraj asked.

'As long as Hallam is a free man, he's a potential danger to Meech. Men like Meech don't like risks and Hallam's loose lips are a risk. He knows the gory details about their previous crimes and probably a hell of a lot of stuff that isn't on record.'

'What are we talking about here?' Denning asked. 'Apart from armed robbery.' He'd looked Meech up on the PNC: a list of crimes and convictions stretching back years. But he was more interested in what wasn't on record: what had Meech been rumoured to have got away with over the years. Kinsella was the best man to ask. He'd been a copper for years; since the days when police officers got most of the information from informants and fellow criminals willing to do deals to save their own sorry skins.

'There's what we know about,' Kinsella said, 'and then there's all the other stuff. The stuff we could never make stick.'

Denning hated the expression 'make stick': good policing was about ensuring a case was solid enough to put before the CPS, relying on evidence rather than having to make it stick.

'Anything specific?' Denning asked.

'There was a nasty rumour Meech was part of the Security Direct robbery,' Kinsella said, 'though obviously nothing was ever proved, just like for most of the major players involved in Security Direct.'

Denning knew about Security Direct: twenty years ago, a warehouse was robbed at gunpoint by several armed men. Millions of pounds were stolen. Only part of the proceeds was ever recovered and a handful of men sent down. Former crime boss Alfie Kane had always been suspected of being the brains behind it, but Kane had gone to great lengths to be considered a respectable businessman now and any mention of his alleged involvement in the Security Direct job was met by a firm rebuttal from his lawyers.

'Assault and robbery?' Denning asked. 'But there's no mention of murder?'

Kinsella looked blank. 'There's nothing on record, admittedly. But let's be honest, it's not a great leap from that level of violence to murder.'

'What about Hallam?' Trudi asked. 'How does he fit into it?'

'Small league compared with his brother-in-law,' Kinsella said. 'Mostly hanging on Meech's shirt tails. His background is mostly petty crime: shoplifting from an early age; car crime. It was only after he married Meech's sister that he started running with the big boys.'

'Might be worth finding out exactly what it is Hallam has on Meech and why Meech feels the need to silence him,' Denning said. 'Dave, can you look into the history between Meech and Hallam. Find out why they fell out. And get on to the prison where Hallam was serving his sentence... find out if he had any visitors or received any letters around the time he changed his mind about spilling the beans on Meech.'

Kinsella nodded. 'I can ask around. I've got a contact in CID who should be able to point me in the right direction.'

Trudi Bell was shaking her head. 'I can't see it somehow.'

'Why not?' Kinsella responded as though she was challenging him personally.

'Whatever lies behind their falling-out, Tony Hallam is still married to Declan Meech's sister. Would he really be prepared to put his own sister through that?'

'Families,' Kinsella said. 'I've known families do far worse to each other for much less.'

'Besides,' Neeraj added, 'they're separated.'

'They've still got children, though. A boy and a girl. They're Meech's nephew and niece. Would he really be prepared to leave them without a father just because he's worried Hallam might say something he shouldn't?'

'We can't rule it out as a possibility, Trudi,' Denning said. He turned to look at the whiteboard behind him. There were photographs of Kieran Judd and the murder scene, but little else at this stage. 'In the meantime, what else have we got?'

'We're chasing up any CCTV from the area,' Neeraj said. 'However, the street itself doesn't have much, and there's bugger all in the way of doorbell footage.'

'I'm working my way through our witness statements,' Trudi added. 'Though apart from the report of a "hooded figure running down the street", we've got Jack Shit to go on.'

'OK, then we keep looking and keep asking.' Denning nodded at Molly, who was waving a Biro at him.

'About this witness statement,' she said. 'Going by our, admittedly vague, description: could it be a woman?' Her comment was met with silence by her colleagues.

'I spoke to Cassie again last night,' she continued. 'She mentioned an ex of Kieran's who might be worth talking to. Seems she had issues about Kieran leaving her for Cassie. She calmed down eventually, but Cassie thinks it's possible she might have got in touch the other day. Just before Kieran was murdered.'

Denning wasn't convinced, but he knew they had to keep all options on the table. 'Could just be a coincidence, but probably better to look into it anyway. Have you got contact details for the ex?'

'I've got an address.' Cassie had provided the inform-ation, though she'd kept insisting she wasn't sure it had been Scarlett on the other end of the phone.

'Then have a word with her. At the very least we want to rule out Judd as the intended target.' He looked at the team. 'I'm expecting the post-mortem details to be emailed through later this morning, so that might offer some possibilities. Let's hope we get a lucky break soon.'

Chapter Twelve

Scarlett Rennie lived in a small flat beside a bus stop on St Paul's Road in Islington. She was in her early twenties, short and blonde. She pulled a face when Molly explained who she was and why she was there.

They were sitting in her flat, no offer of tea or coffee. A bus had pulled up at the bus stop outside and the chugging of the engine shook the flat's thin windows.

'I was sorry to hear about Kieran,' she said. 'He didn't deserve that. But I don't see why you think I've got something to do with it. I haven't seen Kieran for more than a year.'

'We're speaking to everyone who knew Kieran,' Molly said. 'So far we have yet to establish a reason for his murder.'

'So why are you speaking to me? I haven't seen Kieran for ages.'

'As I say,' Molly continued, 'we're speaking to everyone who knew Kieran. We need to establish a motive for what, at the moment, has all the hallmarks of a motiveless killing.'

Her jaw dropped open. 'You don't think I had a reason, do you? I loved Kieran. We were going to settle down together. We probably would have if *she* hadn't chanced along.'

'So, Kieran left you for Cassie?'

She pulled a face. 'It wasn't quite as simple as that. Kieran and I went through a bit of a bad patch. Well... it wasn't that exactly. He started behaving oddly. Drinking a lot more than he used to and sulking. I didn't know what it was about. It was like he had something on his mind.'

'Did you ask him?'

'Of course I did. If there was something bothering him, then he didn't want to talk about it. Said it was something and nothing. But he changed. I suggested we had a trial separation. I thought the shock of that would bring him to his senses, but it had the opposite effect.'

'That's when he met Cassie?'

'She was a friend of a friend. She'd moved to London to do some course or other. Anyway, the next thing I knew was when I suggested we give things another go and he tells me he's seeing someone else. I thought it was only a flash in the pan, but then he tells me they're having a baby together.'

'Cassie claims you harassed them. Is there any truth in that?'

'She's a liar. I never "harassed" them. Me and Kieran had stuff to discuss; there was unfinished business between us, but he didn't want to know. He said it was over and he didn't want to talk to me.'

'So you didn't phone them on the night in question?'

'No. He changed his mobile number, so how could I?'

'They kept the same number for their landline?'

'Why would I bother? I mean, what would be the point?'

'You tell me? You said you and Kieran had unfinished business. What exactly was that business?'

'Private business, that's what.'

'Kieran's dead,' Molly reminded her. 'This *is* a murder investigation. If this "unfinished business" has any bearing on the case, I need to know.'

Scarlett looked at the floor, shook her head and signed. 'OK. Kieran had a credit card still registered to this address.' She raised her arms by her head, frustrated, and looked Molly in the eyes. 'They kept sending stuff here. I didn't know if he owed them money. I didn't want to find myself on a credit blacklist, did I?'

'Were they threatening?'

'I don't know, do I. I didn't open his sodding mail.'

Debt, thought Molly. If Kieran owed someone money and wasn't able to repay them then that could be a reason for wanting him dead. But a credit card company would have sent bailiffs round rather than hire a contract killer to hunt him down. But if he owned other people money...

'What happened in the end?'

'I went to Citizens Advice. They said if I contact the credit card company and tell them he's moved then they'd stop bothering me. I did and they did.' She gave an indifferent shrug. 'I should have thought of that in the first place.'

'And that was it? You didn't have any reason to contact him after that?'

She huffed. 'Me and Kieran said all we needed to say. I accepted it was over and he'd found someone else. I can't say I was happy about it, but there's no point trying to flog a dead horse, is there?'

'OK, so just for reasons of elimination, can I ask where you were yesterday evening?'

She shot Molly a withering look. 'Seriously? You really think it was me who stabbed Kieran?'

'I'm happy to let you prove me wrong,' Molly said.

Scarlett Rennie sighed. 'I was working. I work in a pub in Stoke Newington and I was on late shift last night. The Jolly Kinsman on Chatton Road. You can check with the manager.'

Molly made a mental note. Despite her claims to the contrary, she wasn't so sure Rennie had got over Kieran quite as easily as she was claiming. 'Tell me about Kieran,' she prompted. 'How long were the two of you together?'

She looked at Molly for a moment as though unsure whether to answer her questions.

'About two years. Maybe a bit longer.'

'And you were happy together?'

'What kind of question is that? Of course we were happy. We wouldn't have stayed together for so long if we weren't.'

Molly wasn't so sure. Couples sometimes deluded themselves into believing they were happier than they actually were. Sometimes they stayed together for convenience rather than any other reason. 'I'm sorry,' she said. 'I'm not prying. I'm just trying to build a clearer picture of Kieran.'

'Well, what can I tell you? We were together and then we weren't.'

'What kind of man was he?'

She shrugged. 'A normal bloke. Never in any trouble. There's no reason why someone would want to kill him.'

But the fact was that someone had killed Kieran Judd and, until they knew for certain that he hadn't been the intended target, Molly and the team had to explore every possibility. 'When you said he always seemed unsettled... why was that?'

'I just got the impression he wasn't happy with his lot in life. He was always unsettled. He had wanted to be a teacher for a while, but suddenly changed direction for no reason and seemed unhappy. I think this was one of the reasons we split up.'

'A teacher?' Molly was beginning to build a picture of Kieran Judd. 'What happened?'

Scarlett stared at her for a second. She clearly resented the intrusion into her life and the questions about someone who was no longer a part of it. After a moment she shook her head and said: 'He changed his mind. I don't know why. We were living together at the time, but we were spending most of our days arguing. Money, mostly. I think the main reason he wanted to be a teacher was because the money was better. But then again, it could have been anything. He was always restless.'

'But it was money you argued about? Nothing else?'

She gave Molly another look. 'Mostly, yeah. The usual stuff couples argue over.' She gave her another look, which said *I'm sure you know what I'm talking about.*

'When was this?'

'About two years ago. It was just after that he left. Just walked out one day and never came back.'

'No reason?'

'If there was, he didn't tell me. Next thing I know he's shacked up with someone new and they've got a kid together. He left me to manage the rent on this place on my tod. Luckily, my mum helped out with the rent, then I changed jobs. I'm assistant manager at the Kinsman, so the money's not too bad.'

Molly was thinking things over. Something clearly happened two years ago to make Kieran Judd suddenly up sticks and walk out of a relationship. She had a feeling that whatever that was, it was somehow relevant to his murder.

'And you have no idea why he left? There was no big argument? No moment that sparked his decision to walk out?'

'Like I've already told you, no. The only person who could answer that question is Kieran and you're too late to ask it now.'

Chapter Thirteen

Declan Meech was a difficult man to track down. Of course, it was possible he wanted it that way. They knew he was no fan of the police and his record showed he was someone who was happy to treat the law with a lack of respect.

They eventually found him in a breaker's yard in Dagenham, sourcing spare parts for a car he claimed to be restoring.

'What is this?' he asked when Denning and Neeraj approached him, eyes searching them warily, as though anticipating trouble. He wasn't a tall man, Denning reckoned just over five feet, which tallied with the only description they had of Kieran Judd's killer. But what Meech lacked in height, he more than made up for in bulk. He was stocky and compact, and looked like he could easily handle himself in a fight. His skin was badly pockmarked. He was dressed in a pair of oil-stained jeans and a grubby T-shirt with a faded logo on the front.

'We'd like to speak to you about your brother-in-law,' Denning said. 'Tony Hallam.'

Meech was holding an old gearbox. He examined it, turning it over in his hands, then threw it back onto a heap of scrap. 'I ain't seen him for months. Not since the twat got himself sent down. And frankly, I'd be very happy if I never set eyes on him again.'

'Why do you say that, Mr Meech?' Neeraj asked.

Meech observed Neeraj for a few seconds as if contemplating whether or not to answer the question. 'The man's a waste of skin. Maria and the kids are better off having nothing to do with him.'

'We have reason to believe his life might be in danger,' Denning said calmly. 'Just wondered if you knew anything about that?'

Meech turned to look at the two men and gave a low, guttural laugh. 'Well, that doesn't surprise me, but I'm afraid I can't help you gents. If someone has got a grudge against Tony, then you need to get looking elsewhere.' He picked up what looked like part of an exhaust and examined it. 'I admit I don't particularly like the geezer, but I don't have any reason to wish him dead either.'

'But the two of you did fall out?' Denning asked, making it sound more like a statement. 'About the time he was sent down? And you blamed him for what he put your sister through.'

He was still examining the exhaust. 'Tony and Maria were none of my business. I know better than to interfere between a man and his missus.'

'Even if the man in question was being physically abusive to his wife and the wife happened to be your sister? And then there's the children? Your nephew and niece. It can't be easy for you knowing their father is a violent man.'

Meech looked at Denning, then glanced over at Neeraj. He was sizing them up, as though tempted to take them both on in a fight. He tossed the exhaust back on the ground and moved over to another pile of scrap, then rummaged through it for something. 'He never harmed those kids. Maria would never have let him. She dotes on them. She'd kill him if he even laid a finger on either of them.'

'Really?' Neeraj asked.

Meech stopped rummaging in the scrap pile and turned to face them.

'Not *literally*. It's a figure of speech. Maria would never harm a fly. That's her trouble. Too damned soft. She's always letting blokes walk all over her.'

'Including Tony Hallam?' Denning asked.

'Doesn't mean she'd try to kill the sod. And nor would I, if that's what all this is about.'

'So, you're telling me you don't know of anyone who would want to harm Tony Hallam?' Denning asked. He could sense the unfriendly vibes coming off Meech, like body odour.

'Like I've already told you both, I haven't seen Hallam since before he went into prison almost a year ago.' He swaggered over to another pile of junk, kicking some of it with his foot. A thin pall of rusty dust blew into the air. 'I still don't see why you lot are wasting your time talking to me. If someone is out to get Tony, you're better off speaking to him.'

'Well, right now we're speaking to you, Mr Meech. Because we think you might be able to come up with some good answers to our questions. The first one being, why did you and Tony Hallam fall out when he went to prison?'

Meech sighed. 'Hallam reckoned I was responsible for him being sent down. He blamed me and threated to run to you lot with all sorts of stories about how I was everything from Jack the Ripper to Reggie Kray. It was all a load of old pony, but since when did you lot ever give a toss about the truth?'

'And were you responsible for getting him sent down?' Denning asked. 'It would certainly get him away from Maria and the children. Could all be very convenient?'

'Except he was only sent down for a couple of years. What was going to happen when he got out?'

'Somebody kills him?' Neeraj offered.

'Look, he's been warned by you lot to keep away from Maria and the kids. As far as I'm aware, Tony hasn't been near them since he got out. She'd have said if he'd been bothering her and she hasn't said a word so, as far as I'm concerned, he's behaving himself. If someone does want to do him, then they'd need a better motive than that.'

'Do you think it's possible he could harm Maria and the children now he's out?' Denning asked. 'It could be she's scared of him and doesn't want to drag you or anyone else into it.'

'How the hell would I know? I can't read that girl's head at the best of times. If she's got a problem with Tony, she either comes to you lot or she asks me. As far as I know, she hasn't done either.'

Denning was weighing things up in his mind. He believed Meech when he said Maria hadn't mentioned anything about feeling threatened by Hallam. But that didn't mean Meech didn't have another potential motive for wanting him dead.

'So what might Hallam have told us if he'd gone ahead and informed on you?'

'What do you mean?'

'It's a straightforward question,' Denning said. 'You told us he'd threatened to run to us with all sorts of stories about you. What kind of stories are we talking about?'

Meech threw a piece of engine on the ground, where it landed with a clang. 'Made-up ones, that's what. Tony was full of shit. Probably still is. I reckon you'll find that out for yourselves soon enough.' He stood with his hands in his pockets staring at both men, willing them to defy him. 'The guy's a loser; a waste of space. We're all glad he's out of our lives.' He fixed Denning with a heavy stare. 'But that doesn't mean I wanted him dead. If you think that, you're off your heads. Are we finished?'

Denning smiled at Meech. 'For now, Mr Meech. But if anything does happen to Tony Hallam, then I have a feeling we'll need to speak to you again.'

With that, they turned and headed back to the car.

Chapter Fourteen

Molly had had no luck tracing the call that Cassie suspected might have come from Scarlett Rennie. The tech team had traced it back to a pay-as-you-go mobile. They could try and track the mobile through the service provider, but it would take time. Alternatively, Molly could just ask Rennie if she owned a pay-as-you-go mobile phone. She wasn't sure exactly how much time and effort she was supposed to be investing in this. Denning had asked her to look into Kieran Judd's life and see if she could find anything that either didn't make sense or raised alarm bells, even though she'd got the impression from the briefing that he was convinced Declan Meech was behind this and Tony Hallam the intended target. But whatever the case, it really did feel like searching through a haystack for the proverbial needle. Kieran Judd seemed to have led a blameless life. According to his employers he ran several sports sessions for young children during the school holidays and half-term. He didn't get paid for them and organised the events himself in his own time. He also supported a couple of local children's charities: children with special needs and a charity that supported the children of single parents. Molly had briefly considered exploring the uncomfortable possibility that Kieran might have had closeted paedophile tendencies – it would certainly have given someone a motive for killing him – but nothing had come up on the database and there had never been any complaints made about him all the time he'd worked at the leisure centre. She did think about digging deeper: previous employers; other places he'd lived… but she sensed she was heading straight for a dead end. There was nothing to suggest Kieran Judd was a paedophile. She had the distinct impression that Denning was still convinced Tony Hallam was the intended victim, and wanted little more than a token bit of digging into Kieran Judd's background. Of course, she could be misreading that. Denning was a shrewd detective; she trusted his judgement, but even clever coppers got it wrong from time to time.

There was still the question of the mystery caller: someone had specifically asked for Kieran Judd by name, at least according to Cassie. Despite her being the obvious candidate, she didn't think Rennie was the caller in question. Unless she was a very good actress, she'd made a convincing effort at persuading Molly she was over Kieran. But did people really get over relationships that easily? She thought about Jon. She'd noticed another message from him on her phone. She hadn't bothered reading it; she knew what it would say.

Was it fair to compare Rennie with Jon? Molly reckoned she still had feelings for Judd, despite her claims to the contrary. But none of this suggested she was responsible for killing him. They'd split up over a year ago. Why would she wait until now to kill him? It didn't make any sense.

She was sitting at her desk, reading over the witness statements. The description given of the person running away was suitably vague. The witness – a woman in her late seventies – wasn't sure if the person running away was male or female.

It was possible that CCTV had thrown something up. 'Trudi,' she shouted over, 'have we got any useful CCTV from the night of the murder yet?'

Bell shook her head. 'There's something from one of the main roads. A bloke seen acting suspiciously, but it turns out he was waiting for a lift. He's been traced and spoken to by uniform. He was buying a kebab at the time of the murder. Both CCTV from the kebab shop and the guy who works there have confirmed it.'

'Cheers, babe.' Great. That didn't help. She read over more witness statements. Despite it being a well-populated residential street, with people returning from work, no one had seen or heard anything. The only description they had wasn't much use to anyone.

And then there was Kieran Judd himself. No one had a bad word to say about him. Even his ex-partner admitted he was an all right bloke.

She began to think Denning must be right, and Kieran wasn't the target. In which case, she was wasting her time looking into his life. But something niggled at her. Something Rennie had said about how Kieran had suddenly changed…

She rubbed a hand over her eyes. What did that matter? People changed all the time. She had. A year ago, she would have defended her relationship with Jon to the hilt. Now she had to admit she'd got it wrong. But what had happened to Kieran Judd to turn him into a different person? Somehow, for some reason, she thought this was relevant.

Chapter Fifteen

Jasper Avenue was an upmarket street not far from Alexandra Palace. A street that was dominated by impressive, semi-detached Edwardian villas with tidy gardens and bay windows. Only the blue-and-white police tape that dangled between a lamppost and a tree outside number fourteen that morning indicated anything wrong inside.

Denning was greeted by Sheila Gorton, whose face was grave. 'Another one for you, Inspector,' she said dryly as he climbed into his protective suit.

'Why did you specifically ask for me?' His initial thought had been to pass this over to one of the other MITs as they were already running round in circles trying to find Kieran Judd's killer. The last thing he needed on his plate right now was another murder.

'You'll see,' she said, and led the way into the living room in the front of the house. The room was tidy, smartly decorated with high ceilings. Pictures on the walls and light furnishings. The body on the rug in front of the fireplace was the focus of attention. Blood was drying on the light-coloured rug.

'Susan Elliot,' Gorton said. 'A primary school teacher. Cleaner found her this morning. She's been stabbed in the abdomen. Same as Kieran Judd.'

Denning knelt down next to the body. Susan Elliot was in her early forties. Smartly dressed, with a grey skirt and white blouse, most of which was now stained red with her blood. 'Robbery…?'

'Initial evidence would suggest not,' Gorton replied. 'It doesn't look as though anything's been taken. We've found her bag. There's money and credit cards in her purse.'

Denning looked around the room: the TV was in the corner and there was a laptop on a desk by the window. 'They could have been disturbed? Fled empty-handed?'

'There's no sign of a break-in. It's likely she let the killer in, suggesting it was someone she knew.' She gestured for Denning to join her in the hallway while the CSIs worked around her and the photographer took pictures. 'A single stab wound, Matt,' she said. 'The same as Kieran Judd. This can't be a coincidence.'

He thought about this. People being stabbed to death in London was hardly news. But he couldn't ignore the significance of two people being stabbed to death so close to each other in worryingly similar circumstances.

'Did she live alone?'

'Husband's in Aberdeen at a conference on sustainable energy. Police Scotland have notified him. Two grown-up children, according to the cleaner. She's in the kitchen, still in shock. Probably not too much she can tell you. Her name's Linda Feltham, by the way.'

Denning headed into the kitchen, which was as spotless as the living room. Smart white units and polished grey tiles on the floor. The cleaner was sitting at a table staring into a mug of tea that one of the uniformed officers had probably made for her. Denning sat down next to her.

'Mrs Feltham?'

She nodded, still clutching her tea.

'I'm Detective Inspector Denning from the Met's Homicide Command Unit. I need to ask you a few questions about Mrs Elliot.'

She placed the mug of tea on the table. 'I've told the other man everything I can,' she said. 'I don't know what happened.'

'I appreciate that,' he said calmly, 'but if you could just tell it to me, it would help.'

She took a deep breath. 'I arrived for work as usual...'

'What time was that?'

'Eight-thirty. Well, just after. The bus was late. I let myself in and everything seemed normal. I usually start work in the kitchen, but I noticed the sitting room door was open, usually it's shut. They don't like the cat going in there as he scratches the furniture. I looked in the room and Mrs Elliot was lying there... I thought at first that she'd maybe fallen and hit her head, but then I could see she was bleeding from her stomach. It was horrible.' She covered her face with her hands. Denning waited until she'd regained her composure. 'Sorry. It was just so horrible. I've never seen anyone dead before.'

'I understand. It isn't nice for anyone.' Denning had been a copper for a long time and he still struggled with seeing people murdered. It didn't get any easier as the years passed. 'Did you see anyone when you got here this morning? Either hanging around the house or in the street outside?'

'No. Mind you, I'm in a world of my own when I'm walking down the street. But no, there was no one else here... I haven't even seen the cat today.'

She looked around her as though suddenly aware the animal wasn't where he should be.

'It's all right,' Denning said. 'He's probably just in the garden somewhere.' He glanced out the glass doors into the wide expanse of greenery that was the back garden. 'Was Mrs Elliot usually here when you arrived for work?'

A shake of the head. 'No. She always left for work early. She's a teacher at a primary school in Finchley. Our Lady of the Sacred Heart, or something like that. She's usually in first thing. The only time I really see her is during school holidays.'

'Do you know if the Elliots have any children?' he asked.

She shrugged. 'Mr Elliot had two kids from his first marriage, but they don't live at home anymore. I don't know where they live.'

'And Mr Elliot: what's he like?'

'I hardly ever see him. He works away from home a lot. He's an IT consultant. I'm not sure exactly what it is he does. I think he advises people on their IT systems. I've only met him a couple of times. He seems all right. He's going to be devastated.'

Denning tried to reassure her. 'Specially trained police officers will speak to him. Can you give me your contact details please, Mrs Feltham. I may need to speak to you again. And I'm afraid I'm going to have to ask you to leave. The house is now a crime scene.'

'Will I still get paid for today?' she asked nervously. 'I need the money.'

'I'm afraid I can't say. You'll probably have to take that up with Mr Elliot, though he may well have other things on his mind right now. How did Mrs Elliot pay you?'

She looked sheepish. 'She gave me cash at the end of the week. I mean, I always declare it,' she added quickly.

Denning suspected he was witnessing an example of the black economy at work, but at the present moment in time, that wasn't really of concern to him. 'Look, don't worry. Your working arrangements with your employer aren't any of my concern. I only want to find out who murdered Mrs Elliot. Anything else isn't relevant.'

She scribbled her contact details on a Post-it note and handed it to him. He asked a uniformed officer to show her out the back door, after he'd taken her fingerprints. He assured her this was for nothing more than elimination purposes. He was pretty confident she wasn't their suspect.

Back in the hallway he was joined by Gorton and Neeraj. 'Did you get anything useful from the cleaner?' Neeraj asked.

'She didn't see anyone when she got here, which means whoever did it must have been quick and here early.'

'Body's still warm,' Gorton confirmed, 'she's been dead for less than a couple of hours.'

'So, whoever did it must have got here early,' Neeraj said. 'I'd say that suggests it was planned.'

'If this wasn't a random attack, then they must have been familiar with her movements,' Denning said.

'You think she was deliberately targeted, boss?' Neeraj asked.

'Right now, Deep, I don't know what I think.'

'Obviously it's for the post-mortem to confirm it,' Gorton added, 'but I would say the stab wound is almost identical to Kieran Judd's.'

He looked at the house. A smart, middle-class property owned by a professional couple. There was nothing here to link their victim to either Kieran Judd or Tony Hallam. Their worlds were poles apart. Despite Sheila Gorton's claim, this had to be a coincidence. But he didn't believe

86

in coincidences. Two people stabbed to death in their own homes in the past week – this couldn't be a coincidence. But right now, he couldn't imagine it being anything else.

Chapter Sixteen

Denning called another briefing. His gut feeling still told him this was down to Declan Meech. He was certain Meech was somehow key to all this. But that was assuming the two murders were linked. There was, as yet, no evidence to support Sheila Gorton's assertion that the two murders were in any way connected. But even Deep Neeraj had insisted the chances of two people being stabbed to death in their own home and there not being a connection, had to be slim. *A coincidence…?* They couldn't rule it out, at least not until they'd exhausted every other option.

'Susan Elliot,' he said, addressing the room. 'Aged forty-two. A primary school teacher, married, no children.' He hadn't yet spoken to Laurence Elliot, the husband, but they had managed to get some information from him, despite him being in a state of shock. 'Her husband will formally identify her when he gets back to London later this afternoon, but the cleaning lady is certain our victim is definitely Mrs Elliot. We have no motive for her murder, and can rule out sexual assault and robbery.'

'Unless they were disturbed?' Trudi Bell said. 'Threatened her into telling them where her valuables were, she refused to comply and was stabbed as a result.

Before they have a chance to ransack the place, the cleaning lady turns up for work.'

'The crime scene people seem to think that isn't how it happened, Trudi,' Denning said. 'They reckon it was quick and neat. Someone knew what they were doing... killed Susan Elliot and then were straight out of there.'

He gestured at the whiteboard. There were the usual victim photos framed by general pictures of the crime scene, plus a plan of the ground floor of the Elliots' house.

'So, what have we got?' Dave Kinsella asked.

'The post-mortem will give us a clearer indication, but it looks like a single stab wound to the stomach, puncturing the abdominal aorta resulting in significant blood loss,' Denning said.

'Same as Kieran Judd,' Kinsella said.

'And just like Kieran, our killer was either very lucky or knew what he was doing,' Denning added.

'Yet we're still treating these two murders as unconnected?' Molly said.

'Until we can find an obvious link,' Denning said, 'then yes.'

'But we can't ignore the obvious similarities,' Kinsella said. 'At least we'd be pretty stupid if we did.'

'What does her husband say?' Molly asked.

'He claims his wife hadn't been threatened by anyone recently and, to his knowledge, had never been in any kind of trouble. So we have to ask ourselves why someone would want to kill her.' He looked at his team, hoping to find some answers, but he suspected they were as much in the dark as he was.

'We're certain she let the killer into the property?' Trudi Bell asked. 'There's definitely no sign of a break-in?'

'The CSIs have been over the house… back door locked, windows shut and the cleaning lady has confirmed that the front door was locked when she arrived at work that morning.'

'So we're assuming the killer was let into the house, then locked the door when they left?' Kinsella asked.

'The front door's on a latch, Dave,' Denning said. 'It would have locked automatically when they shut it.'

'Did the killer know her husband wasn't at home?' Molly asked. 'If so, perhaps she was deliberately targeted? An attempted sexual assault. She fights back, he kills her?'

'Possible, but the crime scene manager couldn't see any signs of sexual assault. Obviously if the post-mortem says otherwise, then we look at that possibility.'

'I take it there's the usual lack of witnesses,' Kinsella said.

'Despite the fact the time of death suggests the murder happened early on, when people would have been leaving to go to work. There would have been people around. But, so far, door-to-door enquiries haven't come up with anything. Obviously we'll keep going, but so far our killer seems to have been very lucky.'

'Especially with their timing,' Molly said. 'They were in and out before the cleaner called round.'

'They must have been watching the place,' Trudi said. 'They knew there was a window between her leaving for work and the cleaning lady calling round.'

'Then there's the big question we're all thinking,' Kinsella said. 'Does this tie in with Kieran Judd, and if so, how?'

Denning turned to the two whiteboards: one was laid out with the details of Kieran Judd's murder, the other, which had been hastily assembled that morning, was devoted to Susan Elliot. Photos of her home and her blood-stained body. He looked at the two boards and the two victims: what, if anything, linked them? A middle-aged woman and a man in his twenties? Then there was Susan Elliot and Tony Hallam: certainly, they were closer in age, if that was relevant. Poles apart socially, but that was probably even less relevant than how old they were. But his gut was still saying this was where the link was. It *had* to be…

'I think we should be looking for something that connects Tony Hallam with Susan Elliot,' he said. 'Or Susan Elliot with Declan Meech.'

'What about Kieran Judd?' Molly asked. 'We still haven't confirmed that he wasn't the intended target.'

Denning thought about this. Everything told him this wasn't an avenue worth pursuing, but a nagging voice in the back of his head said they weren't yet in a position to conclusively rule it out.

'OK,' he said reluctantly. 'As you're already on the case, Molly, see if there's anything that connects Susan Elliot and Kieran Judd.'

Though in his heart he hoped there was nothing that linked them.

Chapter Seventeen

Laurence Elliot was a mild-mannered man in his mid-fifties. He had neatly trimmed brown hair and a pale complexion, and was dressed in a navy jacket and open-necked pale shirt with a motif on the lapel. He'd told Molly he was staying with a friend in Twickenham until Forensics had finished in his house, so he agreed to meet her in the lounge bar of The St Margaret's Hotel, halfway between Twickenham and Richmond.

'Susan and I have only been separated for a few months,' he said. 'It was a second marriage for both of us but, in hindsight, we probably rushed into it. I work away from home a lot, so we agreed Susan was to stay in the house until we could sell it.' He gazed at Molly through a pair of horn-rimmed glasses, the sort she hadn't seen anyone wear for over a decade.

A waiter hovered nearby and Molly ordered a pot of tea for them. 'Had you been together long?' she asked.

'That's the tragic thing,' he said. 'We'd only been married for about a year.'

'Sometimes these things just don't work out,' she said, as much for something to say.

'Susan was never really happy. At first I thought it might be me. My first wife always complained that she found me dull. I actually thought that was something in my favour with Susan.' He smiled awkwardly. 'Well, maybe not "dull", but reassuring. Safe.'

The waiter arrived with their tea, placing the pot and two cups on the table. 'Tell me about Susan?' Molly asked.

'I don't really know what I can tell you. We met through mutual friends. We'd both been single for some time and were looking for company more than anything else. Initially we clicked, but then after a few months we realised we'd probably made a mistake. I had secretly been hoping we might agree to give things another go. That's one of the reasons I wasn't in any hurry to sell the house. Susan, however, was adamant it was over. She was already looking at buying a flat nearer to where she worked.' He poured out two cups of tea, asking if Molly took milk and sugar.

'Just milk,' she said.

He handed her the cup and added milk and two lumps of sugar to his cup before stirring it.

'She was a teacher?' Molly asked.

'Yes. A primary school in Finchley. She hadn't been there for very long. A couple of years, I think. She was very conscientious. She was hoping to make deputy head soon.'

Molly sipped her tea. Earl Grey, she noted. 'And she had no enemies that you knew of? There were no issues at work that concerned her?' Molly asked, but couldn't imagine the politics of a primary school were the sort that would result in murder.

'No. She enjoyed working at the school. She got on with everyone: staff, pupils and parents. It's a good school with a good reputation.' He stared at his cup. 'She did say something strange about a week ago… a couple of days before I left for Aberdeen.'

'Go on,' Molly prompted.

'She said she thought someone had been following her. I asked her to be more specific, but she said she thought she was probably over-reacting.'

'She didn't report this to anyone?'

'I don't think so. I said that if she was worried to contact the police. She said she thought she was just being paranoid.' He sighed and rubbed a hand over his face. 'It feels very odd speaking about Susan in the past tense. I know we weren't together anymore, but I still cared about her. It was horrible having to identify her body at the mortuary. I don't think that's something I'm ever going to get over in a hurry.'

Molly smiled sympathetically at him. There was something very likeable about Laurence Elliot, despite, or maybe because of, his self-professed dullness.

'You said Susan had been married before. Do you know if her first husband is still around?'

'I never knew much about him, to be honest. He died shortly after they split up. A heart attack, I believe.' His forehead wrinkled. 'You don't think it's got anything to with...' He looked awkward as if he was struggling to say what he was thinking. 'Relationships? Susan had had other relationships before she met me. Nothing serious, just casual flings. At least that's what she told me.'

'At this stage we're keeping an open mind about Susan's murder, Mr Elliot, but if you happen to have names or contact details of anyone Susan had been involved with, it would be very helpful. At the very least we'll need to eliminate them from our investigation.'

'Yes. Yes, of course.' He paused and sipped his tea before placing the cup back in the saucer. 'There were only a couple as far as I know. I don't want to give you the impression Susan slept around. Far from it. I think she just wanted a bit of company. Nothing more than that.'

'Of course. I'm not suggesting anything. It's just we've got to look into every aspect of her life, especially if there's no obvious motive for her murder. It's entirely possible this could have been a random attack... an opportunist who was frightened off, or a casual thief. However, we think there's a good chance Susan knew her killer and let them in to the house.'

'It's just...' He took another sip of tea, finished it, then placed the empty cup and saucer on the table. He was clearly struggling to say something else. 'I think Susan might have been seeing someone else, though I can't be certain.'

Molly was suddenly paying more attention. 'Recently, you mean?'

He looked embarrassed; uncomfortable at the thought of talking about a woman he clearly still had feelings for, even if those feelings hadn't been reciprocated for a long time.

'I can't be certain. It's just... little things, you know. Phone calls and she would tell the person on the other end of the line that she would call them back. Disappearing for weekends, supposedly staying with friends, but then being vague about where she'd been and who these friends were.' He gave a diffident smile. 'I could have been imagining it, of course, but sometimes you just get a feeling, don't you?'

Molly nodded. He was right. When it came to relationships sometimes it was almost possible to second guess what your partner was thinking. She used to do it with Jon all the time. It was one of the reasons she knew the spark had gone out of their relationship for both of them.

'You don't know who it was?' If she was seeing another man, then this was definitely something worth chasing up. 'Someone from work, maybe? A neighbour?'

But Laurence Elliot didn't seem to know. He looked like a man who had just lost the last few strands of hope that had kept him going. The faint possibility he and Susan might get back together – however slim – had been dashed for ever in the cruellest of ways. Combined with the knowledge there was a real chance his wife was already seeing another man. She couldn't help feeling sorry for him.

'I wish I could say I knew Susan well enough to answer that.' He sighed. 'Perhaps if I'd been a better husband, or if I hadn't pressurised her into marriage, she might still be alive now.' He looked at Molly. 'You think she was murdered because she was having an affair?'

But Molly didn't know that. The more she discovered about Susan Elliot, the less obvious the answers seemed.

'It really is too early to say at this stage, Mr Elliot. But whatever the reason for your wife's murder, I really don't think you should go blaming yourself. There's only one person to blame for her murder and that's the person who killed her. And I can promise you we'll do everything we can to find them.' She took another sip of tea, enjoying the tangy taste. 'What about Susan's family, any friends? Perhaps they might be worth talking to?'

'Most of her friends were through work. She wasn't especially close to her family. Her parents are both dead and she was an only child. Perhaps that was her problem… she was looking for that sense of belonging.'

She smiled at him. 'Thank you, Mr Elliot. I appreciate everything you've done. I'll be in touch when I have some news.

He thanked her, promising to get in touch if he could think of anything else, adding that he would be staying in London for another couple of days and then heading back to Aberdeen at the end of the week.

Molly watched him head out of the hotel to the car park. She waited for a few minutes, trying to attract the attention of the waiter, who was busy chatting to an elderly couple who had just come in. She watched Laurence make his way across the car park and into a Jaguar before driving off. Safe but dull, she thought. A few years ago, she couldn't have imagined anything worse than being saddled with a man who fitted that description, but right now that sounded exactly like what she wanted. Reassuring and dependable.

At least now she felt she had something positive to focus on. If Susan Elliot was having an affair, then Molly had to find whoever it was she'd been seeing and speak to them – just to eliminate them from their enquiries if nothing else. She would look into the claim that Susan Elliot thought someone was following her. It could be nothing, but it could somehow be linked to the man she may or may not have been seeing from the website.

However, like Kieran Judd, there didn't seem, on the surface, to be anything about Susan Elliot's life or her past that indicated she should be the victim of a crime. They couldn't both have been killed in a case of mistaken identity...

She started to wonder about Kieran again: there was nothing about him that rang any bells, which was in itself strange. But maybe Denning was right and this was all really to do with Tony Hallam.

She finally got hold of the waiter and paid for the tea. Technically, she should ask for a receipt and claim it back on expenses, but was it really worth the hassle? Part of her had actually enjoyed sitting in a hotel lounge chatting to someone over a cup of Earl Grey. Sometimes there were some perks to the job. Then she sighed and thought about what Laurence had said about Susan being lonely. That was something she could – reluctantly – admit to feeling herself at the moment. Splitting up with Jon was more painful than she'd thought, but although she knew she'd done the right thing, she missed him.

Chapter Eighteen

Denning waited for Maria Hallam to answer her front door. She glanced either side of her, ensuring that her neighbours' curtains weren't twitching, then opened the door fully to let him in.

'Declan called me,' she said once they were settled on a couple of bar stools in the kitchen. 'He said you've been asking questions about Tony.' She said it like a statement rather than a question. Her eyes boring into his.

'As part of an ongoing investigation into a recent murder, yes, we've spoken to your brother as well as your ex-husband.'

'I told you there was no reason to speak to either of them. I haven't seen Tony for months and Declan...' She stared at her fingernails, painted a dark-ochre colour. 'Declan doesn't like to be bothered by things.'

Denning wondered what she meant by that, but sensed he was going to have to wait until she was more forthcoming.

'We have good reason to believe your ex-husband's life may be in danger,' Denning said. 'Therefore, we have a duty to warn him.'

She looked like she was about to break down. 'You really think someone is trying to kill him?'

'Right now, I think it's a definite possibility.' He looked at her. 'Does the name Susan Elliot ring any bells?'

She pulled a face. 'No. Why? Who the hell's Susan Elliot?'

'Tony's never mentioned her?'

'No. Never.' She shot him a curious look. 'What's this about?'

It was a long shot on his part. If could find some connection between Susan Elliot and Tony Hallam, then he might actually start making some progress with this case. 'It doesn't matter. I got the impression, the last time I spoke to you, that you thought Tony was seeing someone. I wondered if it might have been Susan Elliot.'

'I said I thought he was seeing someone before he went inside last time. I have no idea who he might be seeing now. You think this woman could be Tony's new girlfriend?'

He had to admit, it didn't seem likely. Professional, educated Susan Elliot and career criminal Tony Hallam... but love was meant to be blind, and lust seemed to play by its own rules, so anything was possible. 'And you're sure you haven't heard from Tony since his release from prison?'

'I told you last time you were here – I haven't seen him and I don't want to see him.'

'So he hasn't tried to make contact?'

There was a pause before she answered. 'I didn't say that.' She looked at her nails again. 'He texted a couple of times a few weeks ago. He told me he wanted to see the kids. He said I didn't have any right to stop him seeing them as he was their dad.'

'Did he threaten you?'

'He didn't need to. He knows I know what he's capable of.'

'So he *did* threaten you, just not in so many words.'

'Like I said… Tony's used to getting his own way.'

'Did you report this?'

She laughed. 'What would be the point? You lot never do anything anyway. No, I phoned Declan. He said he'd have a word with Tony.'

'And did he?'

She shrugged. 'I don't know. But he stopped texting.'

'When was this?'

'About a week ago.' She looked at Denning, frowning. 'Look, the most Declan would have done was have a word with Tony, put the frighteners on him. There's no way he'd harm him. Well, certainly not *kill* him.'

Denning scratched his head. If Declan Meech had gone after Tony Hallam, he would have made sure he had the right man. Unless he'd paid someone else to do it. A professional killer who wasn't as professional as he'd anticipated and they'd got the wrong man. It seemed far-fetched, and yet…

'Maria, if Tony's life is in danger, you need to tell me everything you know. He's still the father to your children.'

Whether his words had pricked her conscience, or she just wanted him off her back, she suddenly became animated. Shuffling uncomfortably on the narrow barstool at the raised kitchen table.

'Declan would never harm Tony. Declan thinks more of Tony than he does of me. Oh, yeah, he talks tough when it comes to looking after me and the kids, and don't get me wrong, if Tony ever pushed his luck Declan would put him straight, but he and Tony have been mates for years. Long before me and Tony got together. There's no way Dec would ever risk his friendship with Tony, no matter what anyone might tell you.'

Denning was surprised to hear what she was telling him. From what they knew it was the opposite. 'I thought Tony blamed Declan for being sent down last time?'

She shook her head and laughed. 'Tony agreed to take the rap for their last job as he's got a lighter record than Dec, so he'd be looking at a shorter stretch. There was no suggestion that Dec had stitched Tony up.'

It took Denning a minute to digest what she was saying. If she was telling him the truth, then her husband had clearly committed perjury in order to protect her brother's guilt. It was a serious case of obstructing justice, and Maria Hallam was clearly complicit. But this was a murder investigation: he needed to prioritise what was important now, and right now catching their killer was his main priority.

'So they're friends?'

'As close as brothers. Well, when me and Tony got together they were as good as brothers, weren't they?'

He didn't know if she was telling the truth. It would certainly get Declan Meech off the hook if someone was trying to kill Tony Hallam. But somehow none of this rang true with Denning. 'Are you telling me that Tony and Declan are still working together?'

She nodded slowly as though she was talking to an idiot. 'They've never stopped working together. They were planning something big when Tony was sent down. I expect his time inside was little more than an inconvenience. Whatever it was they were planning is probably still on the cards. They're not going to let something like prison stop them.'

Chapter Nineteen

Molly was following up on a hunch. Perhaps not even a hunch, more of a niggling feeling that had wormed its way into her brain and refused to budge. She decided to follow it up in her own time rather than clock it as part of the official investigation, all too aware that Denning was pushing for a quick result.

She was glad Cassie was in when she called round unannounced at Beth's flat.

'It's not like I've got anywhere else to go,' she said, greeting Molly with a warm smile. 'At least not yet.'

'It shouldn't be for too much longer,' Molly said, trying to be helpful. 'They've almost finished in there.' Molly declined the offer of tea or coffee this time. She was still savouring the taste of the Earl Grey from The St Margaret's Hotel.

'I'm sorry I haven't got anything more positive to tell you,' she said. 'I could fob you off with the usual crap about "following up a useful line of inquiry", but I'm not going to lie to you. You deserve better.' She sat down on the sofa. 'How are you coping?' She nodded at baby Arthur, who was playing with some coloured building blocks on a patchwork rug in front of the mock-marble fireplace. The baby smiled at Molly and held out a painted block for her to examine. She smiled back. He continued to look at her for a moment, still slightly uncertain about her presence in his life, but accepting she was now somehow a part of it.

'We're doing all right,' Cassie said. Then, blushing, she added, 'At least as well as we can under the circumstances. I've spoken to Kieran's parents. They want his funeral to be held in Ireland. I don't know why – he hadn't lived there since he was a boy. The only family he has left over there are distant cousins. His parents moved back there when he was sixteen, but he probably only visited them a couple of times a year.' She smiled awkwardly at Molly. 'They were asking when the funeral would be? I said I didn't know. I was only repeating what the woman from Family Liaison told me, but I think they thought I was trying to fob them off.'

'We'll release Kieran's body as soon as we can, Cassie. But I have to warn you, even once we've arrested someone for his murder, there's always the chance the defence could ask for another post-mortem.' She saw Cassie's face contort into a pained expression. Little Arthur made a noise part-way between a grunt and a chortle, though he couldn't possibly have understood the significance of what they were discussing, which was probably just as well. 'Your FLO should have explained that to you,' Molly added. 'Though I appreciate it's a lot to take in when all you want to do is grieve and get on with your life.'

'I spoke with the woman from Family Liaison yesterday afternoon,' Cassie said. 'She said she'd try to find out from you when Kieran's body would be released.'

'I can have a word with my DI, see if we could hurry things along. But honestly, Cassie, at the moment, I don't think they're going to be releasing Kieran's body anytime soon. If we can find evidence proving Kieran wasn't the intended target, then we might be able to hurry things along. However, there has been one development that might have an impact on our investigation.' She told Cassie about the other murder and how there might be some link with Kieran's death.

'You still think the intended victim was the man who used to live upstairs? Tony?' Cassie asked. 'Was it him?'

'No. It was a woman called Susan Elliot.'

Molly watched Cassie to see if her face gave away any kind of recognition at the name, but she just looked blank.

'There was something on the news about that. You think her murder is connected to all this?'

Molly wasn't sure what she thought. Susan Elliot's murder threw up more questions than answers and was potentially turning the case in a different direction, even if Denning was refusing to see it.

Arthur started banging some of his building blocks together and shouting noisily. Cassie knelt down on the rug and lifted him up, kissing his head as she placed him on her knee. 'He'll want something to eat soon. To be honest, I think we're going to have to move out of the flat. I can't afford the rent without Kieran's wage coming in. The rent's paid up until the end of the month, but after that I don't know what I'm going to do. Trying to find somewhere decent to rent in London is almost impossible.'

Molly knew exactly what it was like trying to find somewhere affordable to live. Searching online for flats and bedsits that were both in her price range and fit for human habitation. At least she had some money coming in. Cassie didn't even have that to fall back on. 'Maybe your parents could help out?' she said.

Cassie sighed. 'They'd probably suggest I move back home. I can't think of anything worse than living with them again. My mum would just take over, try to bring

Arthur up her way.' She kissed his head again. 'I wouldn't want that. He deserves better.'

Molly didn't like to ask what she meant: what could have been so bad about her own upbringing that Cassie would rather risk homelessness than live with her parents? But then families had always been something Molly had struggled to understand. Her own was pretty dysfunctional – who was to say other people's weren't as complicated.

She stood to leave. 'I'll be in touch, Cassie. But you've got my card. If you need to speak to me, just give me a call. Any time. I mean that.' She paused, worried that she might be in danger of overstepping the line. 'Even if you just want to talk.'

Cassie nodded and smiled. Molly knew she had to remain professional. Cassie Bane was the relative of a murder victim, and there were people trained to help her. Molly's job was to find her partner's killer.

Chapter Twenty

Denning wasn't even sure McKenna was listening to him. She was sitting behind her desk glancing every so often at the pile of papers in front of her. She would cast the occasional glance at the clock on the wall behind him when she thought he wasn't looking. He could sense she was still sticking to the theory that Hallam was a non-starter. He had to admit, the more time passed, the more he began to think she might be right, even if it pained him to admit it.

'What Maria Hallam says throws a new light on things,' he said, when he was sure he had her attention. 'We'd previously been working on the assumption Hallam and Meech had fallen out. Now, from what she's saying, they're still thick as thieves, if you excuse the pun. I think this is something we should be looking into.'

McKenna's focus was now fixed on him. 'Why are we speaking to Maria Hallam? You should be looking for the killer of Kieran Judd and Susan Elliot. We are assuming their murders are linked?'

'I still think Tony Hallam was the intended victim. We're looking for anything that connects Hallam with Susan Elliot. Both were single, to all intents and purposes, so that avenue's worth exploring.'

'So we're ruling Declan Meech out as a suspect in Kieran Judd's murder?' Denning could tell from the look on her face she was going to take some convincing on this line of thought.

'Taking into account what Maria Hallam has said, combined with what Meech told us, then I'd say it's unlikely. Unless there's more to it, or there's something she's not telling us.'

'Like…?'

Denning was thinking on his feet. At the present moment in time, he wasn't entirely sure where he was going with this. And McKenna didn't like wild theories. She wanted hard facts and solid leads. She was a boots-on-the-ground copper rather than a cerebral ideas officer.

'From what she's said,' Denning continued, 'I think Hallam and Meech are planning something.'

'Planning what? A round-the-world balloon race? A cake-baking contest? What do you mean "planning something"?'

Denning took a deep breath. Sometimes McKenna tried his patience. But then, to be fair, he suspected the feeling was mutual. 'A crime. And I would reckon a fairly serious one, judging by their past records.'

McKenna fixed him with one of her gimlet stares for a second. 'Well, unless they're planning on committing a murder, it's not really relevant to this investigation,' McKenna said coldly. She continued the stare. 'We've got two murders, Matt, probably linked. With the distinct possibility there could be more, unless we find out what the hell this is about. Right now, any connection to Tony Hallam and Declan Meech is looking tenuous at best.'

'None of this detracts from the fact I still believe Hallam's life might be in danger. If not from Meech, then someone else. I still think he's the intended target rather than Kieran Judd.'

'And where does Susan Elliot fit into this? Was she a case of mistaken identity too? Because I can't see a respectable school teacher and a hardened criminal having much in common.'

Denning wanted to say that it was surprising what seemingly disparate people had in common. Instead he went with: 'There's a possibility Susan Elliot was having an affair. According to DS Fisher, her husband suspected as much. This means he could be a suspect.'

'Except he has a solid alibi for the time of her murder. He was in Aberdeen at the time, wasn't he?'

'It's not too difficult to get a flight from Aberdeen to London and back without many people realising you're missing,' Denning argued, 'However, I accept he's an unlikely candidate, but at this precise moment I don't think we're in a position where we can afford to rule out anything.'

McKenna seemed to give the matter some thought. Eventually her gaze returned to the paperwork that littered her desk. 'OK, I accept we keep our options open for now. What else have you got?'

'We're looking at anything that connects Susan Elliot with Tony Hallam. And anyone Hallam was in prison with, or has pissed off since he got out.'

'And Susan Elliot? Apart from a possible affair, what do we have on her so far?'

'Right now, very little. I think the affair angle is worth pursuing.'

'Susan Elliot and Tony Hallam? Seems unlikely.'

Denning didn't want to admit that he agreed. 'I strongly suspect the answer lies with Hallam. I really think we need to explore the possibility Hallam and Meech are planning something illegal. Perhaps Susan Elliot got inadvertently tied up in it? Or she was killed to stop her from talking.'

'Which would bring us back to Meech being a suspect again. But would Hallam really want to risk yet another stretch inside?' She pursed her lips in thought. 'Meech, on the other hand...'

'Agreed. I would put money on Meech being the brains behind whatever it is they're planning.'

McKenna sat back in her chair. 'At the moment, all we have is the possibility Tony Hallam's life could be in danger. Anything else isn't really our bag. If he and Meech are planning something then I need to pass it over to the appropriate body. Meech has been on the National Crime Agency's radar for some time. It might be worth having a word with them. At least flag up that we think there's something going on. Chances are, if there is, they'll already have an indication, but it won't do any harm to let them know we suspect something is afoot.' She looked directly at Denning. 'But, in the meantime, you need to find the killer or killers of Kieran Judd and Susan Elliot. I can't overemphasise this, Matt. I'm getting earache from upstairs. And then we've got the media running panic stories about a knife killer slaying people at random. It piles the pressure on. This isn't about Tony Hallam or Declan Meech, and we don't have the luxury of chasing shadows down the wrong avenue.'

'That's if it does turn out to be a wrong avenue,' Denning said. But even he knew she had a point. Despite his misgivings about the man, and despite the fact he *knew* Hallam was up to something, this was beginning to feel like a red herring. Only how was he going to tell the team?

Chapter Twenty-One

Molly was in her bedroom in Trudi and Charys' small flat.
The room was barely bigger than a decent-sized prison
cell, with a double bed taking up most of the space, and
an Ikea wardrobe/drawer combination occupying the wall
behind the door. Her over-sized suitcase was precariously
placed on top of it. A short wooden three-legged stool sat
beside the bed and doubled as a bedside table, which was
already cluttered with a reading lamp, alarm clock and the
novel Molly just didn't seem to be able to finish.

Trudi and Charys were in the living room, curled
up on the sofa with a bottle of Chardonnay, watching
some slushy chick-flick-type rubbish on Netflix. Molly
had made her excuses and retired to her bedroom.

She opened her laptop, and settled down to browse flats
to let.

She didn't know whether she was depressed or
surprised by what she saw listed. The ones she could afford
were either so remote they might as well be in another
part of the country altogether, or else they were just plain
horrible. The ones that did hold any appeal were too far
outside her price range to even consider, unless she was to
share, and that was something that definitely didn't appeal
to her. She enjoyed staying with Trudi and Charys, and
they'd meant it when they told her to treat the flat as her
home. But it was their place and she constantly felt like she

had to fit herself in around them. The inevitable queues for the bathroom and the rota for the tiny kitchen reinforced her conviction that she needed to find somewhere of her own soon.

She briefly thought about what Cassie had said about no longer being able to afford the rent on her flat without Kieran's money coming in. Life could be undeservedly cruel sometimes: in the blink of an eye and through no fault of her own, Cassie's life had been torn apart. It wasn't just losing her partner in the most horrific of circumstances, it was the loss of the security and stability she'd taken for granted. Now she faced the unwelcome prospect of losing her home and having to find somewhere for her and her son to live when the choices of what was available were clearly very limited.

Another thought was buzzing round her head, one she was trying hard to dismiss. She was pretty sure Cassie's flat would be in her price range, and a good size for her. Not too big, but not too cramped either. It was an OK area, by London standards, and she wasn't in a position to be too picky. Trudi and Charys were cool about letting her stay, and there was certainly no question of either of them hassling her to move out, but she knew she couldn't live there for ever. But how would she feel if she took advantage of Cassie Bane's misfortune? Then there would be the knowledge of knowing what had happened in that flat. Molly wasn't squeamish, but living somewhere a murder had taken place, especially if she knew about it, would freak her out more than a little. Plus, it would be hugely insensitive to Cassie: sympathising with her circumstances one minute, then taking advantage of her misfortune the next.

She could hear Trudi and Charys laughing in the living room. Every time she looked at them, she saw a happy couple, comfortable around each other. They had their own shorthand when it came to communicating, even finishing each other's sentences on occasions. It was the kind of comfortable relationship Molly had so desperately wanted with Jon, but just never seemed to achieve. She tried hard not be envious of their relationship.

From what she could hear, they were still watching whatever it was on Netflix. Charys was commenting which other TV shows she'd seen various actors and actresses in. Molly smiled to herself and closed her laptop, having decided she was too depressed to spend any more time that evening looking for properties she couldn't afford. She glanced again at her phone. The messages from Jon had finally stopped, but earlier that evening she'd spotted a text message from Rowan, Jon's daughter. She had recently come back into Jon's life having been estranged from him for years after her parents had divorced. She'd married her fiancé that summer with Jon as the proud father-of-the-bride.

According to Rowan, Jon was unhappy and she was worried about him. She wanted to meet Molly, but Molly wasn't sure. The last thing she wanted was pressure from Rowan to get back with Jon; though to be fair, it was unlikely she would be placing that kind of pressure on Molly. Rowan was sensible. She understood the state of play between Molly and her father. She knew Molly wasn't going to go back to Jon for the wrong reasons.

Molly sighed. Jon had been such a huge part of her life for over five years. For so many of those years she'd tried hard to focus mostly on the good times – and there were many good times: Jon could be kind, supportive, good fun. But so often she'd found herself blinking away the bad times, pretending they didn't matter, or weren't indicative of the real Jon. It had all changed when he'd lost his job. With it, he'd seemed to lose his purpose. He struggled to fill his days with enough to keep his brain busy. She would come home from a stressful day at work and the breakfast dishes would still be sitting in the sink unwashed. Or he would be stoned out of his brain. Any discussions would lead directly to an inevitable argument, for which she invariably felt the need to apologise.

But she was aware of what she'd sacrificed. Not just her relationship, but her home. She'd had a nice life: safe, comforting. Somewhere she could call home. Even if the house did belong to Jon, he'd never been proprietorial about it. It had been his house, but her home.

She'd moved out of Jon's nice big house in Crouch End and was reduced to living in a pokey box room in a friend's flat. When she thought through her options, she knew her choices were limited. Rent a room somewhere? Or a house share? The prospect of living like a student at her age wasn't something that filled her with joy. But the alternative, kissing and making up with Jon just so she could get her old life back, filled her with even less joy.

Chapter Twenty-Two

Claire wasn't too happy to see Denning when she opened the front door to see him standing on the doorstep. She still lived in what had been their marital home: a neat but bland 1980s townhouse halfway along a quiet cul-de-sac in Surrey Quays.

'You should have called,' she complained, when she showed him into the kitchen. 'I'm trying to get dinner ready.'

'Sorry. It was kind of a spur-of-the-moment thing.' He smiled, hoping she would see that he came with good intentions. 'Where's Jake?'

'He's upstairs, playing on one of his computer games in his bedroom.' Denning could hear the sounds of electronic gunfire coming from upstairs.

Claire was standing by the oven, stirring something in a pot. It smelled sweet. Claire had always enjoyed cooking, unlike Sarah, who considered it a chore and often joked about preferring to live in a hotel, where the meals were cooked for you. If she moved to New York, Denning mused, she may well get her wish.

'Can I see him?' he asked.

'He'll be down in a minute for his dinner. You can see him then. But not for long. I don't want him getting over-stimulated this close to bedtime.' Claire added some seasoning to the pot, and turned to face him. 'What is it you want, Matt? This isn't a great time to call.'

'I appreciate that.' He sat at the kitchen table, already laid out for two places. 'I won't stay for long. And don't worry, I'm not trying to cadge a meal.'

'Good. Because there's barely enough here for me and Jake.'

It had always been a happy home, until their marriage had ended. He'd long since come to terms with the guilt he'd felt when he announced he'd met someone else. It had taken Claire a long time to forgive him. But she had, and relations between them were on a stable footing now, something he was keen to continue.

He realised he hadn't told Claire about Sarah wanting to move to New York. It wasn't important at this point because not only was it not definite, there was no guarantee he would be going with her even if she did decide to go.

'I wanted to see how he was getting on at school.'

In truth, he'd meant to ask the previous week when Jake had actually started at his new school. Sometimes work just took over his thoughts, pushing out important things such as his son. It was thinking about Susan Elliot that had prompted him into remembering that he had forgotten to ask. A murder investigation tended to take over his mind and he had forgotten that the schools had recently gone back. He was due to see Jake that weekend, but with another murder investigation on the go, there was a chance he might have to cancel. He hated cancelling his weekends with Jake. Not only did he look forward to them, he knew Jake did too. He didn't want his son growing up with a father who was only ever on the periphery of his life. Jake needed stability.

'It's early days,' Claire replied, 'but so far so good.' She turned to face him. 'I think he'll like it there.'

'That's great. But, like you say, it's still early days.'

Jake had been in conventional school until that summer, but being autistic and ADHD meant he'd struggled with the other pupils and hadn't received the support he should have. After much discussion, Denning and Claire had agreed to send him to a specialist school.

'You think he'll settle?'

She turned the heat down on the pot and shouted for Jake to come down for his dinner.

Jake came running into the kitchen and rushed up to his dad, greeting him with a hug. 'Daddy! Are you staying for dinner?'

Denning hugged his son back, feeling guilty that he didn't see him nearly as often as he wanted to. That was partly down to the job and partly down to him feeling awkward around Claire. 'I can't stay for dinner, little fella, but I'll take you out soon.' He usually saw Jake every other weekend, but because Jake had just started at a new school, Claire didn't want him unsettled for the first few weeks. As Denning was now in the middle of a major murder investigation, this suited him. But he still missed his son.

'How are you enjoying your new school?' he asked.

Jake gave an indifferent shrug. 'It's OK.'

Denning reckoned that was probably as good as it was going to get. 'Have you made any new friends?'

'Not yet,' he replied. His father's heart sank a little. Jake had always struggled to make friends; that was part of his ADHD, which meant it was part of him, and Denning wouldn't change that for anything. Jake preferred his own company to that of other children, and usually that wasn't a problem. But school was all about socialising; about establishing who you were in relation to others. Denning worried about Jake, and his torturous journey to adulthood.

'I'm sure you'll make new friends,' Denning said, trying to reassure himself as much as his son. 'It's always a bit scary at a new school.'

After a moment, Jake untangled himself from his dad and sat at the kitchen table.

Claire began spooning their food out of the saucepan and into two bowls. 'Look, Matt, you can stay for dinner if you want to. I'm sure I can make this stretch to another bowl. I'm not very hungry.'

He shook his head. 'Thanks. And don't think I don't appreciate the offer, but Sarah will have made something.' He rubbed Jake's head affectionately. 'I really should be going.'

He said his goodbyes and headed back to the car. He'd gone round to tell Claire that there was a chance he might be leaving the country, but now he'd realised he could never leave Jake. Even if they waited until their son was a bit older, there was no guarantee he would ever come to terms with his daddy living on the other side of the world. Jake needed him and, as he opened the driver's door of the Focus, he realised he needed Jake. It would mean telling Sarah he'd made his decision and the ball was now in her court.

Once he was inside the car, his phone pinged with a WhatsApp message. He assumed it was from Claire telling him not to come round unannounced again, especially at dinnertime. But instead, he was shocked to see that it was from the one person he hadn't expected to hear from again: Anna Klein. Apparently, she wanted to meet.

Chapter Twenty-Three

Denning held another briefing first thing the following morning. So far, they were struggling to find something to officially link the two murders. Or, at the very least, to link Susan Elliot with Tony Hallam or Kieran Judd.

'We have to assume,' Denning said, addressing his team, 'that Susan Elliot was deliberately targeted. There's a chance she knew her killer and let them into the house. The forensics report states that there is no evidence of a break-in: doors and windows were secure. They've checked for prints and DNA, but nothing's come back as a match so far.'

'What about witnesses?' Neeraj asked. 'It looks like the kind of street where neighbours notice things.'

'It seems not,' Denning said. 'At least not on this occasion. We'll keep going with house-to-house enquiries but, as with Kieran Judd, nobody has come up with anything useful so far.'

'So, whoever did this is quick,' Dave Kinsella said. 'In and out without being noticed. Like I said before, they're either very clever or very lucky.'

'There's a park at the back of the houses,' Trudi Bell said helpfully. 'Our killer could have climbed over a fence into the street unnoticed.'

'And then rung the doorbell and blagged their way inside?' Kinsella's tone told them he wasn't buying this.

Denning nodded at the forensics report. 'Unless they're mistaken, then yes, that looks like the only way our killer could have gained entry.'

'But that doesn't make sense,' Trudi argued. 'Unless Susan Elliot knew her killer. Or at least trusted them enough to let them in to her home.'

'So, either someone she knew, or someone she didn't think would be a threat,' Neeraj said. 'Gas man, maybe, or someone similar.'

'There were no reports of anyone hanging round the street,' Kinsella said. 'If this was an opportunist crime, one of the neighbours would have seen something suspicious.'

'In which case, we're assuming she knew her killer.' Kinsella looked around the room for support. A couple of heads nodded.

'Her husband would be an obvious choice,' Trudi said.

Denning explained about the alibi.

'That could almost be described as a perfect alibi,' Neeraj said with a grin.

'Yeah,' Kinsella added. 'Too bloody perfect.'

'Obviously we'll check flights and ANPR to see if he flew or drove between Aberdeen and London, and ask the hotel he's staying at for confirmation that he was where he said he was. In the meantime, we keep looking into Hallam. Have you spoken to the prison where Hallam served his last sentence?'

'Nothing to report there, boss,' Neeraj said. 'While Hallam couldn't exactly be described as a "model prisoner", there were no issues with other prisoners. Or staff. He gets a bit lippy sometimes, but no more than most.'

'OK,' Denning said. 'That doesn't let Hallam off the hook. I still think he was the intended target.'

'So we're definitely linking Susan Elliot's murder with Kieran Judd's?' Kinsella asked.

'It could yet turn out to be a coincidence, but both were stabbed in their own home. Single stab wound. The post-mortem confirms the knife wounds are similar, suggesting the same killer. So, yes, at the moment, I'm working on the assumption both victims were killed by the same person. The motive being something we need to establish as a matter of urgency.'

'But you still reckon Tony Hallam was the intended target?' Kinsella asked. 'Rather than Kieran Judd?' Kinsella stroked his chin. 'It's just, I can't for the life of me see a connection between Tony Hallam and Susan Elliot. One's a respectable school teacher, while the other's a scumbag.'

There was sniggering at his comment, and Denning waited until it passed. 'Susan Elliot's husband believes she was having an affair,' Denning said. 'Let's consider the possibility the person she was having an affair with was Tony Hallam.'

Kinsella was shaking his head, while the rest of the team looked blank. He could tell they weren't buying this, and he had to admit it was stretching credulity somewhat.

'OK, Dave, I accept what you're saying about the obvious differences between Susan Elliot and Tony Hallam, and I know it's a bit of a long shot, but work with me here. We can't conclusively rule it out, and until we know what this is about, we have to consider all the options. We know Hallam was effectively single and was believed to have been seeing other women during his marriage to Maria Hallam. This would give us a possible connection between Hallam and Susan Elliot.'

'Which gives Susan Elliot's husband a strong motive,' Trudi said. 'For argument's sake, let's say he discovered his wife was playing around with Hallam – she fancied a bit of rough, nothing wrong with that, we've all been there. But her husband, who still wants to give the marriage another go, decides to take matters into his own hands. He goes after Hallam then his wife.'

'Except he has an alibi,' Molly said.

'OK,' Denning said. 'Check his alibi. Make sure he didn't slip back from Aberdeen unnoticed. And check his mobile phone records. It's possible he could have hired someone to do the job.'

'All this is, at best, tenuous,' Kinsella said. 'Be honest, boss, it's little more than a hunch. There's nothing to substantiate the theory Susan Elliot *was* having it off with someone, and there's certainly nothing to suggest that person was Tony Hallam.'

Denning had to accept Kinsella had a point. Right now, all they could do was toss theories around the team and try to find one that sounded credible. 'All I'm saying is that it's one possibility, but that doesn't mean we shouldn't blind ourselves to others.' He looked round the room at the sea of faces that were clearly unconvinced by his theory. 'OK. What do we all think? Any other theories we should be exploring? I accept what Dave is saying about there being little to link Susan Elliot with Tony Hallam, but, equally, we have nothing to link her with Kieran Judd either.'

Molly had her hand in the air. 'It might be tenuous, but Kieran Judd once worked as a TA. I haven't got any further details and there's nothing to suggest he worked at the same school as Susan Elliot, but it's something.'

Denning thought about the significance of this. 'OK, that's interesting.' He looked around the team, trying to gauge their rection. 'This gives us a possible connection between our two victims.' If they could find something that connected Susan Elliot to Kieran Judd they might actually feel like progress, even if it did shoot his theory about Hallam down in flames.

'It still doesn't give us a motive,' Neeraj argued.

'Disgruntled pupil,' Kinsella offered, though the cheesy grin on his face suggested he wasn't being entirely serious.

'They worked in a primary school,' Molly replied coldly.

'Youth crime,' Kinsella responded, with the same cheesy grin. 'They're starting younger these days.'

There was a general groaning from the team. Denning waited until they'd finished. 'Right, well we've got enough to be getting on with. Molly, find out which school Kieran Judd was a TA at. See if there's any overlap between him and Susan Elliot.'

'Where does this leave the Tony Hallam/Susan Elliot love-tryst-theory?' Kinsella asked. 'Are we now dropping that and chasing this new angle?'

'We keep all options on the table, Dave,' Denning said. 'Until we know for certain why these two people were killed, we can't afford to rule out anything.'

'If Susan Elliot was having an affair,' Trudi Bell said, 'then we need to find out who with. At the very least, we need to eliminate them as a possible suspect.' She shot Denning a pathetic look. 'Assuming her paramour wasn't Tony Hallam.'

Chapter Twenty-Four

Greg Lawton was in his early fifties. Tall and elegant, he was what her Great-Aunt Mim would have described as 'suave'. But Mim was a romantic novelist and, as such, prone to depicting men heroically. Molly was more prosaic and would have simply described him as smooth.

He lived in Primrose Hill, in a large flat with an impressive view of London that stretched out the wide bay window in the elegantly furnished sitting room.

Laurence Elliot had been more forthcoming than she'd expected. He'd accessed his wife's laptop and checked her emails. It seemed she'd met Greg Lawton about three months ago on a dating website. They'd met up a few times, but there was no suggestion the relationship had developed beyond friendship at this stage. Laurence Elliot had also confirmed he hadn't discovered any mention of reference to anyone called Tony Hallam.

'Yes, Susan and I were close,' Greg Lawton explained. He was dressed in a pale-pink cashmere sweater and a pair of grey slacks, and sat back comfortably on his sofa, smiling warmly at Molly. 'Susan explained that she'd married Laurence on the spur of the moment. He'd proposed out of the blue and she couldn't bring herself to say no. She admitted she'd made a mistake, but didn't want to hurt him.'

'So, Laurence knew she was unhappy?' Molly was certain he was mentally undressing her. There was something slightly sleazy about Greg Lawton, which even Great-Aunty Mim would struggle to polish.

'I imagine so. She certainly made it clear she wanted out. Despite his feelings, I think Laurence accepted that.' He smiled again at Molly. 'When it's over for one party it's effectively over for both. Only a fool would fail to see that.'

Molly nodded her agreement, knowing that only too well.

'I have to ask you where you were yesterday morning,' she said.

'Of course. I was here, then I left for work. My neighbour saw me leave and my secretary can confirm I arrived at work at the usual time.' He offered Molly a cheesy grin, flashing his immaculately white teeth. 'I didn't murder Susan, if that thought's running loose inside your head. Do I look like a killer?'

She fixed him with a look that made it clear she wasn't prepared to put up with any crap. 'Nobody's suggesting you murdered Susan Elliot, Mr Lawton. But if she felt her life was in danger, then there's a chance she might have given some idea as to why and from whom. Can you think of anyone who would want to harm Susan?'

He rubbed a hand on his slacks as he thought about the question. 'Off the top of my head, no. I suppose you have considered Laurence?' He gave another toothy smile. 'Well, of course you have. I imagine he's the obvious suspect here, though from what I know about him, he's no more a killer than I am. But no, to answer your question, I can't think of anyone who would want to harm Susan. She never mentioned feeling threatened and she wasn't the sort who made enemies easily. I wouldn't dream of telling you how to do your job, but if I were you I'd be looking for some maniac who attacks women. If you read the newspapers, the world seems to be full of them.'

'Did she ever mention someone called Kieran Judd?'

Again, he rubbed his leg as he gave the question some thought. 'Not that I recall.'

'Or did she say anything about being followed, or having received any strange phone calls?'

'Strange phone calls…? No, nothing like that. I know I keep saying it, but no one was threatening her. People liked Susan… she was good at her job and she was popular. I can assure you that whoever did this wasn't someone Susan knew.'

Molly was beginning to think the main thing Susan Elliot and Kieran Judd had in common was that they didn't seem to have any obvious enemies. Was being too nice a reason to murder someone?

She stood to leave, thanking Greg Lawton as he showed her out. She didn't leave her card to ask him to get in touch if he thought of anything; it was obvious he knew very little about Susan Elliot's life and Molly didn't feel particularly comfortable at the thought of being contacted by Greg Lawton.

As she headed back to her car, she wondered what women saw in a man like that. But people had so often said that about her and Jon. Sometimes Cupid behaved in a way that wasn't obvious.

She was on the point of reaching into her bag for her car keys when her phone rang. It was the school where Susan Elliot had worked.

'Hello, DS Fisher?'

'Hello,' the voice said, 'I'm returning your call from earlier. This is Hazel Kelly. I'm the principal teacher at Our Lady of the Convent School. You left a message with a colleague asking about Susan Elliot?'

Molly confirmed this and asked how long Susan Elliot had worked at the school.

'Susan had only been with us for a couple of years. She was initially known by her maiden name of Milton when she first started there. She was known as Mrs Elliot after she married. I did suggest she kept Milton, at least for a while, as the children knew her by that, but it was almost as though she was keen to be rid of it.'

Susan Milton, Molly thought to herself. Was that significant? They'd run the name Susan Elliot through the PNC on the off-chance that something might come up, but nothing had. Perhaps the name Susan Milton might produce something.

'Could you do me a favour, Hazel?' Molly asked as she dug in her pocket for the car key. 'Could you get me a list of all the schools where Susan Milton worked previously?'

There was a pause from the other end of the line. 'Well, I don't know about all the schools where she worked, but I could certainly find the last two. It would have been on her application form. We've still got a copy. She would be registered with the teaching authority of England, and the local authority would have a record of her employment if you want to go further back than that.'

'OK, thanks. I'll start with the last two schools. If I need to dig further, I'll contact the relevant authorities.'

Molly thanked her and rang off. Now that it looked like they could discount Susan Elliot's love life as the reason for her murder, she had a feeling that the answers might lie in her professional life. And if she could find a definite link between Susan Milton and Kieran Judd, then they might just finally start making some progress with this case.

Chapter Twenty-Five

Denning was surprised to get a call from Maria Hallam. He was in the car at the time, so he answered on hands-free. Her voice reverberated around the small space until he adjusted the sound and could hear her without his ears hurting. She told him she wanted to meet, but away from her home. Her neighbour had agreed to look after the children, so she suggested they meet in a park not far from her home.

Denning's first thought was that this was some kind of trap. What – and who – would he find waiting for him when he got there. But curiosity got the better of him and he agreed to meet her.

When he got there, he found her sitting on a bench near some swings. She looked like she'd been crying.

'Tony's been round,' she said, fixing Denning with a doleful look. 'He came to see me this morning.' She bit her lower lip. 'He knows I've been talking to you.'

'Did he threaten you?' Denning could tell something wasn't right. 'If he has, we can speak to him, warn him off...'

'No. He didn't threaten me, at least not in so many words. He just made it clear he didn't like me talking to the police. He still reckons you framed him the last time he was sent down. I told him about the murder, and about how you think his life is in danger, but he said it was all rubbish. Well, he didn't say "rubbish", but you get my drift…'

Denning did. All too clearly. Hallam was obviously rattled, and it wasn't entirely down to the death threat. 'We do believe his life may be in danger,' Denning said, trying to reassure her. 'It's not "rubbish", and because of that we had a right to warn him to be careful.'

Maria Hallam bit her lip again. 'He thinks you're playing games with him. He thinks it's some kind of ploy to catch him out.'

'Catch him out? Catch him out at what exactly?'

She didn't answer, and Denning sensed that she'd said more than she'd wanted to. He tried to reassure her, or at least get him to tell her more. 'Maria, what's going on between Tony and Declan? As far as I was aware, they hated each other. Now you tell me that's not the case. What's really going on here? What are they up to?'

'They're not up to anything.' She paused. 'At least not far as I know.' She blew her nose on a paper hankie. 'Declan doesn't speak to me. And today was the first time I've seen Tony since he got out. Neither of them would be happy if they knew I was here talking to you.'

She seemed frightened, like a caged animal knowing it was facing threat. But getting her to open up to him wasn't going to be easy, even if she had taken the first big step of agreeing to meet with him. 'Maria, do you know something's going on? Is that why Tony's so agitated about us speaking to him?'

She looked at Denning. 'I need you to keep away from Tony. And Declan. If they knew I was speaking to you now…'

'What, Maria? What would they do? If you're scared of them…'

'It's not that. I can handle Declan and Tony. They'd never hurt me. Or the kids. It's just that sometimes they don't think of the consequences. Like I told you last time, they've been mates for a long time, way before I came on the scene.'

'I think you're scared of him. We can protect you. There are places you can go.'

'Some awful shelter, where I'd be living in constant fear that he could track me down. No thank you. I'd rather take my chances with him. But those chances would be a lot better if you left him alone.'

'I can't make empty promises. If Tony is planning something – something illegal – then we'll arrest him, simple as that. I can try to keep your name out of it and I can offer you police protection if you think you're in danger, but I can't turn a blind eye to law-breaking. If you really want me to help, let's make this official.'

She looked at him pleadingly, her face twisted, tortured, her eyes meeting his. 'Well, don't say I didn't warn you. Whatever happens next, I tried my best to stop you. None of this is on me.'

He opened his mouth to say something, but Maria Hallam was already on her feet and walking away. He could go after her, but would there be any point? She was clearly not going to tell him anything useful. As he watched her walk away, he wondered what that had really been about? Was she genuinely scared about what her husband might do, or was that some kind of warning? And if she was frightened of Tony Hallam, what was it that made her so scared of her ex-husband? There was a court order out against him, ensuring he kept away from his wife and children. If he was in breach of that, then he could be recalled to prison in a moment.

And then there was the biggest question of all: what exactly were Tony Hallam and Declan Meech planning that was making them so nervous around the police?

Chapter Twenty-Six

Molly had convinced herself that this visit to Cassie Bane was purely professional. She needed to clear up the details about Kieran's work history. If the FLO was around – which seemed unlikely as they were more overstretched than the rest of them put together – then she would fob her off with a good story. Molly sometimes alarmed herself at just how good a liar she'd become over the years.

Though to be fair, it wasn't a lie. She *did* need to ask Cassie some further questions. This case was unravelling faster than a ball of wool being toyed with by an eager kitten. She now knew the answers lay with Susan Elliot and Kieran Judd, and Cassie was best placed to help answer some of those questions.

But, if she was being completely honest with herself, there was more to it than that. She was concerned about Cassie. And Arthur. She knew the FLO would put Cassie in touch with various organisations who would be able to help her out financially as well as with any grief counselling and emotional support she might need.

However, Molly just couldn't help feeling sorry for her on a personal level: she was a young woman who was struggling to come to terms with having her life suddenly and brutally torn apart, all the time trying to keep things as normal as possible for the sake of her son.

As she rang the bell for Cassie's flat, she knew what Denning's reaction would be: accusing her of getting too involved with a victim. Overstepping a boundary that was in place for a reason. Subtly implying a lack of professionalism. But she couldn't help how she felt...

Cassie smiled when she opened the door. 'DS Fisher. Come in.'

'As I've already told you,' she said as Cassie showed her into the tiny flat, 'call me Molly.'

Cassie looked tired. Molly suspected she wasn't sleeping, which was understandable under the circumstances. She wondered just how much help the FLO was being. 'Can I get you something to drink?' Cassie asked. She showed Molly into the tiny living room and indicated for her to sit down. Molly sat herself on the sofa opposite the fireplace, while Cassie took her usual chair in the corner.

'No. Thank you, and I really can't stay long.' Molly didn't want to put Cassie to any more trouble than she had to. And it really was true that she didn't have a lot of time. If she'd been honest, this could have been done by phone. 'How are you getting on?'

'OK, I suppose. It still feels very strange. I do appreciate everything you're doing for me.'

Molly only wished they were doing more. She had hoped she would have been able to offer Cassie some positive news by now.

'I just need to ask you some more questions about Kieran,' she said. 'I know it must feel like we've been over everything a thousand times, but hopefully this is the last time I'll need to speak to you.'

Cassie nodded. 'If it helps find Kieran's killer, then I don't mind.'

'Did Kieran ever work as a teaching assistant in a primary school?'

She thought for a moment. 'I'm not sure. It's possible... He did mention something about having once worked in a school and he'd thought about training as a teacher, but he decided it wasn't for him.'

'Did he say why he changed his mind?'

'He just said teaching was too much responsibility and he didn't think he was suited to it.'

'I'm not saying this is significant, but it might be worth looking into anyway. Do you know which school he worked in, and when?'

She rubbed a hand over her cheek. 'I don't know. It was before we met. All I know is that he wasn't there for very long, just a few months. Which wasn't like Kieran: he usually stuck at a job, even if he didn't always enjoy it.'

'But you can't remember the name of the school?'

'No, sorry. And he never said why he left.'

She thought about something, but looked like she wasn't sure what to say.

'Go on,' Molly prompted. 'Anything you can tell me might be useful.'

Cassie drew her legs up on the chair and tucked them under her. 'He told me he left a job a couple of years ago because of something that happened. He wouldn't go into detail, and I assumed it was something like bullying, but it could have been the school he worked in.'

Could have... 'But you can't be sure?'

She shook her head. 'Look, I really don't know what I'm talking about. We've all left jobs we hated for all sorts of reasons. It doesn't mean something bad happened.'

'But you think it's possible Kieran might have once worked in a school?'

'Yes, it's possible.'

'Cassie, I know this is a bit of a long shot, are you sure the name Susan Elliot doesn't ring a bell? Kieran might have known her as Susan Milton.'

'Susan Milton... No, I don't recognise the name. Wasn't Susan Elliot that woman who was stabbed to death the other day? Do you think that's got something to do with what happened to Kieran?'

Molly tried to reassure her. 'We don't know at this stage. But it is possible they might have known each other.' She smiled at Cassie. 'If you could think of the name of the school where Kieran worked, it would be a great help.'

'I could look for his CV,' she said. 'He might have had a copy on his laptop.' She looked at Molly. 'It does feel a bit like prying though.'

Molly tried to reassure her. 'It would help, Cassie.'

She headed over to a corner beside the bucket chair. Kieran's laptop was sitting with the lid closed. She picked it up, carried it over to the sofa, and sat down next to Molly before opening the lid. There was a photo of Kieran, Cassie and Arthur taken at Bodiam Castle, smiling with the ruined building behind them. 'That was taken earlier this summer,' Cassie said, reading Molly's thoughts.

Molly smiled. The screensaver on her laptop was one of her and Jon, but she'd recently changed it to a more generic one of a lake.

Luckily Cassie knew the password to get in. There were several icons indicating Windows folders. One said Work underneath and Cassie clicked on that. One of the Word documents said CV. She opened it and read over it. It outlined Kieran's educational and work background: he had a degree in Sports Science and a certificate in life-saving and another in CPR. Under Work Experience it listed half a dozen jobs, about average for someone his age.

Molly studied the CV carefully. If he'd hated the job and left under questionable circumstance, then it was possible he may not have listed his time as a teaching assistant. But it was there: just over two years as a TA at Thomas Blake Primary School in Chiswick. There was no reason given for his leaving.

Thomas Blake Primary School... Not the same as Our Lady of the Convent, but if Susan Elliot had worked there then they might finally be on to something...

'What do you think?' Cassie asked. 'Could it be relevant?'

'I don't know. But I think it's worth looking into.'

Chapter Twenty-Seven

The young woman introduced herself as Alice Hennicke. Sporting short, spikey blond hair and a pair of slightly over-sized glasses, she informed Molly that she was the school secretary. She smiled, apologising that Rachel Atherton, the head teacher, was tied up, and would Molly mind waiting. 'She shouldn't be long,' Alice said, pointing at a padded chair halfway down a whitewashed corridor that seemed to lead to a vast, airy assembly hall at one end and a cafeteria at the other. A smell of chips and baked potato emanated from the direction of the cafeteria. 'If you don't mind waiting...'

Molly stubbornly refused to take a seat. It would have reminded her too much of her own time at school – a time she hated so much she'd almost banished it from her memory. Even being back in one now made her uncomfortable.

The name plate on the door said *(Mrs) Rachel Atherton – Head Teacher*. She suspected this was what head teachers did: made people – children and adults alike – wait in the corridor in an attempt to boost their own sense of self-importance. Then again, perhaps she was being unfair. Maybe she was making an important phone call, or in a meeting that couldn't be rearranged just because a police officer was conducting a murder inquiry...

Molly used the time to look around. Thomas Blake Primary School had been built, she guessed, from the sharp lines and white-painted breezeblock walls, sometime in the 1960s, possibly the early 1970s. Children's drawings adorned the walls; there was a smell of pine disinfectant mixing with the mushy aroma of the lunchtime offerings coming from the cafeteria's kitchen at the end of the corridor. Just along from the head teacher's door was a glass cabinet with a picture pyramid of staff members and their job titles. Rachel Atherton's photo was at the top of the pyramid. She had a scrubbed and professional no-nonsense look about her that reminded Molly, very slightly, of Betty Taggart.

Beside the staff board was a cork-tile board, with children's pictures pinned to it: mostly scribbled drawings of happy family scenes. Molly thought about her own fractured childhood. And then she found herself thinking about Arthur and what the future would hold for him.

Her thoughts were disturbed when the head teacher's door opened suddenly and a child of about five walked out, his face a mask of injured innocence. A few seconds later, Rachel Atherton stuck her head out the door and asked Molly to come in.

The office was neat, professional and lined in stained wood. There was a framed picture on the wall of a severe-looking woman in a bun, whom Molly assumed was the school's original headmistress. The woman currently occupying that role had her hand outstretched and she shook it, acknowledging the steely grip she received in return. Whilst Rachel Atherton didn't look quite as severe as the woman in the painting, there was certainly a superficial resemblance.

'I'm Rachel Atherton,' she said with a stern smile. She was an efficiently dressed woman in her early forties, with neatly styled hair. She had an air about her of someone who disliked having her authority challenged. 'How can I help you, DS Fisher?'

Molly sat opposite Mrs Atherton, trying her best not to be intimidated. Up until now any dealings she'd had with a head teacher had not been on favourable terms.

'I'm enquiring about two people who may have worked here. A Susan Elliot – though she might have been known by the name Milton – and a Kieran Judd. Judd would have been a teaching assistant, and Susan Elliot or Milton a teacher.'

Rachel Atherton stared at her for a few moments, possibly sizing her up. But Molly Fisher had toughened up over the years and wasn't about to allow herself to be intimidated easily, especially not by someone who was more at home bullying young children than squaring up to world-weary adults. 'What, exactly, would you like to know, sergeant?'

'Anything you can tell me about them would be helpful. For instance, how long did they work here? Why did they leave? Did they have much contact with each other?'

She sat back in her chair and seemed to give the matter some thought. 'It was some time ago and there's really not much to tell. Susan Milton certainly worked here as a teacher. However, she was only here for a couple of years and, I'm sorry to say, failed to make much of an impression. I don't really remember much about her.' She steepled her fingers together and observed Molly. 'And as for the other name… remind me?'

'Kieran Judd. He would have been in his early to mid twenties at the time he worked here.'

She shook her head. 'No, I'm sorry that name doesn't ring a bell.'

'Maybe you could check your records? According to his CV, he definitely worked here. He would have left about two years ago.'

Rachel Atherton pressed her fingers against her lips. 'Oh yes, I remember now. He left at about the same time as Susan Milton.'

'Really?'

She dropped her hands and gave Molly a pleasant smile. 'There was nothing strange about that. Schools often have a high turnover of staff, including teaching staff. If I remember rightly, Susan wanted a promotion and it was made clear to her there were no sufficient opportunities here for that. Kieran, again if I remember rightly, decided the job wasn't for him. Not uncommon. As much as we like to try to attract men into teaching assistant posts – it's always good for young people to have positive male role models – it generally tends not to be the kind of job that appeals to young men.'

'So that was it. There was no other reason why they left?'

'There were certainly no disciplinary matters, if that's what you're suggesting. Both had a solid work record: turned up on time, did the job. From what little I remember, both were very professional, and well regarded by their colleagues.' She stared unblinkingly at Molly. 'Can I ask what this is about?'

'Both Kieran Judd and Susan Elliot have been murdered,' Molly said. 'Stabbed to death. We have reason to believe they were deliberately targeted.'

Molly watched her reaction. Just for the briefest of seconds there was a slight flinch, as though Rachel Atherton had received a mild electric shock. But she quickly regained her composure. 'Oh my gosh. I did see something on the television about a couple of people being stabbed, but I must admit I didn't pay too much attention to the names. I assumed it was just down to some maniac on the loose.' She gave a slight heft of her shoulders as though an attempt at a shrug. 'Is there anything tangible to suggest their murder is in any way connected to this school, DS Fisher?'

'Apart from both victims having worked here...?'

The head teacher gave Molly a tight smile. 'As have many people over the years. This could be nothing more than a coincidence, do you not think?'

'Perhaps. But it does prove that there's a connection between Susan Elliot and Kieran Judd. That raises the possibility that someone killed them because of something they knew or something they did.'

Rachel Atherton offered another tight smile. 'I really wish I could help you more. But while I'm very sorry about what happened to Kieran and Susan, I really don't think it has anything to do with anything that happened at this school.'

Molly was slightly shocked by her apparent detachment. They were discussing the murder of two former staff members and Rachel Atherton was presenting a face of efficient professionalism. There was something about Rachel Atherton's demeanour that she found slightly disconcerting.

'Did anything happen while they were working here?' Molly asked. 'For instance, were any allegations ever made about them?'

The head teacher looked impassive. 'As I've already told you, there were never any disciplinary matters against either Susan Milton or Kieran Judd. And just to emphasise, there have never been any allegations made about any member of staff at this school.'

'I wasn't implying that...' Molly took a breath and regained her composure. 'I wasn't suggesting that anything had actually happened. But sometimes allegations are made about teaching staff, which have to be taken seriously, even if they subsequently turn out to be false.'

Molly waited for Mrs Atherton's response. Eventually she said coldly: 'Neither Susan Milton nor Kieran Judd were ever the subject of any allegations – false or otherwise – while they worked at this school. Now, I'm afraid if you don't have any further questions, I'm actually quite busy, as I'm sure you must be.'

She picked up the phone, pressed a number and asked the secretary to come to her office. A few seconds later, there was a tap at the door and the secretary appeared. 'Alice, would you show DS Fisher out, please.'

Molly stood, nodding politely at the head teacher, who was already busying herself with some paperwork on her desk. 'Thank you, Mrs Atherton,' she said with as much sincerity as she could muster, 'you've been very helpful.'

The secretary smiled at Molly and gestured to follow her into the corridor. She knew when she was being fobbed off, but Molly knew when and how to pick her battles, and this particular battle could wait until she'd found out more about Thomas Blake Primary School and its icy head teacher.

She walked along the corridor, quickly falling into step with Alice. 'Have you worked here long?' Molly asked, mostly by way of small talk but also to see if it was worth quizzing the secretary on the real reason Susan Elliot née Milton and Kieran Judd had left the school.

'Not long,' she said breezily. 'Actually, I've only been here a few weeks. Mrs Atherton's been great though. She's really shown me the ropes.' She turned and looked at Molly. 'I know she probably came across as a bit of an ogre, but she's actually very nice when you get to know her. I think she just puts on this tough front because she's so determined to appear efficient and professional. By all accounts, she's really transformed the school.' She stopped talking, as though suddenly aware that she'd said too much.

'Yes,' Molly agreed blandly. 'It looks like a lovely school.'

But she was thinking about Rachel Atherton. There was something she hadn't wanted Molly to know. Her reaction when Molly had told her what had happened to two of her former colleagues: shock, yes, but something else: *fear*...?

Despite her cool detachment – her efficiency and professionalism – Molly reckoned Rachel Atherton had a pretty good idea why Susan Elliot and Kieran Judd had been murdered, and she would bet her pension that reason was somehow connected with something that had happened at this school.

They reached the main door that led out into the car park. Alice pressed a large button beside the door, which unlocked with a click. Once Molly was outside, the door closed behind her with another firm click.

Chapter Twenty-Eight

Denning was unhappy at the lack of progress. He knew murder investigations took time, and despite the relentless detective work along the way, often you had to rely on a lucky break that came at you out of nowhere and pushed the investigation in the direction it needed to go. What he didn't need was another setback, and yet suddenly, that was exactly what he was facing.

Helen Livingstone was sitting in her kitchen, crying into a clean hankie and sipping a mug of strong, sweet tea that had been made for her by one of the two uniformed officers currently keeping her company in her kitchen. A tall, awkward-looking man hovered nearby: a neighbour apparently. And, it seemed, their only witness to what had happened.

The kitchen looked new: smart white units and marble tops. Not too dissimilar, Denning mused, to the one he and Sarah had in their flat.

Helen Livingstone's husband Euan was lying dead in the hallway of their detached house on a modern estate of 'executive homes' in Swiss Cottage. He'd been stabbed to death when he'd answered his front door.

By the time Denning arrived, the road had been cordoned off. Sheila Gorton and her CSIs were already suited up and going about their business.

'Just like Susan Elliot,' Gorton had said as soon as she saw him walking up the driveway. 'And Kieran Judd...'

Euan Livingstone had died where he fell: on the doorstep in full view of his neighbours. Only, nobody had seen anything. It was late afternoon. Although the Livingstones were retired, most of their neighbours were at work. However, someone in the house opposite worked from home. He'd heard a scream, and looked out of his window to Euan clutching his stomach, bleeding. The neighbour had glimpsed someone running down the street: hoodie, fast, average build. The description as vague as before.

The neighbour had phoned 999 and then rushed over to the Livingstones' house. He was presently standing in the kitchen anxiously trying to comfort Helen Livingstone, and looking like he'd rather be somewhere else.

'Same MO as the others,' Gorton said, standing next to Denning in the kitchen. 'I know that doesn't necessary prove anything, but it suggests we're looking for the same person.' This was why she'd asked for Denning, even though Swiss Cottage technically fell under the jurisdiction of another team. As much as he didn't want to admit it, this was down to their killer.

'Mrs Livingstone,' Denning began, 'I'm DI Matthew Denning. I'm terribly sorry for what's happened... I will need to ask you some questions in a minute.'

She looked up at him, her eyes red and glistening, and nodded. Denning turned to the neighbour. 'You live opposite, I believe? I understand you may have witnessed what happened, Mr...?'

'Wilde,' the man said, extending a nervous hand, clearly not someone who was used to dealing with the police, thought Denning. 'Charlie Wilde. I've already told one of your officers what I saw, which, I'm afraid, wasn't much.' He repeated what he'd already told the uniformed officers, apologising for not being able to add more. Denning could sense the man was uncomfortable, and probably wanted to return to his own home, having only come over to check on Helen Livingstone out of courtesy and concern.

Denning turned to Helen. She had stopped crying and was staring blankly at a cup and saucer on the draining board by the sink.

'Are you OK to talk now, Mrs Livingstone?' Denning asked gently. 'I need you to go over what happened.'

'The doorbell rang, he went to answer it. We were getting ready to go out. We were due to meet friends for dinner this evening. I was upstairs in our bedroom getting changed. He went downstairs and then I heard him scream. When I ran downstairs, he was lying in the hallway bleeding. Mr Wilde from across the road came over. He told me he'd phoned for an ambulance. They told me he'd been stabbed and had lost a lot of blood. They said it was too late. By that time the police had arrived and they took me in here and made me a cup of tea. But I just wanted to be with Euan.'

'Did Euan say anything?'

She thought for a moment. 'No. He was just lying there. He tried to say something, then he passed out.'

'You don't know what he was trying to say? I know it's difficult, but anything you can tell us will be helpful.'

She shook her head. 'He wasn't making any sense. He was just muttering. If he was trying to say something then I couldn't make it out. Then he just…' She couldn't finish the rest of the sentence. She started crying again and Denning realised he was in danger of pushing her too far. He felt guilty pressuring her like this, but the situation

147

was getting serious. If it was the same killer, there was now an even greater urgency about this case. According to Gorton, Mrs Livingstone's GP had been contacted and was on his way. It was likely he would give her a sedative. But in the meantime, Denning needed to gather as much evidence as he could while events were still fresh in her mind.

'I am sorry, Mrs Livingstone, and I realise this isn't easy, and I won't keep you much longer.' He paused, waiting for her to compose herself. 'Did you hear anything on the doorstep? Any conversation?'

'No. I told you... I heard the doorbell ring. Then I didn't hear anything until Euan screamed. I was in our bedroom. It's at the back of the house. I thought it might have been a delivery or something. Euan's always ordering things from Amazon. Rubbish mostly. I'm constantly having a go at him about it...' She realised what she was saying and stopped abruptly. 'Why did this has happen to us?' She looked at Denning when she asked the question, but he knew it wasn't addressed at anyone specifically. 'We're good people,' she continued. 'Things like this shouldn't happen to us.'

Denning didn't have the heart to say that crime happened to anyone. You could make your home as secure as possible; ensure your life was as free from risk and danger as it could be, and still be a victim of crime. Crime didn't discriminate. 'I know it's distressing, but we don't believe this was an entirely random attack, Mrs Livingstone. We believe it's possible your husband was targeted by someone he knew. Can you think of any reason why someone would want to kill him?'

She looked at Denning as though she'd asked an impertinent question. 'Of course not. Euan was a good man.

There was something on the news the other day about a man being stabbed on his doorstep somewhere in east London. The press seem to think it's the work of a maniac. This could be the same person. Killing innocent people in their own homes for no reason at all.'

He'd read the stories in the press. The more sensationalist papers were running stories along the lines of there being killer on the loose in London targeting householders at random. McKenna's refusal to condemn the stories merely added fuel to the fire. It was a double-edged sword: on the one hand it meant the press were being kept on the back foot as far as the murders were concerned, but it also served its purpose as far as newspapers were concerned and helped to spread fear and panic among its readers.

'We don't know anything for certain at this stage,' Denning said calmly, 'but we believe the murders are linked. And we believe there's something that links the victims.'

She shook her head, trying to focus on what Denning was asking her. She looked at him like he was talking nonsense. 'I don't know,' she said. 'I'm sorry I can't be of more help.'

'I won't keep you any longer, Mrs Livingstone. I just need to ask you one more question. What did Euan do for a living? Before he retired?'

'He used to work in a primary school,' she said. 'He was a headmaster.' A flicker of a smile twitched at her lips. 'Although I believe they're referred to as head teachers these days.'

'Which school was that?' Denning asked.

'Thomas Blake Primary School,' she said. 'It's in Chiswick.'

Chapter Twenty-Nine

'This is turning into something of a shitshow,' McKenna said the next day.

They were in her office; McKenna behind her desk, her right hand clutching a tuft of her raven hair; Denning sitting opposite trying to look as though he was more in control of the situation than he felt. The atmosphere in the office was grim. 'Now we've got a third murder on our hands,' McKenna continued, 'and still no idea as to who's responsible or why.' She removed her hand from her hair and started drumming her fingers on the desk. Both the hair clutching and finger drumming were a visual sign that McKenna wasn't happy. 'Are we certain these killings are linked, Matt? I mean, can we say for sure we're dealing with the same killer?'

He repeated what Sheila Gorton had told him about the MOs being the same. And then there was the other piece of information that pretty much told them these murders were connected. 'We know that Euan Livingstone had been head teacher at the same school where Kieran Judd and Susan Elliot née Milton had worked,' Denning said. 'That gives us something to work with.'

'So we can now assume the school is the link?'

He nodded. 'DS Fisher was there this afternoon, talking to the current head teacher, a Rachel Atherton. Apparently she confirmed that both Susan Eliot and

Kieran Judd had worked there, though both left the school around two years ago. From what I can gather, Euan Livingstone retired not long afterwards.'

'We're assuming this isn't a coincidence?'

'According to Molly, the head teacher was deliberately vague, insisting Susan Elliot and Kieran Judd left of their own accord and weren't involved in anything that resulted in a disciplinary matter. Naturally she's following this up as we speak, but it does raise the question of why the head teacher was so evasive.'

'You think she's hiding something?'

He thought about this. 'Possibly. Or it is just possible this has nothing at all to do with the school.'

McKenna stopped drumming her fingers on the desk and fixed Denning with one of her gimlet stares. 'OK, let's focus our attention on the school. We'll need to speak to the head teacher again: find out what happened that could have resulted in three former staff members ending up getting stabbed to death in their own homes.' She dropped the gimlet stare and resumed the finger tapping. 'I presume we can now rule Tony Hallam out as being the original intended target?'

Denning tried not to feel too sheepish. 'It looks like Hallam has nothing to do with any of this. If the school is the link, then we can assume Judd was the target all along.'

'So we've wasted a considerable amount of time running round after a man who wasn't even part of this investigation in the first place?'

It was asked as a question but came across as a statement. 'Hallam is still up to something. I'm absolutely certain of that.' Denning felt he had to fight his corner. Even if Tony Hallam wasn't directly involved in their murder investigation, he was still a man who needed watching.

'Unless he's planning to murder someone, or he already has, then it's not really any of our concern, is it?' She sighed. 'Look, I've spoken to someone at Serious Crime... they say they'll keep an eye on Hallam and Meech but, without anything concrete, there's not a lot they can do. And this is not our call.'

They were disturbed by a knock on the door and Denning was glad of the distraction. Molly Fisher entered the office and looked from Denning to McKenna and back again, as though uncertain which of her senior officers she should speak to first. Out of deference, she addressed McKenna.

'As I suspected, Rachel Atherton lied,' she said. 'Well, OK, maybe she didn't exactly *lie*, but she wasn't entirely honest.' She turned to look at Denning. 'Technically, I should arrest for obstructing a murder investigation.'

'What are you talking about, DS Fisher?' McKenna asked, the exasperation clear in her voice.

'Thomas Blake Primary School,' Molly said. She looked at them as though it was so obvious it didn't need to be spelled out. 'I should have realised. In fact, I think I remember reading something about it at the time.'

McKenna looked at Molly. 'Any chance you could let us in on it? Sometime today, preferably.'

'I googled it,' Molly continued, ignoring McKenna's sarcasm. 'About two and half years ago a child was killed.'

Chapter Thirty

'We now know what happened at Thomas Blake Primary School,' Denning said as he addressed the team first thing the following morning.

They sat at their desks, bleary-eyed. Three murders, which meant the pressure was mounting to get a result.

Denning gestured at the whiteboard behind him. Photos of the victims were pinned to it: Kieran Judd, Susan Elliot and now Euan Livingstone. Underneath was a photo of a park along with a map. The photos of Tony Hallam and Declan Meech had been removed.

'During a school outing to a local park in early April two years ago, five-year-old Noah Daniel, a pupil at Thomas Blake Primary School, ran out of the park and into the path of an oncoming car. He was killed. His death was a tragic accident. The car's driver, a seventy-six-year-old woman called Marion Haynes, hadn't been speeding. In fact, according to the traffic police, she had barely been doing the speed limit. But it didn't made a difference. Noah Daniel hit his head against the kerb and died later that day in hospital from a bleed on the brain. The traffic report of the incident had been emailed through and the team had read it. The coroner's report stated it was an accidental death, and Marion Haynes was cleared of any culpability. There were claims that the school had been negligent and there was an official inquiry into its handling of the events that led up to the accident. It was argued that the children were not fully supervised at the time, an accusation the school strenuously denied. There are printed copies of both the coroner's report and the ensuing inquiry on your desks. It's worth reading over them to get some background to the case. But as always, don't take everything at face value; these situations aren't always black and white.'

'So this is about revenge,' Kinsella said. 'Someone's going after the teachers who were on duty that day. Surely that makes the kid's parents our number one suspects?'

'Not necessarily, Dave,' Denning said. 'Obviously we will be speaking to Adam and Peta Daniel, Noah's parents, but let's not start jumping to any conclusions just yet.'

'Not even obvious ones…?' Kinsella asked.

Denning ignored him and continued. 'We have a list of all the teachers who were on the school outing that day, and we need to arrange police protection for the surviving ones. Uniform are speaking to them now. Obviously we'll need to interview them.'

'What about Euan Livingstone?' Trudi asked, leafing through the inquiry report. 'he wasn't there on the day.'

'He was head teacher at the time, Trudi,' Denning said. 'He was the one who authorised the trip. Ultimately it was his responsibility.'

'But the school must have authorised dozens of these kind of trips over the years. He wasn't to know what was going to happen.'

'None of them were,' Molly added. 'Despite the inquiry's findings about shortcomings regarding the children's supervision, it does conclude that it was a terrible accident. Ultimately no one was responsible.'

'We have to assume our killer thinks otherwise,' Denning said. 'But, like I said, let's not jump to any conclusions until we've spoken to all the staff members who were there that day. We also need to speak to Rachel Atherton again. She's the current head teacher at Thomas Blake Primary School, but according to the inquiry findings, she was working at the school at the time as deputy head, so she would have been aware of the facts.' He paused and looked over at Molly. 'Despite this, when DS Fisher spoke to her yesterday, she failed to mention any of this. It might be worth our while finding out why.'

Dave Kinsella was looking disgruntled. 'If this really is all to do with this kid's death, then you'd go after the driver of the car.' He looked directly at Denning. 'I presume we have checked that she hasn't been knifed too.'

'Uniform are speaking to Mrs Haynes this morning, Dave,' Denning said. 'But there have been no reports of anyone else being killed in similar circumstances.'

'She could have moved away,' Neeraj said. 'No longer be living in London.'

'I've checked HOLMES 2,' Denning said. 'Ignoring the usual random knife crime that seems par for the course these days, the only murders matching ours are the ones we already know about.' HOLMES 2 gathered and collated information relating to all major crimes committed in the UK. It wasn't fool-proof, as no system was, but it was a helpful tool for cross-checking any similar crimes to the ones they were currently investigating and finding useful connections.

Kinsella sounded like he still needed some persuading. 'All these people left the school ages ago. If this has got something to do with what happened, why is our killer offing people who no longer work there? And why now?' He folded his arms across his chest. 'For argument's sake, let's say these murders have sod all to do with what happened to that kid, then we have to consider other motives. I mean, up until the other day we thought this had something to do with Tony Hallam and Declan Meech?'

'We don't know, Dave. We don't even know for certain that this *is* to do with the incident in the park. But right now, it's the best lead we've got.'

'Does this mean we're now officially ruling out any link with Hallam?' Kinsella asked.

'If our theory is right, then we have to assume Kieran Judd was the intended target all along. Naturally, we'll keep all options open and if anything comes to light that suggests Hallam *was* the intended victim, or if we find anything that links Hallam with either Susan Elliot or Euan Livingstone, then we'll reconsider. But for now, let's focus on Thomas Blake Primary School, and Noah Daniel's death.'

Denning was sure he could see a smug look pass over Kinsella's face, even though it was Kinsella who'd pointed them in the direction of Tony Hallam in the first place. He could have mentioned that fact, but this wasn't the time or the place for petty point scoring.

'We're assuming our killer is going to go after someone else?' Neeraj asked. 'Do you know who the most likely victim could be?'

'It could be anyone who was supervising the children that day,' Denning said. 'Which is why we need to speak to them all.'

Denning noticed Trudi Bell was shaking her head very slightly. 'Trudi?'

'I have to reluctantly admit, Dave may have a point about why they've waited until now. This all happened over two years ago.'

'Something's made our killer strike now,' Molly said. 'Something significant.'

'An anniversary, maybe?' Neeraj suggested. 'His birthday? Or something's happened within the family to trigger this reaction?'

'Or something else…?' Molly suggested.

'Let's face it,' Kinsella said. 'Until we speak to this Adam and Peta Daniel, then we're pissing in the dark. We should bring them in.'

'We need to be careful, Dave,' Denning said firmly. 'We don't know they're responsible, and they did lose a child in tragic circumstances. The last thing they need right now is for us to go after them accusing them of murder, with little or no evidence to back that up.' He looked around his team. 'We'll speak to Mr and Mrs Daniel, but we'll do so with kid gloves.' He looked at Molly when he said this. 'But right now our main priority is to protect the surviving staff members who were in the park on the day. Because if there's another murder, then it's going to be on our watch.'

'Exactly what kind of police protection are we talking about here?' Neeraj asked.

'At the moment, Deep, whatever we can get. We'll warn the potential victims, issue them with an Osman warning if necessary, and ask them to take obvious precautions. In addition, we'll see what uniform can spare, though we'll be lucky if we have the resources to offer round-the-clock protection.'

'We don't even know for certain that they are being targeted,' Kinsella said.

'We can't take that risk,' Dave. 'The first three victims are directly involved with what happened in the park that day. We have no option but to ensure the safety of the others involved.'

Denning wished he had something more constructive to offer, because he had a horrible feeling that their killer wasn't going to stop until they'd finished the job they'd started.

Chapter Thirty-One

Peta and Adam Daniel lived in Hammersmith. They were still living in the same neat, bay-windowed, terraced house they had called home when their only son had gone off to school one morning and never come back.

It was two-thirds of the way along a quiet side-street off Fulham Road. At one end of the road were a row of shops: an off licence; a florist; and a newsagent. At the other end, the District Line trundled past.

The Daniels looked to Molly to be in their mid-forties. Peta was wearing a flowery dress, with her hair tied back in a loose pony tail; Adam was slightly older, with a greying beard, long, wispy hair, slowly edging from black to grey, and large Eric Morecambe-style glasses. They showed Molly and Trudi into a cluttered living room awash with books and esoteric artwork on the walls.

There was a dusty old chaise longue in the bay of the window, which reminded Molly of the grotty old one Jon used to have mouldering in his sitting room, until it collapsed under the bulk of an overweight neighbour during a party earlier in the year. She hadn't mourned its passing.

The room was comfortably furnished, with what looked like a hessian mat and a couple of heavy bookcases, overflowing with books. There was a faint mustiness about the house; it was in need of a good airing. She spotted a framed photograph on a table beside the fireplace of a dark-haired child in glasses with an unsure smile, who she took to be Noah. It looked very much like a school photo, probably one of the last ones ever taken of him.

'He's still in our hearts,' Mrs Daniel said, noticing her looking at the photo. 'We think about him every day. It would have been his birthday in November. He'd have been eight.' She stared impassively at Molly and Trudi when she spoke as though she was talking about someone distant that he barely knew. She suspected this was her way of coping.

'He was a lovely, bright lad,' Adam added. 'I don't think that school was the best environment for him. I don't think they challenged him enough. In hindsight, we should have chosen another school for him.'

'I'm very sorry about what happened to Noah,' Molly said. 'I can't begin to understand what it must be like to lose a child. As much as I hate having to do so, I must ask you some questions about the accident.'

They looked at each other. Molly could read from their faces that even though it happened over two years ago, the wounds had yet to heal. Remorse radiated off them like a pungent smell that no amount of scrubbing would ever remove. She understood their anger.

'He wasn't being properly supervised,' Peta Daniel said coldly. 'It was as simple as that. If they had been properly looking after him, he would never have run out onto the road into the path of that car. He knew about roads and the dangers of traffic. It wasn't his fault.'

'The school claimed it was an accident,' Trudi said. 'According to them all the correct procedures were followed at all times.'

'They never admitted it was their fault he was killed,' Adam said quietly. 'But they were entirely responsible. They should have ensured Noah was being watched at all times. I fail to see how the school wasn't to blame.'

'I understand how you must feel,' Molly said. 'But there was an official inquiry into the incident. It established that the school had followed all the procedures as they claimed: a full risk assessment had been carried out before the trip, and there were sufficient staff members to look after the pupils.' She realised this wasn't what they wanted to hear, but it was the truth, however unpalatable for the Daniels. 'The coroner declared it was an accidental death.'

'The whole matter was covered up,' Mr Daniel said abruptly. 'We wanted to take the school to court and charge them with corporate manslaughter, but were talked out of it by our solicitor. He said we didn't have a case. The school *claimed* the children were being fully supervised, but it's clear that wasn't the case. If it had been, Noah wouldn't have been able to run out onto the road.'

'They closed ranks,' Peta said darkly. 'And don't tell us you understand how we feel. You don't. You can't.'

Molly let the comment pass. They were angry. And their anger was understandable. They had to deal with pain of losing a child every day of their lives. Molly's questions were adding to that pain. 'If you'd felt that strongly, you could have taken out a private prosecution against the school,' Molly said. She wasn't sure what it would have achieved, but it might have offered the Daniels some sort of closure.

'They said if we made an issue out of it then it would come out that Noah was a difficult child. It was lies but they had the upper hand. We were helpless against them.'

Molly suspected they were exaggerating, though it was just possible there may well have been a grain of truth in what they were saying. She could imagine the school would be keen to protect its reputation, even if it meant fighting dirty with two grieving parents. 'You must have been resentful,' Molly said. 'Angry even.'

'We were at the time,' Adam said. 'But there's no point in carrying all that anger round with you. It won't bring Noah back.'

It was difficult not to feel sympathy for them. Grief and pain still washed over them like a rainfall. Molly did briefly wonder if they really could be responsible for killing three people in cold blood: the animosity towards the school still festered, and she couldn't blame them for that, but she didn't think they were capable of murder. She couldn't see them inflicting the kind of suffering that had been visited on them on to other people. But she had to push, just to make sure. 'Did you blame the school? Or did you blame specific people in the school?'

'What do you mean by that?' Peta Daniel looked at Molly quizzically.

'I mean, for argument's sake, did you ever feel like taking revenge against anyone involved? Specifically the members of staff who had taken Noah to the park that day? You're right when you said I can't imagine what it's like to be in your situation. I can't, but I'm trying to understand the emotions involved. Has that anger ever spiralled since, I wonder?'

'I don't understand what you're saying.' Adam Daniel looked like someone had just slapped him on the face. He looked at his wife who just shook her head slowly. Then he turned to look at Molly and Trudi. 'Yes, we were angry at what happened to Noah, but we wouldn't take our anger out on other people.' A realisation seemed to spread over his face as the penny dropped. 'Oh, I see where you're going with this. That man, the one on the news last night. The one who was stabbed to death…' He looked over to his wife again. 'He was the headmaster at Noah's school. I told you I recognised the name. Remember, he came round to see us after it happened. Oh, he was very sorry and offered us his sympathies, but what he really wanted was to make sure we didn't hold him responsible.' He was still looking at his wife. He turned to face the two detectives.

'In the end,' she said calmly, 'we asked him to leave.'

'We didn't murder that headmaster,' Adam Daniel said. 'I can see what you're thinking, and I know you have to ask these things, and I suppose I can understand why we might be suspects, but we're Quakers. We don't believe in violence or in retribution.' He shook his head, looking at the photo on the table of the child he'd never see again. 'Yes, we were angry at the way he handled the situation. At the way they *all* handled the situation, but we would never take our anger out on anyone else. Yes, we wanted the school to pay for what happened to Noah, and yes, we felt they got off lightly after what happened. But if you're seriously suggesting that we were angry enough to actually kill someone over it, then you're wrong. Very wrong.'

And Molly believed them. Whoever was killing the people involved in Noah Daniel's death, it wasn't his parents.

Chapter Thirty-Two

Alice Hennicke greeted Denning and Neeraj with a warm smile when they pitched up at Thomas Blake Primary School and showed her their ID, asking to speak to Rachel Atherton. They'd phoned ahead to make sure she was free to see them; neither had the time nor the inclination to wait outside her office like a pair of naughty schoolboys. This was a murder investigation and Denning was already suspicious as to why the head teacher had felt the need to deliberately mislead Molly.

'I'll show you to her office,' Alice said, still smiling. 'I believe she is expecting you.' She led them along a short corridor that smelled of boiled cabbage and beeswax. Alice tapped lightly on the door and waited until a voice shouted to come in.

Rachel Atherton was sitting behind her desk, unsmiling and looking annoyed. Denning and Neeraj showed her their ID and explained why they were there.

'I went over all this yesterday,' she said, indicating for both men to take a seat. 'I spoke to a DS...' She shook her head trying to remember.

'DS Fisher,' Denning said. 'And I appreciate that. However, you didn't actually tell DS Fisher the whole story, did you?'

She pulled a puzzled face. 'I don't know what you mean. I confirmed that the members of staff she mentioned worked here and all had now left the school. I was sorry to hear about what had happened to them, but I don't see what more I can tell you.'

'You could tell us exactly what happened two-and-a-half years ago,' Denning said. 'The accident in the park. Noah Daniel being knocked down and killed.' He looked directly at her, ensured he held her gaze. 'You worked here at the time, Mrs Atherton, as deputy head teacher, so you must have been aware of exactly what happened that day.'

She stared back at Denning; an intimidating look that probably worked with young children, and possibly their parents, but its effect was wasted on Denning. McKenna had perfected the gimlet stare and this wasn't even in her league.

'I really don't know what you're insinuating,' she replied icily. 'It was a terrible accident and a member of staff resigned as a consequence. As far as I'm concerned, the matter was handled appropriately at the time and the school was in no way responsible. It was also over two years ago. I don't want to lecture you on your job, Inspector, but as I told DS Fisher yesterday, these awful murders have nothing whatsoever to do with this school. The connection is nothing more than circumstantial. I would be looking elsewhere for your motive.'

Denning had read up on Rachel Atherton and Thomas Blake Primary School before coming round to see her today. The school certainly had a reputation to be proud of: it had been judged Outstanding by Ofsted the previous year, while Rachel Atherton had generally been credited with turning the place around after two or three years of average results and mixed grades. She had a trenchant reputation: both for getting results and for running a good school. Although there had been some minor grumblings about her on social media and intemperate letters to the local newspaper, parents liked her. She was strong on discipline and attendance. There was no suggestion she was anything other than a hundred per cent professional and dedicated to her job. But there was something about her approach to the school that he'd found uncomfortable: there seemed to be almost too much of an emphasis on discipline and following the rules, and not so much focus on enjoyment and creativity. Rules were all well and good, but it was his belief that children – particularly young children – should be allowed to express themselves and be encouraged to be individuals rather than well-turned-out robots. He was glad Jake didn't go to Thomas Blake Primary School.

'Well, thank you for your advice, Mrs Atherton, but I'll conduct the investigation into the murder of three of your former employees as I deem appropriate. And that means exploring all the possible motives behind their murders. We now believe the day in question is significant. Perhaps you could talk me through exactly what happened in the park that afternoon.'

She tried to outstare him again, but eventually acknowledged defeat. 'I imagine you know the basics,' she said. 'Most of it was covered in the very public inquiry that followed the death of Noah Daniel.' She looked at Denning and Neeraj, a steely glint in her eye. 'There was a full inquiry. The school was found not to have breached any health and safety regulations. There were sufficient teaching and support staff supervising the children on the day. The school had undertaken numerous trips to that park before Noah Daniel's accident, all without incident. The inquiry absolved us of any blame.'

'I've read the inquiry findings. I accept that officially the school was found to have done nothing wrong. But it's now clear someone feels otherwise. Perhaps you could fill in some of the blanks for us. Tell us what the inquiry left out.'

She sighed heavily and sat back in her chair. 'Our year one teachers had decided to take the children to the park as a treat. This was something they often did, though usually towards the end of the summer term. But we'd been enjoying a spell of pleasant spring weather and someone had suggested to Euan that the children might benefit from a trip to the local park. I was against the idea and said as much at the time. I don't think it's good to take the children out of school too often, unless it's directly beneficial to their education. I've personally organised trips to the Natural History Museum and the Science Museum. We were even talking about a trip to the London Transport Museum later this year. But these trips need to be properly organised. Parents notified; risk assessments undertaken and obviously an assurance given that we have sufficient members of staff to supervise the children. We have a duty of care towards these children.'

'I don't see how taking them to a nearby park was placing them in danger,' Neeraj said. 'Especially as what happened was an accident.'

'I take it you don't have children, sergeant?' she said witheringly. 'It only takes a couple of disruptive influences and the whole group dynamic changes. Believe me, I have a degree in child behavioural psychology, and I've worked in schools all my life. I know what I'm talking about.'

Neeraj didn't answer. Denning, who was very familiar with the sometimes-challenging behaviour of children, spoke for both of them. 'I'm sure my colleague wasn't trying to question your running of the school, Mrs Atherton. We just need to get a clear picture of what happened that day and how someone might have come to the conclusion that the school was in some way to blame for a child's death.'

His comment seemed to propitiate her and she even offered a wintry smile. 'I'm sorry, Inspector, I don't mean to come across as unhelpful, but I really feel we're in danger of going round in circles here. The school did nothing wrong. You've said yourself the inquiry absolved us of any blame. I can't see how this discussion is helpful.'

'Three people who were on that school trip are now dead, Mrs Atherton. You yourself may yet be in danger. We don't know why this person is doing this, but they clearly have some kind of vendetta against the school, and it would appear to relate to the incident in the park. Anything you can tell us will help us catch this person.'

She gave another heavy sigh. 'Like I told you, I was against the decision to take the children to the park that day. It's different in the summer: the school year is coming to an end, the children are naturally getting restless and can't wait for the holidays. It's especially difficult for the youngest ones: Years One and Two. School is still is a relatively new experience for them. OK, I know a lot of them have been to nursery and pre-school, but primary school is very different. We're preparing them for life in a grown-up world. Yes, I know what you're thinking. I can read it in your faces. They're children. But the devel-opment from childhood to adulthood is a process. This is where that process starts. They learn the basic skills that will hopefully see them turn into fully rounded adults: social skills, discipline, the desire for knowledge. A solid work ethic. This is where that all begins.'

Denning thought about Jake. These were the things he wanted for his son, but these factors didn't take into account the children who couldn't understand them. The children who were in danger of being left behind. Children like Jake. And Noah Daniel.

'I know you probably see me as some kind of monster.' She offered another cold smile. 'I'm not. I just believe in getting the best from the children in my care. Nurturing their potential. Giving them hope.'

'That's all very laudable, Mrs Atherton. But can we get back to the day in question. You've made it clear you were against the decision to take the children to the park, but you were obviously over-ruled by Euan Livingstone. Can you tell us what happened next?'

'I admit that this particular trip might have been planned, but it was poorly organised. No arrangements were put in place to deal with…well, to put it bluntly, to deal with children like Noah Daniel. Noah could be difficult. Well, perhaps that's unfair. Maybe difficult is not the right word. Challenging would be the correct term.'

'Challenging?' Denning asked. 'In what way?' Though he could already sense which direction the conversation was heading in.

'Minor behavioural issues. For instance, if you asked him to do something, he wouldn't do it. Equally, there would be times you would tell him not to do something and he would deliberately do it to spite you. In a classroom environment such behaviour can be managed, but outside, with more children than staff and numerous stimulants that can distract a child, it can be much harder to manage that behaviour.'

Denning found himself starring at a novelty mouse mat on her desk when she was explaining this. To hear about children with special needs referred to as though they were nothing more than an inconvenience was slowly making his blood boil. But he was here to find answers that would help him catch a killer before they struck again; his personal feelings were not relevant. 'But he never received a formal diagnosis of autism or ADHD?'

'The school contacted Noah's parents on numerous occasions about his behaviour, but nothing was ever done beyond empty promises about how they would speak to him.'

'How come?' Neeraj asked.

'Noah's parents were what I suppose we would have called hippies in days gone by. I imagine "free spirit" would be the modern equivalent. They didn't want their son labelled or stigmatised. They insisted he should be free to develop at his own rate and not be saddled with something he might not have that would dictate the direction his life would take.'

'So, what exactly happened the day he was killed?' Neeraj asked, drawing everyone's attention back to the matter in hand.

She looked at Neeraj, throwing him what Denning suspected was the look she used when dealing with a child whose behaviour she defined as challenging. But the effect was lost on Neeraj, who just stared back at her, mouth open slightly.

'The TA who was responsible for looking after Noah was momentarily distracted. Before anyone could react, Noah was running towards the gate that led on to the road which ran along the western edge of the park. It wasn't a particularly busy road – it even, I believe, had a 20mph limit.' She rubbed a hand over her eyes, then continued. 'The other TA on duty that day – Kieran Judd

– ran to try and stop him.' She rubbed her eyes again. 'He wasn't quick enough. Noah was out the gate and straight on to the road before he had a chance to catch him. He'd spotted an ice cream van in a nearby road, apparently. It was just bad luck that there was a car going along the road at the time. The driver wasn't going fast – as the inquiry clearly stated – but Noah ran straight into her path. He bounced off the car and hit his head on the kerb. The whole thing only lasted a matter of seconds. An ambulance was called, naturally, but the paramedics couldn't save him. Laura Grieve, the TA who was supposed to have been looking after Noah, resigned from her job shortly afterwards. Although she wasn't directly to blame for what happened, she felt responsible.'

'It seems a lot of the staff on duty that day left the job in the wake of the accident,' Denning said. 'Susan Elliot and Kieran Judd both either left teaching or went to another school. Euan Livingstone took early retirement.'

She looked impassive, sitting behind her desk, making it clear what had happened was nothing to do with her decision-making. 'It's not uncommon for staff to either leave the profession or to move to other schools. Euan had been talking about retiring before the accident, and felt no reason to change his mind.'

And I bet you were quick enough to jump into his shoes, Denning thought.

'When you say Laura Grieve was distracted, how exactly was she distracted?'

'Laura had personal issues going on at the time. I understand her marriage had recently ended and she was struggling to cope with it. In hindsight, we – Euan – should have either offered her more support or even insisted she took some time off until she was better able to cope with her situation. However – and again, against my better judgement – she insisted she was coping OK, so it was agreed she could carry on working.'

'Although you stated she wasn't directly to blame for what happened, I get the impression the school didn't try to dissuade her from resigning?'

'She admitted that her mind wasn't fully on the job. She accepted that it was her momentary lapse in concentration that resulted in Noah's death. She took responsibility for what happened, even though there was no suggestion that the school held her personally responsible. Euan was very clear that he didn't blame her.'

The school still accepted her resignation, Denning thought, suggesting an element of blame had been apportioned.

'You should seriously think about accepting police protection yourself,' Denning said.

'Me?' She sounded incredulous. 'I had nothing to do with what happened. I wasn't anywhere near the park that day. As I've already told both yourselves today and your colleague yesterday, the members of staff involved have all now left the school. The school itself is now under new leadership. As far as I'm concerned, this has got nothing to do with me.'

'You were deputy head at the time,' Denning said. 'Whoever's responsible for these killings was prepared to go after Euan Livingstone. It's possible our killer may feel this makes you as responsible as the staff members who were there on the day. Your life could be in danger, and I would advise you to take some precautions.'

'But that's different. Euan was head teacher at the time. He took overall responsibility for what happened. I was against taking the children to the park. If I'd been listened to in the first place, then none of this would have happened.' Her tone was indignant, but Denning was firm.

'All the same, it's possible the person responsible for these killings is unaware of that.'

'I'm sorry, but I can't have my life disrupted. Or the running of the school for that matter. We've got an assessment coming up next term and we need to prepare for it.'

'Your life might be in danger, Mrs Atherton, so I would advise you to put up with a little inconvenience for now, just to ensure your personal safety.'

She smiled another wintry smile. 'I appreciate your concern, Inspector. Believe me. But I don't scare easily. And I'm certainly not about to go into hiding at the exact time this school needs me.'

'OK. In that case, I suggest you take some precautions. Change your route to and from the school. Keep an eye out for anyone acting suspiciously. Maybe have a word with your local crime prevention team about beefing up your home security. The school's too, if necessary.'

She gave an awkward laugh. 'My husband and I have more than adequate security at home, and as you would be aware from when you arrived on the school premises, entry and exit to the main building is by key fob, and all visitors have to be buzzed into the building by the school secretary. There's CCTV covering the main entrance, which is supervised by at least two staff members at the start of the day, the end of the day and during playtime and lunchbreak. Short of having armed guards patrolling the corridors, there's not much else we can do.'

It all sounded very impressive. 'OK, Mrs Atherton. My colleague and I have made you aware of the situation. If you choose not to accept our suggestions, that's entirely up to you. I don't think there's any more we can say.'

'Of course, the best thing you could do to guarantee my safety, and that of the remaining staff members, is to catch the person responsible as quickly as possible,' she added cuttingly. 'And I would very much appreciate it if you try and keep the school's name out of it. What happened was so long ago it's hardly relevant.'

'I'll do my best, Mrs Atherton,' Denning said politely. 'Of course, I can't promise the press won't make the connection. In which case, the matter is out of my hands.'

When they were back in the car, Neeraj turned to Denning. 'Blimey, she was a bit scary. You gotta feel sorry for those kids. I read somewhere that she used to make them walk round the playground for fifteen minutes every morning, in all weathers.'

'Why?'

'Something to do with tackling childhood obesity. Apparently, she won some award for it.'

Hmm, no fat kids here, Denning thought to himself. Or children with developmental issues… There was something too quaintly authoritarian about Thomas Blake Primary School for Denning's liking, or, more to the point, about Rachel Atherton's approach to running the school. OK, she got results, but at what cost to the children's overall wellbeing.

'I'm more curious about why she kept things from us,' he said.

'You think she was lying?'

Denning thought about this. 'Not lying, just holding something back from us. Whatever happened that day, I don't think we've been told the whole story.'

Chapter Thirty-Three

The Laughing Parrot restaurant was located on Westow Hill, the main road that ran between Crystal Palace and Gipsy Hill. The area was officially known as West Norwood, though it was pretty much just a continuation of Crystal Palace. Molly remembered the area from when an old school friend had moved there almost twenty years ago. It had been a different place then: rougher with a slightly tawdry feel to it. The only thing that stood out for her was how much cheaper house prices were in that part of London compared to where she was living at the time. Poor transport links were the main reason, combined with the fact the area had an overlooked feel, as though it wasn't really part of London at all.

But, like so much of the capital, the area had been transformed in recent years. As prices in the more fashionable parts had risen, professionals looked further afield for affordable places to live. Gipsy Hill, with its amazing view of London, had developed a charm all of its own.

The outside of the restaurant was painted green and had brightly coloured menus in the window. It looked, at first glance, like it belonged in some piazza in southern Europe.

When Molly pushed the door open, she was greeted by a tall, willowy woman wearing a white cotton dress.

'Can I help you?' She smiled at Molly, assuming she was an early customer.

'I'm looking for Penny Garnett,' Molly said, showing her ID.

The woman looked at the card and then peered at her. 'I'm Penny Garnett,' she said. 'Can I ask what this is about?'

'Perhaps if you took a seat,' Molly said, indicating a table. The interior was painted in a slightly lighter shade of green that the exterior. Wood panelling ran along one wall, with abstract art work on the others. At the far end was a wooden counter and above it a ceramic cage with a stuffed parrot in it. Molly couldn't tell if the parrot was actually laughing.

It was still early so the restaurant wasn't busy: just a couple sitting in the window enjoying a pot of tea and some homemade carrot cake; a man sat near the counter, tapping away on his laptop, a large glass tumbler of coffee cooling by his elbow. Another hour and they'd be gearing up for lunchtime.

'Can I first confirm that you're the same Penny Garnett that previously worked as a teacher at Thomas Blake Primary School in Chiswick?'

She looked slightly taken aback, as though Molly had just pricked an open wound. 'Yes. I did… I left just over a year ago. I…' She rubbed a hand over her face. 'Look, can I ask what this is about?'

Molly was about to tell her when another woman appeared from what looked like the kitchen area. She was slightly shorter than Penny, and wore a chef's apron.

'This is my partner, Freya,' said Penny.

Molly introduced herself. 'If you're not too busy, maybe I could speak to you both together. This does concern both of you.'

Once the women were seated, Molly told them what they knew so far. 'I understand that the local CID will have spoken to you,' she said. 'They'll have advised you on the situation.'

'Yes,' Penny said. 'Two police officers came round earlier. They mentioned issuing something called an Osman Notice.'

'Yes. It probably sounds more alarming than it is,' Molly added. 'We have a legal obligation to make you aware that your lives may potentially be in danger, and advise you to take suitable precautions. And I have to stress that at this stage we don't know for certain that our killer is going after everyone involved in Noah Daniel's death, but we're working on that assumption. In which case, we have a duty to warn you.'

The women looked at each other. 'I must admit,' Penny said, 'when I heard what happened to Kieran and Susan. I did wonder. I didn't make the connection at first. I'd forgotten all about Kieran – he was only at the school for a short time – and Susan had changed her name. And, to be honest, I was trying not to think about it too much. I hoped it had to be a coincidence.'

'I still can't get my head round this,' Freya said after a moment. 'Pen had nothing to do with what happened that day. She was just one of the teachers who happened to be there. Nobody can think she's in any way responsible.'

'Like I said, we don't know for certain that is the case,' Molly said. 'But obviously I have to make you aware of the situation and advise you to take precautions. The CID officers will have informed you that we can offer you police protection if you feel you need it.'

'This is insane.' Freya looked at her partner for feedback, but Penny Garnett just shook her head.

'I can't honestly say I'm surprised, Freya. OK, I know I wasn't to blame for what happened, at least not directly.' She looked from one woman to the other. 'We were all responsible, but only one person ended up taking the actual blame.' She looked at Molly 'Laura Grieve, one of the TAs. She took what happened badly and was persuaded to resign. Looking back, it really wasn't fair, but we just all sort of went along with it because, well I suppose it let the rest of us off the hook.' She wrinkled her brow. 'I don't mean legally, but morally. At the end of the day, Laura was no more to blame then the rest of us.'

'So, she was asked to leave? Who by?'

Penny shrugged. 'Euan Livingstone I imagine. He was the head at the time. A nice man but slightly out of his depth. Mind you, it could have been Rachel. She was pushing hard to take over Euan's job at the time. It's the kind of thing she'd do, get someone to take responsibility, just in case there was any comeback on the school.'

'Rachel Atherton?' Molly asked, although she already knew the answer. 'Yes, I've met her. I got the impression she wasn't someone to be messed with.'

Penny laughed. 'That's certainly one way of putting it.' She rubbed a hand though her mane of hair. 'The whole thing was unfair. Laura genuinely thought she might be charged with manslaughter. You see, Noah was in her care. I mean we were all responsible for the welfare of the children that day, but the TAs all had specific groups of children they looked after. Noah was part of Laura's group.'

'But there was no real possibility that Laura Grieve would have been charged with manslaughter,' Molly said. 'The inquiry made it clear that it was an accident. There was no liability attributed to any one individual.' She'd read the inquiry report. It named the staff members on duty that day, but it had been very clear that no one staff member was found to be responsible. 'Why would she have thought otherwise?'

'The inquiry took around eight months to reach its conclusions,' Penny said. 'Laura had left by then. No one was in a position to second guess the inquiry's conclusions at that point.' She pursed her lips and shook her head. 'I don't know why Laura thought what she did. Like I say, she blamed herself. Maybe part of that self-blame involved a need to face some kind of legal redress.'

'So she lost her job? Forced to resign? It seems a bit harsh.'

'To be honest with you, DS Fisher, I think it was only the job that was keeping her sane at the time. I did hear a rumour that she had some kind of breakdown after she left.'

Molly wasn't surprised to hear it. The guilt that went with the responsibility combined with having so much time on her hands to think about what had happened would inevitably have done untold damage to her already fragile mental health. She knew it was imperative that they spoke to her soon.

'If she'd just waited for the outcome of the inquiry,' Penny said. 'Noah's parents weren't happy about the outcome, and I can't really say I blame them, but it meant the school's reputation survived intact. It was a difficult time for everyone though. Especially those of us who were there when Noah was killed.'

'What did you mean about the job being the only thing that was keeping her sane?'

'Laura had been having personal problems at the time after her marriage had ended. She was drinking. There were days she'd turn up with a hangover and could barely function. We all used to cover for her; make sure Euan and especially Rachel didn't find out how bad things were. If anyone is to blame here then it's me. Looking back, I should have told them Laura wasn't coping. But she promised me she was sorting herself out and turning her life around. She swore blind she was off the booze and seeking therapy.'

'What are you saying here, Penny? Laura Grieve wasn't in a fit state to be looking after children?'

Penny Garnett looked uncomfortable. 'She'd lied to me. It turned out she wasn't off the booze at all. The day of the school trip, she turned up for work with the most appalling hangover. I should have insisted she went home; said she was ill. I mean she *was* ill. But it would have meant we wouldn't have had enough staff to cover the outing. We were already down a couple of TAs; a combination of staff shortages and the Year Twos being on some dull trip Rachel had organised to the National History Museum. Anyway, whatever the case, Laura went on that school trip when she should never have been near the park or supervising children that day. I did think the fresh air might help sharpen her up a bit, but she was in such a state.'

Molly was struggling to take it all in. 'So, you're saying Laura Grieve was distracted because she had a hangover?

That's why Noah Daniel died?' If that was the case, Molly thought, then Laura Grieve *was* responsible.

'If I'd just told the truth in the first place,' Penny said. She was fighting back tears; dabbing at her eyes with her knuckles.

'None of that changes the fact this isn't your fault.' Freya reached out and placed a hand on her partner's arm.

'I stood back and let Laura take the blame for this,' Penny said. She looked at Molly. 'You think Noah's parents are behind this? Maybe if I had a word with them…?'

'I don't think that's a good idea,' Molly said. 'There's nothing to suggest that they are responsible. If anything, this has brought everything back for them.'

'So we just sit around waiting for some murderer to come after us?' Freya asked.

'No. We'll arrange for you to have a police officer with you at all times. We can provide you with an alarm linked directly to your nearest police station. Keep an eye out for anyone strange or suspicious.'

'We run a restaurant,' Freya said, 'we have strangers in here all the time.'

'If you're worried, you really should think seriously about closing the restaurant,' Molly said. 'Just until we catch the person responsible.'

'Yes. The local CID officer who spoke to us earlier today advised us to close for a while. But he didn't stipulate how long we should close for. This is our livelihood. If we close this place then we can't pay our mortgage.'

Molly was picking up on the aggressive tone from Freya. She understood where it was coming from, but it wasn't helpful. 'I appreciate this is difficult. I accept this is not a situation either of you wishes to be in. However, it's happened. We need to do what we can to keep you both safe.'

Penny sighed. 'Don't take it out on her, Freya. I already feel guilty about what happened. Not just that a child was killed on my watch, but at how we treated Laura. She was no more to blame than any of us.'

'Are you saying that justifies someone wanting to kill you? It was an accident, for Christ's sake!'

Penny turned to Molly. 'We would appreciate any support the police can give us. We'd rather not close the restaurant if we don't have to. But if it comes to it and you really think my life is in danger then we'll consider it. We've already made arrangements to stay with some friends for a while. But we'd like to keep the restaurant open if we can.' She offered a smile. 'I appreciate everything the police are doing for us.' She looked over at her partner. 'We both do.'

Freya looked like she was about to say something, then just smiled at Molly too.

'Just let us know what you need us to do,' Penny said. 'If it turns out it's easier for us to shut the restaurant, then we'll definitely consider it.'

'Thanks,' Molly said. She accepted that they wanted to carry on as normal. It was also possible, as with many people who felt their lives were in danger, that there was something unreal about the situation, as though the threat only really existed in the minds of the police. Molly wished that were the case. 'I'll give you my card,' she said. 'Call me anytime you need to.'

As she left the restaurant, she had the strangest feeling that someone was watching her. She looked behind her but there was no one there. *Jumping at shadows now*, she thought. But it was an eerie feeling, a prickling on the back of her neck. If someone was planning to kill Penny Garnett, then there was a strong chance they weren't going to let Molly get between them and their ambition.

She stopped and turned round. If someone was watching her then the best thing she could do would be to confront them head on. But there were just people walking up and down the pavement, going about their everyday business, and taking no notice of her. There was nothing to worry about except her own paranoia.

Chapter Thirty-Four

Denning wasn't sure what he was doing there. It was a pub by the river in Wapping that he'd been to before with Sarah on leisurely Sunday afternoons, sometimes for lunch, sometimes just for a drink and the chance to unwind while looking out onto the river. The Pear and Partridge had character, atmosphere and real ale. Despite its quirkiness, it was slightly off the tourist track so it wasn't busy in summer.

This evening was the first time he'd been here in several months. There was a very good reason why he hadn't been here and she was striding towards his table.

'Hello, Matt.'

He hadn't seen Anna Klein since the last time he'd been here back in June. He offered a weak smile, which he knew didn't reach the rest of his face. DS Anna Klein, to give her full name and rank, had previously been a member of the CID in Islington. Until it had been discovered that she had been involved with a criminal. A fact she had deliberately kept from her employers. On one level, he felt sorry for her but, on another, he wished she would just go away.

She scraped the chair opposite towards her and sat down.

'How have you been?' she asked.

He was determined to keep the conversation light; two old friends catching up over a drink after work. Except they'd never really be what could be described as friends exactly.

'Good, Anna. You?'

'How do you think?'

If he'd been surprised to get her call the other day, he'd made sure his voice said otherwise. His first thought had been to fob her off, telling her he was in the middle of a major murder investigation. He knew she wouldn't buy it. It was easier just to agree to meet, listen to what she had to say, make his excuses and wish her a nice life. However, he had a feeling it wasn't going to be that straightforward. Nothing with Anna ever was.

'I wasn't sure if you'd agree to meet me,' she said. She picked up a menu and began perusing it. She was wearing in her trademark raincoat, except rather than the smart business suit he was used to seeing her in when she was working, she was dressed in jeans and a casual top.

A waiter hovered by their table. Denning ordered a steak and green salad; after spending some time perusing the menu, Anna ordered linguini and a glass of white wine.

'There's still no word on when my hearing will be,' she said as soon as the waiter was out of earshot. 'I'm still suspended.'

'On full pay, Anna. Some people would say you're not doing too badly.'

She shot him a withering look. 'That's not really the point, is it?' She tried for a smile, an attempt to soften the rougher edges of what had become their relationship. 'I've explained the situation to them and argued my case, but they won't take me off suspension. It's ridiculous: the Met is seriously short-staffed and they won't let me work.'

'Those are the rules, Anna. Look, you'll be given an opportunity to argue your case. Your Federation rep must have prepared well. That, taken alongside your years of good service, are bound to count for something.'

'But there are no guarantees, Matt. I could be chucked out the Met for something silly that happened before I even became a police officer. It's so unfair.'

'And you'll have the opportunity to argue your case.'

'You've been there. You know how these things work. They twist things.'

Denning had been subject to an IOPC investigation earlier in the year when a suspect he'd been pursuing had been killed. The investigation had cleared him of any blame, but the circumstances had been very different. He still had to live with the guilt though; knowing someone had died as a result of his actions. 'It was a formality in my case, Anna. My actions weren't intentional. And I certainly never lied to my superiors about it.'

'I didn't lie. I just didn't mention something I didn't think was relevant.'

'Then tell them that. Be honest. Tell them you made a mistake. I'm sure there are plenty of colleagues who would speak up for you.'

She looked awkward for a moment. 'That's why I'm here. It would help if you gave me a reference. You're a DI; that would hold some sway.'

'Me? What about your own DI at Islington? Or your DCI?'

'I don't want to ask them. They've already said they don't want to get involved. It's difficult... besides, it would be better coming from you as you work in a different department. It would look good.'

'I don't know… I mean, it's not as if we worked together much. I mostly know you socially. That's probably not going to have much influence.'

'You owe me.'

He tried to hide his surprise. 'How do you work that out?'

'You were the one who told me to work with Molly Fisher. If you hadn't put me and her together in the first place, she wouldn't have gone running to Professional Standards with her stories. All because she didn't like me.'

'It wasn't quite like that though, was it?' He'd asked Molly and Anna to work together on a murder investigation a few months back. Anna Klein had been familiar with the background to the case, which had concerned the murder of a teenage girl who had become involved in a gang, and he'd naively assumed Molly and Anna would have worked well together, having much in common. It had turned out, however, that their working relationship was anything but harmonious. Denning sensed Molly now regretted the decision to report Klein and had never intended to get another officer into serious trouble. It was too late now though: once it became official, an IOPC investigation took on a momentum of its own. When the wheels started to turn, nothing was going to stop them.

'She stabbed me in the back.'

'You lied about your involvement with a known criminal, Anna. Molly had every right to report you.'

'I just don't think it's fair I'm being punished for something that happened long before I joined the Met.' She stared at her hands. 'I love that job, Matt. It means everything to me. If I'm forced to resign, what am I going to do?'

'It probably won't come to that. A slap on the wrists; possibly a demotion. You're a good officer. It'll go in your favour.' Denning didn't know this and was merely guessing.

'I can't face being demoted. Do you know how humiliating that would be?'

'You don't have to stay at Islington. There are other stations. It happens. Officers get demoted all the time for various reasons.'

'Matt, can't you just put a good word in for me? It would help.'

He sighed. 'I'm in a difficult position, Anna. How can I give you a reference when it was one of my team that reported you to professional standards? Please appreciate how this looks from my standpoint.'

He could tell from the look on her face that she didn't agree with him.

'Don't you see?' she said. 'It would carry more weight if it came from you. It would tell them that you don't agree with Molly's accusations.' She leaned in closer to him. 'In fact, Matt, you'd be doing me a massive favour by trying to persuade Molly to withdraw them.' She looked at him pleadingly.

He felt some sympathy for her: at the end of the day, she was a good copper who'd just messed up. He wasn't even entirely sure of the facts behind the case, except that she'd failed to declare a connection to a suspect in an assault case. Naturally, there was bound to be more to it than that. However, Molly had felt it necessary to formally report the matter to the IOPC. That was a tough decision for any police officer to make: to have to place another officer's career in jeopardy like that was never easy. Molly had done it and he respected her for it. Even if he knew she secretly regretted the decision, he was still going to stand by her.

'Anna, I'm sorry you're in this mess. Really. But you have to appreciate the difficult situation this puts me in.'

'I'm only asking for a reference. Just speak up for me. I would do the same in your position. It can make all the difference.'

He knew she was right. A word from him could be the difference between a formal reprimand and her P45. As an ex-copper, she'd struggle to find a job that paid as well... 'Let me think about it, Anna. I'm not going to be pressured into anything.'

She offered him a smile. 'Thanks, Matt. I would owe you, big time.'

He didn't know why she was thanking him. He hadn't actually agreed to do it. There was still a chance he'd change his mind. He wanted to change the subject. 'Let me think about it. In the meantime, have either Declan Meech or Tony Hallam come up on your radar at some point? Local villains.'

'Declan Meech is known,' she said. 'He's got a lengthy record, but seems to have been keeping his nose clean of late. Hallam...' She shrugged. 'I don't recognise the name, but I could look into him for you.'

Denning knew this was her way of saying any favour would be carefully considered. But he wasn't even sure there was anything Anna Klein could say that would be useful, nothing that couldn't be gleaned from the Police National Computer database. Mind, she had contacts and heard things that hadn't been made officially. Denning was certain that was where the likes of Tony Hallam operated.

'Thanks,' he said. 'That would be helpful.' He only hoped he wasn't going to regret his decision.

Chapter Thirty-Five

Molly hadn't seen Jon for several months. She was already regretting agreeing to meet him. At least they agreed to meet on neutral territory. Babushka was a trendy coffee shop in Crouch End, near the Broadway. They used to frequent it on weekend mornings, whenever Molly wasn't working. During happier times, they would sit in the window and people-watch.

He looked tired, like he wasn't sleeping. Part of her felt sorry for him, but another part of her just didn't want to know. So much of their relationship had involved her mothering him: making sure he ate and didn't drink too much or abuse too many substances. She enjoyed her freedom too much to want to return to those days.

'It's good to see you,' he said as soon as she sat down. 'I ordered a latte for you.'

She spotted the long, thin glass of frothy white coffee on the table. 'Thank you. How have you been?'

'Yes, good. I've been OK. You?'

It was strained small talk, the kind people made at the start of a first date, but they were both well beyond that stage now. 'I'm fine, Jon. Very busy at work. In fact, I can't stay long.'

She knew there was an element of her that wanted a 'normal' family life; a husband and kids and a house in the suburbs. She also knew Jon could never give her this, at least not in a way that she would have been comfortable with. This was all part of why they'd split. Since she'd moved out, she'd had a chance to reassess her life: she knew what she wanted, and what she didn't.

He looked crestfallen, but what had he been expecting? Some kind of reunion? 'I thought, maybe, we could go for dinner afterwards... talk properly...'

'There's nothing to talk about, Jon. I'm staying with Trudi and Charys for now. When I've found somewhere permanent then I'll collect my stuff from your place.'

'*My* place. That used to be our home.' He shook his head. 'I just wish I knew what I'd done wrong.'

'You betrayed my trust, Jon. You spoke to a journalist, telling her about a case that could have jeopardised a murder investigation.' She was trying to keep her voice level. There was no point rekindling old arguments and chasing after old fights. They had to focus on the future. 'But it's not just that, is it. It's us: we were never right for each other.' She sighed, silently berating herself was being so abrupt. 'Sorry. I didn't mean for it to come out like that.'

'You mean the age difference? That never used to bother you.'

Jon was nearly fourteen years older than Molly. It had never been an issue initially, and, if she was being honest, it wasn't the main reason they split up. 'It's more than that. I can't trust you. And then there's everything else. You've never really accepted what I do for a living. I'm proud of my job. I enjoy and I feel I'm doing something useful for society. But it's always been a bit of a joke for you. Jokes about uniforms and handcuffs.'

'That's not true. I've always respected your job. And I've supported you. When you wanted to join MIT, I encouraged you.'

She sipped her latte and felt like she was fighting a losing battle. 'Jon, we can analyse every aspect of our relationship and who said what to whom... try to work out what went wrong and what didn't. But it isn't going to change anything. It wasn't working out and we can't make it work now.'

He looked like he was going to cry. She wanted to say something reassuring but there was no point in making false promises.

'I still miss you,' he said. 'The house is so empty without you.'

'Then get a lodger.' She shook her head. 'I'm sorry. I didn't mean that to sound so brutal. I just meant you have to accept we've both moved on. Sell the house if necessary. Buy somewhere smaller. It would free up some capital. You could use the money to travel.'

But she could see he wasn't persuaded.

'We could try couples' therapy?'

She shook her head. 'What would be the point.' She sighed. 'Jon, I wish you well, but you've got to accept that it's over. For both our sakes.'

His face dropped. The same hang-dog crestfallen look he used whenever they'd had an argument and he couldn't bring himself to apologise for his behaviour or justify his actions. She was so used to falling for it, it had almost become her default way of thinking. But she knew she'd changed. The same old rut just wasn't working.

'We end up going round and round in circles,' Molly said. 'It's like some kind of perverse dance: you piss me off, I forgive you. Repeat ad infinitum.' She paused. 'Or

I piss you off, you pretend not care. Then same as before. It's not doing either of us any favours.'

'I just wonder who put this thought in your head in the first place. You were happy enough for a long time. We both were. Then, suddenly, you tell me the relationship's over. No warning... it just ends.'

She sighed. He just wasn't getting it, and – she suspected – he was never going to. 'Nobody put the thought in my head. I have, and have always had, the ability to think for myself.'

'I've never tried to change you. Why would I? I thought we worked...' His voice trailed off. For a moment she thought he was going to cry, but he quickly composed himself. 'So where do we go from here?' he asked. 'Your stuff is still in my house.'

'There's no room for it at Trudi's. I'm looking for a place, but it's not easy. I'm up to my eyes at work and there's very little available in my price range. I know that sounds like an excuse, but it's going to take time to find somewhere to live.'

'There's no hurry on my part. If you're stuck, you could always move back in. Take the spare room. We'd stay there as friends, nothing more. At least you'd have a bit of space and you'd be living somewhere familiar.'

Her step-father had once told her, if an offer seemed too good to be true then it probably was. She knew there would be a catch to Jon's offer – the constant pressure to reignite their relationship. It was clear that everything she'd said had fallen on conveniently deaf ears. Jon had no intention of moving on and she was going to have to live knowing he wasn't going to let go. Deep down, part of her knew this had all the makings of a long-term problem.

Chapter Thirty-Six

As it was a warm evening, Molly suggested they met in the park. Cassie seemed happy with the suggestion. 'I was beginning to feel like I was in prison,' she said, as she and Molly chatted while Cassie pushed Arthur in his pushchair. He looked up at Molly, a flicker of recognition on his face. Molly was beginning to feel like part of his extended family now and that wasn't necessarily a good thing. 'I thought if I didn't get out the flat, I was going to go slightly insane,' Cassie said. 'And it's good for Arthur to get a bit of fresh air. I think he's looking a bit peaky. What do you think?'

Molly had no idea how babies should look, but if she had to take a punt, he looked fine to her.

'I think you should stop worrying,' she said, offering Cassie a warm smile. 'But I know what you mean about getting some fresh air.'

The weather was still pleasant; summer seemed reluctant to relinquish its cheery grip. Molly was glad to get away from the MIT office. The atmosphere had been growing increasingly stifling as the detectives struggled with the case. Three murder victims on their call, all somehow linked to an incident in a park similar to the one they were in now. Molly wanted to offer Cassie something more than kind words and vague promises. She understood how she felt, or at least she could sympathise with what Cassie was going through. There was some common ground between them: both were being forced to face up to major changes in their lives. But Molly's feelings about her recent split with Jon were nothing compared with what Cassie was experiencing.

'Cassie, I've spoken to Scarlett. We don't believe she was involved in Kieran's murder.'

Cassie nodded her acceptance. 'To be honest with you, I didn't really think she was. I suppose I was clutching at straws.'

'That's not to say she wasn't the person who phoned that evening. It's possible she still had feelings for Kieran, but not enough to want him dead. I can't go into too much detail about an ongoing murder investigation, Cassie, but we now have a lead. We think we know why Kieran was murdered, and hopefully it won't be long before we catch the person responsible. I know that isn't going to bring him back, but at least it will offer some kind of closure for you.'

'You know why he was killed...?' Her voice was brittle. For Molly this was about a murder victim, but for Cassie this was her partner they were discussing. The man she'd decided to spend the rest of her life with and bring up a child with. To her, Kieran Judd was more than just another anonymous body on a mortuary table. 'I still can't believe that someone would deliberately kill Kieran. It was different when I thought he'd been killed by mistake, that the man upstairs had been the intended target... But Kieran. He was the gentlest, kindest man... There can't be any reason why someone would want to kill him.'

Molly told Cassie about Noah Daniel's death, but kept the details light. At the very least she felt Cassie deserved to know the truth about why her partner had been killed.

Besides, the story was already appearing in the press. It wouldn't be long before the truth started leaking out.

Cassie sat down on a bench and stared into space. 'Kieran used to have nightmares, but never told me what they were about. Now I realise that might explain it.' She rubbed Arthur's head affectionately. 'I wish he'd told me.'

'He probably wanted to put the whole thing out his mind and make a fresh start. There's no suggestion Kieran was to blame, but I imagine he would still have felt at least partly responsible.'

'Then why didn't he tell me? I'd have been sympathetic. It was an accident.'

'I don't know, Cassie. Guilt can affect people in different ways. Even when they have nothing to feel guilty about, it still affects them, deep down.'

'I keep going over it in my head,' Cassie said. 'What happened that day. I can't imagine what that poor little boy's parents must have gone through.'

Molly had tried not to think too hard about it, but, like Cassie, she just couldn't chase the thoughts from her head: an enjoyable trip to the park; children and teachers both looking forward to it. Some welcome spring sun and a chance to have some fun. Then the day ending in tragedy. So many people's lives ruined because of one brief moment.

'I just can't believe Kieran kept it to himself. I wish he'd told me. Maybe I could have done something to help.'

'I doubt there was much you could have done,' Molly said softly. 'You were there for him. You and Arthur.'

Cassie was staring into space. Arthur was making noises in his pushchair.

'Have you found somewhere else to live yet?' Molly asked. She wanted to convince herself that her concern was genuine rather than motivated by her own desire to take over Cassie's tiny flat. But she couldn't ignore the fact that she'd found herself thinking about the flat more and more. Knowing that if Cassie and Arthur had to move out, then someone was going to take the place over, and if it wasn't Molly then it would simply be let to someone else...

'I'm going to move in with a friend,' Cassie said. 'She said I can stay for as long as I like. She and her husband have just split up, so in a way it's probably more about her needing a bit of company as much as her doing me a favour. And the rent will come in handy too.'

'And she's OK with Arthur coming too?'

'Oh yes, she loves kids. Arthur will be spoilt rotten.'

Molly was happy for her. After what she'd been through, she deserved a lucky break. They stopped by a pond and Cassie took a clear plastic bag of breadcrumbs out of her handbag and gave a handful to Arthur, telling him to throw them at the ducks. It took him a moment or two to understand, and it was only after he saw his mummy do it that he followed suit. Molly stood and watched for a few minutes. The normality of it. The reassuring nature of a child enjoying life.

'And you're sure this has something to do with what's happening now? *Why?*'

'We don't know why it's happening now, but we're pretty certain it's connected to Noah Daniel's death. Cassie, can you think of anything that happened in the run-up to Kieran's murder, apart from the phone call, that might be relevant? Was he behaving any differently? Did he seem concerned about anything?'

She stared into space before answering. 'No. Like I've already told you, there was nothing. This whole thing happened out of the blue. A ring on the doorbell one evening and then…'

She didn't need to finish the sentence. Molly knew how it had panned out. A normal evening that had ended with her whole life being ripped from under her. And now the endless barrage of questions, though, if she were honest, so much of this could have been done over the phone.

'I know it seems exasperating,' Molly told her. 'But we need to make sure we cover everything. Now we are clearer on what's motivated the murders, we're in a better position to find the person responsible. This might feel like slow progress, but there will be a breakthrough soon. I promise you.'

Cassie looked at her and she saw the pain in her eyes. 'Do you really mean that, Molly? Or is this just you fobbing me off to make me feel better?'

And in her heart, Molly couldn't say if it was.

Chapter Thirty-Seven

Denning called another briefing first thing the following morning. With the team struggling to focus, there were cups of coffee on most desks. Denning had already had two cups and was contemplating a third whilst he waited for the caffeine to kick in.

'OK, everyone, we need to start making some serious progress here. The press now know the murders are linked. It won't take them long to connect the missing pieces.

There was a copy of the *London Echo* on his desk. Predictably, the murders were the lead story. So far, there was nothing to link them publicly with Thomas Blake Primary School, but it was only a matter of time before a clever journalist made the connection. Rachel Atherton would no doubt do her best to keep the school's name out of the media spotlight, but even she could only hold the press at bay for so long. When the truth did come out, Atherton would have to do some serious firefighting to try and save whatever would be left of her school's reputation. The events of Noah Daniel's death would be revisited and questions asked about the school's handling of it.

Denning turned to DS Fisher. 'Molly, you and Trudi have spoken to Mr and Mrs Daniel. What's your take on them?'

'I don't think they're our killers,' Molly said. 'Yes, they have a grievance with the school, and they're certainly still angry about what happened, but I don't think they have it in them to murder three people in cold blood as some kind of revenge for their son's death.' She pulled a face. 'However, maybe we should keep an eye on them, just the same. As Dave says, they are the most likely suspects. And, right now, we don't seem to have a lot of them.'

'So are we ruling them out?' Kinsella asked. 'Yes or no?'

'All I'm saying at this stage, is that I don't think we're in a position where we can rule anyone out,' Molly said. 'But my gut feeling is that they're not our killers.'

'No offence to DS Fisher,' Kinsella argued, looking directly at Molly with an expression on his face that was anything but apologetic, 'but we seem to be accepting her word that they didn't do it. I think we should check them out further. I mean, if my kid had been killed and the school had got away with it, I'd be out for blood. They still seem like the most obvious suspects.'

Denning knew that Dave Kinsella had a couple of kids; both grown up now, but you never stopped being a father. Denning was a father too, and he knew that parenthood was about that inseparable bond. That bond had been broken in the Daniels' case when they sent their son off to school that day and he hadn't returned.

'I agree with Molly,' Trudi said. 'They're not our killers.'

'What about other family members?' Neeraj asked. 'Uncles, aunts. Maybe we need to speak to Noah's grandparents?'

'OK,' Denning said. 'We look further into the family. Check them out, see if any of them have ever made threats before. Also, let's ask around about Adam and Peta. They would have been spoken to at the time and should have been offered an FLO. Find out who it was and speak to them.'

Molly Fisher and Trudi Bell were good detectives, and Denning trusted their judgement on this. But it was true that the team wasn't exactly knee-deep in suspects at the moment. Every possibility had to be explored.

'In terms of what progress we have made, we've now spoken to all the surviving staff members who were at the park that day, with the exception of Laura Grieve. She's no longer living at the address we were given for her and none of her former neighbours knew where she's currently living. However, one of them did give us the contact details for her ex-husband and we've left a message asking him to get in touch ASAP. In the meantime, check the Electoral Register and local authority council tax records to see if she's flagged up anywhere.'

'We have checked the system to make sure she wasn't our killer's first victim?' Neeraj asked.

'There's nothing on the database to suggest she's been murdered,' Trudi said. 'At least nothing yet...'

'We also need to speak to Marion Haynes. She's been staying with her sister in Great Yarmouth for the past few days, but her neighbour says she was due back.'

'OK,' Molly said. 'I can do that.'

Denning nodded. 'Good. Again, kid gloves approach, Molly. She's not going to thank us for reminding her of what happened with Noah.'

'Are we solely focusing on the teaching staff who were in the park when it happened?' asked Dave Kinsella. 'Or are we still planning to speak to everybody who was working in the school at the time?'

'For now, Dave, we're concentrating specifically on the staff members who were in the park that day,' Denning said, 'as we believe they're the only ones being targeted by our killer.'

'Euan Livingstone wasn't there on the day?' Trudi Bell pointed out.

'True, but as the then headmaster he took ultimate responsibility for the school trip,' Denning said.

'What about Rachel Atherton?' Molly asked. 'She was deputy head at the time.'

'We need to speak to Mrs Atherton again anyway,' Denning said. 'I can certainly raise the possibility of police protection with her again.'

'Are we considering her as a possible suspect?' Neeraj asked. 'She's clearly been withholding information about the incident in park. It's possible there's more she's hiding.'

Denning thought about this. Rachel Atherton certainly came across as something of a cold fish, but the thought of her running around London stabbing people she had some perceived grievance with seemed unlikely. However, it wasn't something he felt they could entirely rule out. 'We can take a further look into Rachel Atherton's background, but I don't think she's our suspect here, Deep.'

'Shouldn't we be going bigger with this?' Kinsella said. 'Like some kind of police presence at the school?'

'Wouldn't that freak the little kiddies out?' Trudi Bell suggested. 'Seeing police patrolling the playground might make them think there's something to worry about.'

'There bloody well is,' Kinsella said dryly. 'Obviously we'd need to be discreet. I mean sooner or later it's going to come out about the school's involvement in all this and people are going to freak out.'

'It's unlikely our killer's going to target any of the pupils,' Denning replied. 'This whole thing seems to have been sparked off by the death of a pupil. I can't see how targeting others would do our killer any favours.'

'Though we can't be certain about that,' Kinsella argued. 'We still don't know what's going on in our killer's head. We assume this is about revenge for what happened, but what if it's something bigger?'

The last thing Denning wanted to consider was having to close the school. 'I refer you to my earlier point, Dave. I believe our killer is only targeting the staff who were on duty the day of the accident. And as none of them are still working at the school...'

'Apart from Rachel Atherton,' Kinsella said.

'Rachel Atherton wasn't head teacher at the time. Euan Livingstone was. It makes sense that he'd be a target, but not Rachel Atherton.' Though even as Denning said it he wasn't completely confident. Something was niggling away at him... Something about Rachel Atherton that he couldn't quite put his finger on...

'We need to strike a difficult balancing act here,' Denning said. 'The main focus is on protecting the staff who were on duty that day. There's no suggestion anyone else from the school is in danger. In an ideal world, yes, I'd arrange police protection for everyone in the school, but the truth is we just don't have the resources for it.'

'Let's hope you're right,' Kinsella added drolly, 'because nobody wants a massacre on their hands.'

Chapter Thirty-Eight

Denning and Neeraj asked Rachel Atherton to go over the events in the park on that fateful day again. Denning was certain there was something she wasn't telling them.

'I'm terribly sorry, Inspector Denning,' she said, her voice dripping icy politeness, 'but I have nothing further to add to our previous conversation. And I honestly feel that all this is wasting my time.'

'We have strong grounds to believe your life may potentially be at risk,' Mrs Atherton. 'We therefore have an obligation to protect you. And our job would be made considerably easier if you were to tell us the truth.'

She looked indignant. 'Not this nonsense again. I can assure you, I haven't received any death threats or seen anyone suspicious hanging around my house, or the school for that matter. And I haven't told you anything other than the truth,' she insisted. 'You can check the coroner's report: the school was cleared of any wrong-doing. Or check your own records. The accident was fully investigated by the traffic police at the time and they concluded it was exactly that: an accident.'

'That's not being disputed,' Denning said. 'I'm refer-ring to what happened afterwards.'

Her face frowned. 'I don't understand. We've been over all that.'

'Not the full story, though. Laura Grieve was very much treated as a scapegoat, wasn't she? She was pressurised into resigning. The school was then able to pass the blame on to Laura Grieve should the public inquiry decide it wanted to apportion blame, then Thomas Blake Primary School could absolve itself of any responsibility. It worked out well for the school, but not so well for Laura Grieve.'

'I'm not sure I would agree with your use of the word "pressurise". Nobody was pressurised into doing anything. As I recall, it was Laura's decision to resign. She accepted she was responsible for Noah Daniel, along with other children in her care, on the day. She accepted that she had been negligent in that park. Nobody *blamed* Laura, of course they didn't. As I told you before, these kind of trips need to be properly organised and supervised, and that particular trip was neither. I can assure you that no such events are allowed to occur nowadays, unless they're properly arranged.'

No, thought Denning, you just treat the school like a prison camp so the children meet your criteria for what's acceptable. But it wasn't so much how she ran the school that rankled with him, right now he was more concerned about her obstinance being a hindrance to the pursuit of justice. 'All right then,' he said, 'perhaps persuaded is a better word. She probably felt she had no option but to resign.'

Rachel Atherton stared at Denning for several seconds; it was as though she was trying to dispute his impertinence. 'I can assure you no one put any pressure on Laura Grieve to resign. I don't know where you got your information from, but I would suggest you do your homework more thoroughly in future, Inspector. Laura

Grieve took full responsibility for what happened, and so she should have. She had a duty of care to the children she was responsible for. She failed in that duty. She was negligent and irresponsible, and her actions – or rather lack of them – resulted in the death of a child. The school has its reputation to think of. It does no one any favours to have this opened up again. It was only poor leadership that resulted in that unfortunate accident. That's not something that can be said about the school today.'

'You were part of that leadership at the time, Mrs Atherton,' Denning said calmly. 'Surely you must share some of the responsibility?'

A heavy silence descended on the room. It was broken by a knock on the door. Alice came in with some letters. 'Sorry to interrupt,' she said. 'The mail's arrived. There are a couple of letters for you. One of them looks like it's from the STEM-start funding people. You said you wanted to look over it as soon ASAP.' She handed two brown envelopes to Rachel Atherton, who took them, placed them on her desk and said: 'Thank you, Alice.'

'Can I get anyone something to drink? Tea or coffee?'

'That won't be necessary,' Atherton said coldly. 'The officers are almost finished.'

Alice smiled awkwardly and left the room.

Rachel Atherton picked up a silver letter opener from her desk and opened one of the letters. 'If you don't mind,' she said, pulling out an A4-sized wodge of paper. 'I need to look over this application form.'

Denning knew when he was defeated. Unless they were to formally charge Rachel Atherton with wasting police time, or something similar, there was nothing more they could do here.

He stood, Neeraj followed his lead. 'Thank you, Mrs Atherton. We'll be in touch if we have any further questions.'

Once they were back in the car, Denning's phone rang. It was Molly Fisher.

'Molly? Any luck with Laura Grieve's ex-husband?'

'He's still in the States and won't be back until next week.'

Denning cursed to himself. This was just what they didn't need.

He was about to say something when Molly's voice came back on the line. 'But I've found an address for Laura Grieve,' she said. 'The Electoral Register has its uses.'

'How recent is the address?' Denning asked.

'Last year, but it's worth a try.'

Chapter Thirty-Nine

The address Molly gave them turned out to be for a semi-detached house in Acton, West London. Solid and Victorian, it overlooked a wide street, where pockets of trees sprouted from square holes in the pavement. Denning rang the doorbell and waited for an answer. There was no sound from inside the house and after a couple of minutes it became obvious there was no one at home.

'They'll be at work,' a voice said. He turned round and saw a woman in her sixties eyeing him warily from over the neighbouring fence. 'Are you police?' she asked. She was dressed in a navy jacket and looked like she was about to head out.

Is it that obvious? mused Denning, who had always wondered what exactly a typical police officer looked like, and hoped he somehow didn't fit the profile.

'Yes,' Neeraj said before Denning had a chance to answer. 'We're looking for a Laura Grieve. This is the address we were given for her.'

'They don't live there anymore.' The neighbour looked intrigued, as though she scented there was something interesting going on. 'They split up a couple of years back,' she said. 'Laura moved out, then he sold the place shortly after his new woman moved in.'

Denning and Neeraj looked at each other. Wherever Laura Grieve had moved to, she clearly hadn't got around to updating the Electoral Register. But it was important they spoke to Laura Grieve, and quickly. They were in danger of wasting their time here. 'You don't know how we can get hold of Laura?' Denning asked. 'It's important that we speak to her.'

She looked at him with a twinkle of curiosity. 'I dunno where he moved to after they sold up,' she said, putting her hand to her mouth. 'My husband might know, but he's at work at the moment. Seems his new wife didn't like it round here,' she said, nodding in the direction of the Grieves' former home, a note of disapproval in her voice. 'Not good enough for her probably. Younger woman. I'd be surprised if it lasted.'

'What about Laura?'

'Sorry, I've no idea where she went after she moved out.' She thought for a moment. 'She was always very pally with Sheila Dean at number twenty-two. She might know.'

'Number twenty-two?' Denning looked around the street. They were standing outside number sixty-seven; the neighbour was number sixty-nine. Twenty-two must be back down the street.

'Oh, she won't be at home,' the woman said, reading his thoughts. 'She'll be at work now.'

'Work?' Denning asked.

'She works in a nursery near Hammersmith tube station.'

'A nursery?' Denning asked. 'As in garden centre?'

'As in children,' the neighbour replied. 'Terri's Tots. I'll give you the address.'

'Laura?' There was a note of surprise in Sheila Dean's voice. She was in her mid-forties, and Denning guessed was probably around the same age as Laura Grieve.

A large window in her office looked out onto the main nursery area. Children were running and crawling around the floor, jumping about in what seemed to have been labelled a 'soft play area' or having a competition to see who could scream the loudest.

'I presume you haven't heard then?' Sheila Dean looked at them curiously.

'Laura died, Her son, Josh, told me. It was a few weeks ago. He phoned me up out of the blue and asked if I wanted to go to the funeral. I couldn't, unfortunately, we'd arranged to go to Italy for a week...'

'Dead?' Alarm bells were ringing. 'You say this was recent?'

'Her funeral was last month.' She shook her head.

'Dead?' Neeraj repeated, as though he was a pace behind Denning. He looked at his DI. 'What happened?'

Sheila Dean seemed slightly taken aback by the directness of his question. 'Josh didn't say and I didn't like to ask. He literally phoned up just as I was leaving for work one morning and I was already running late. I said I was very sorry to hear about Laura but I explained we wouldn't be able to make the funeral. Laura and I had been quite friendly for a while but I have to admit, I'd rather lost touch with her after she moved away. I think she wanted a clean break when her marriage came to such an abrupt end, and I can't say I blame her. To be honest with you though, I wouldn't have said we were all *that* close: obviously we both worked with children, but Laura very much kept herself to herself. We'd meet for coffee and chat if we ever bumped into one another in the street, but that was about as far as our friendship went. I was slightly surprised when Josh rang me. I suppose he must have found my number in Laura's address book or something.'

'Do you have contact details for Laura's son?' Denning asked.

She took her phone from pocket and began scrolling through her list of contacts. Denning had taken his phone out and waited for her to give him the number.

'I don't have an address, but he lives in London as far as I know.' She read out a phone number, which Denning noted.

He thanked her and he and Neeraj headed back to the car. As they were driving back to east London, he phoned Molly on the hands-free to fill her in on what they'd just discovered about Laura Grieve. 'Once we have an address for Josh Grieve, I'd like you to have a word with him. He'll be able to tell us what happened to his mother.' She agreed she'd speak to him as soon as they had his address and Denning ended the call. He could trust Molly to handle this with the tact it deserved. As much as Denning admired Neeraj as a detective, it was his work ethic and determination that sprang to mind rather than his subtlety.

Neeraj said, 'If Laura Grieve died just before all this started, then it's possible she could have been the first victim.'

Denning was thinking about this. 'If she'd been murdered, we'd have known about it. If the MO was the same, or even similar, to the other murders then HOLMES 2 would have that information. There's no record of anyone with that name or fitting her description having been stabbed to death.'

He was aware that Neeraj was looking at him.

'But you have doubts, boss?'

Denning was thinking. 'It would make sense. If she resigned because she took the blame for what happened, then she would be the obvious person to go after. But...' He was thinking about things as he indicated and turned on to Fulham High Road and past the turn-off for Thomas Blake Primary School. Denning couldn't help contrasting the happy faces of the children at Terri's Tots with those at Rachel Atherton's school. He knew where Jake would have been happiest. 'If that is what all this is about,' Denning continued, 'then why go after the others too? If Laura Grieve was responsible, killing her should have been enough.'

Neeraj didn't answer; just crunched on a mint.

Chapter Forty

Marion Haynes was in her early eighties. Her hands were gnarled with arthritis and her face lined with age and wisdom. Laughter lines, Molly thought, except Marion Haynes hadn't done much laughing since the day two-and-a-half years ago when, coming home from her weekly shop at Sainsbury's, she'd accidentally knocked down and killed a child.

She'd peered cautiously at Molly, having opened her front door a tiny crack, and only let her in after she'd phoned the number the detective gave her and had it confirmed she was who she said she was.

'Can't be too careful,' she'd said. Molly had agreed, though she silently resented having to waste time standing on a doorstep when she was in the middle of a murder investigation.

Molly was sitting in the frilly living room now, admiring the pretty ornaments that Mrs Haynes clearly liked to collect: Royal Doulton figurines of ladies in long frocks and men in top hats. They were dotted around the place, occupying pride of place on the mantelpiece, as well as a glass-fronted display cabinet that occupied most of one wall. She imagined Marion got few visitors and was glad of the company, so she accepted the offer of a cup of tea. A few minutes later, Mrs Haynes appeared with a teapot, two cups and a plate full of cakes.

'I've tried so hard to put it out of my mind,' she said. 'But it's always there. I see the little boy's face all the time. I often wonder what would have happened to him if he'd lived. Would he become a doctor or a singer. Or a policeman…'

She was looking at Molly when she spoke, but her eyes focused on something else. An image that had been burned into her memory and would stubbornly remain there for ever more. 'I appreciate it's difficult for you, Mrs Haynes,' Molly said, 'and I'm so sorry to have to bring it all back again.'

'It was terrible. He just ran out from nowhere. I tried to stop in time, but I just couldn't avoid him. It was terrible,' she repeated, just in case there was any doubt about the severity of what had happened. 'I've always been a good driver; a careful driver. My late husband always used to say I drove like a little old lady long before I became one.' The ghost of a smile flitted over her face at the mention of her husband. Molly thought it was both sweet and sad at the same time. 'I'd never even had any points on my licence,' Mrs Haynes continued. 'Or a parking ticket or anything. I haven't driven since. I do miss it though. I felt like I gave up some of my independence when I stopped driving. But under the circumstances…'

Molly could see she was still distraught over the accident. What could she say? Any attempt at reassurance would feel like an empty platitude. However, she had to offer up some words of comfort.

'It's important that you know nobody blames you. The police report said there was nothing you could have done and totally absolves you of any culpability. You mustn't blame yourself.'

Mrs Haynes attempted a weak smile. 'My family all said the same thing to me at the time. But still… Whichever way you look at it, I killed a child.' She twisted her arthritic hands together in her lap. 'I wrote to the boy's parents and apologised, but I never heard back from them. Unsurprising perhaps. I expect they blamed me.'

Molly wanted to reach over and hug her. 'I'm sure they didn't. Or if they did at the time, it was because they were angry and ripped apart by grief. They can't possibly blame you now.'

'Thank you. You're very kind. But none of this makes me feel any better and I'm still not sure why you think this is relevant now. Has something happened?'

Molly told her about the recent murders, deliberately trying to underplay the worst of it so as not to alarm her. 'But I do have to ask, has anything happened recently to make you feel worried or concerned?'

'No. Nothing at all. Do you really think someone is going to come after me because I killed that child?'

'I honestly don't know. It's possible somebody is going after the people who were involved but we can't confirm that at this stage.' She paused, looking over at the elderly woman; sitting in her armchair, sewing by her side, her favourite tea set on display. She was still wracked with guilt. Why would someone want to murder her over that? But Molly had been a police officer long enough to know that nice, decent people were murdered all the time, either just by being in the wrong place at the wrong time, or simply because somebody took it upon themselves to end another's life for reasons that made sense in their head and in no one else's. 'I'll give you my card,' she said. 'If you feel vulnerable, give me a call and we can arrange police protection for you.'

Mrs Haynes took the card from Molly and smiled at her. 'Thank you, but I don't think I need to be worrying about police protection at my time of life,' she said. 'If someone is determined to kill me for my part in that accident, then perhaps that's what's meant to be. It would be a lot easier than trying to live with the guilt of knowing what I'd done.'

As Molly left her house, she felt sympathy for her. At that moment, there wasn't much else she could do.

Chapter Forty-One

Denning wasn't sure what Maria Hallam expected from him. She'd phoned saying she needed to speak with him, but hadn't said why. A combination of curiosity and concern had prompted him to call round. Neeraj had been tasked with uncovering the details of Laura Grieve's death and to let Denning know immediately if there was anything suspicious.

When he'd arrived at Maria's flat, she seemed anxious. For a second, he thought she was going to send him away.

'Has something happened?' he asked.

'Tony's been round again,' she said quietly. 'I know he's up to something. He was drunk and talking all sorts of nonsense.'

Denning sat on the sofa. He could hear the children playing in another room. 'Drunk?'

She was staring at her feet. 'Well, maybe not drunk. But he had been drinking.'

'Did he threaten you?'

She looked sheepish. 'Not explicitly.'

'What was it then?'

'He kept talking rubbish about us getting back together soon... how he was planning something.'

'Planning something? Planning what? To harm you?' This all seemed very vague. He wasn't entirely sure he wasn't being played here: a pawn in someone else's

219

damaged marriage; a mouse being batted between two bored cats. 'If he didn't threaten you, there's little the police can do, Maria. But if you do feel in danger, perhaps you could move out for a while. Move in with a friend or family.'

She shuddered and lit up a cigarette. 'It was the way he looked at me. I know what he's like when he gets that look. He's planning something, I know he is.'

'Planning something with Declan…?' Denning wasn't sure what she was talking about. She didn't appear to be making any sense. He was already regretting coming round here, especially now they seemed to actually be making some progress with the murder case.

'No. Well, maybe. He didn't mention Declan.' She took a long drag on her cigarette. 'I meant me and the kids. I'm sure he's got something in mind for us.'

Denning could smell alcohol on her breath and wondered how much she'd had to drink. 'If you're telling me you believe Tony's going to harm you and the children—'

'You read about it, don't you,' she said, cutting him off. 'Fathers killing their ex-partner, then driving off Beachy Head with the children strapped into the back of the car. Tony's capable of it.' Her eyes were darting between Denning, her feet, the cigarette and back to Denning. 'He doesn't like people saying no to him.'

'Maria, this really isn't my area. I'm a murder squad detective, and I'm in the middle of a murder investigation right now.' He sighed, aware he was coming across as uncaring. 'I can pass this over to the relevant authorities and ask them to treat it as a priority. But I can't investigate it myself.' He told her about their investigation, lightly sketching in the details without giving too much information away – nothing that wouldn't be appearing in print – and how they had now established that they'd been wrong about Tony Hallam having been the intended target. How *he'd* been wrong about Hallam having been the intended target. 'By rights, I shouldn't even be here now,' he said. But he felt bad. Here was a potentially vulnerable woman who was frightened for her family and his hands were tied. Although there a voice in his head begging him to get involved, he knew McKenna was right: he was going to have hand this one over.

'You said you could offer us police protection,' she insisted. 'You said if someone was going to kill Tony then there was a chance they could come after us too.'

'That was before we found out Tony wasn't involved. And, even then, we couldn't offer you protection against Tony. At least not police protection.' He offered her what he hoped was a reassuring look. 'We could arrange for you to have a panic button installed in your flat. It would be connected to the nearest police station. If he threatened you, there would be a couple of officers here in minutes.'

She shook her head. 'There's no point. A load of police turning up mob-handed would just make things worse. I can handle Tony.'

He felt sorry for her. She really did seem scared. He just wasn't sure whether that fear was down to her ex-husband or there was something else going on here. He was certain Tony Hallam should still be in prison. The man was clearly dangerous. If what Maria was saying was true, then he was obviously still involved in criminal activities alongside Declan Meech, but proving it would be difficult. And McKenna was not going to welcome him spending time on a case that wasn't his concern and was taking him away from investigation three murders.

'Maria,' he said softly, 'I really can't get involved personally. I appreciate your concerns about your ex-husband, but there's nothing I can do apart from passing this on.'

He left her flat and headed down the stairwell to the area where he'd parked his car. He was on the point of getting his key out of his pocket when he was suddenly aware of a figure moving towards him from the shadows.

Chapter Forty-Two

Molly called round to see Penny Garnett at the restaurant. They had been allocated an officer to look after them, one who appeared to occupy his time sitting at a table drinking coffee, which meant he had to keep disappearing to the toilet at regular intervals.

'He's probably in the loo now,' Penny said, nodding at the empty seat.

'One of the hazards of the job,' Molly said apologetically.

Penny laughed. Molly could sense that she was trying to put a brave face on matters, but was more than likely unnerved by the whole situation. There was clearly a hint of strain behind the cheery smile. 'Look, now the lunchtime rush is over, I was going to put my feet up for ten minutes and have a coffee. Why don't you join me?' She offered Molly a coffee on the house and the two of them sat at a table near the counter.

'To be honest with you, I really don't think all this is necessary. Freya and I are always very careful. We need to be. Shortly after we opened the restaurant one of our neighbours was robbed when they were cashing up at night. Since then, we've always taken great care with personal security. There's CCTV in both the restaurant itself and in the alleyway out the back. We always thor-. oughly check the restaurant before locking up at night.

And the police did a thorough security check of the immediate area when they arranged for protection.'

'This might all come to nothing,' Molly said. 'And I appreciate it may seem a bit over-the-top, but we have to be careful.'

Penny smiled again. 'I'm sorry. I know I sound like I'm being ungrateful. We do appreciate all the trouble you've gone to.'

Almost on cue, the police officer appeared from the direction of the toilets. A young lad, in his early twenties. Molly suspected this was all a bit tedious for him: he'd probably joined the police thinking of car chases and nicking villains. He would quickly discover just how much of the job simply involved standing – or sitting – around waiting for things to happen. He looked over at Molly and Penny and blushed his apologies. He asked if everything was OK. Molly explained why she was there.

'Why don't you take a break for ten minutes,' Molly said. 'Stretch your legs. I can look after the situation here for a bit.'

He smiled and said he would stretch his legs, and would be back as soon as he could.

'I feel a bit sorry for him, truth be told,' Penny said. 'Stuck in here for hours on end. How exciting can it be to watch endless coffees being made or plates of walnut and lentil Bolognese being served. That's today's special, by the way,' she said, pointing at a blackboard by the counter. 'There's still some left if you fancy a late lunch.'

Before Molly had a chance to politely decline the kind offer, Freya appeared from the kitchen. 'Apologies, no more walnut and lentil Bolognese. I've put what was left into a doggy bag for Beckett.'

'That's our neighbour's hound,' Penny said, coming to Molly's rescue. 'He seems to have a preference for vegetarian food, for some strange reason.'

'It's probably good for him,' Molly said, unable to imagine anything a dog would like less.

'If you don't mind his chronic flatulence,' Freya added. 'Our neighbour's nearly ninety and swears blind he can't smell a thing.'

Molly laughed. She enjoyed their company. And she needed to laugh after visiting Marion Haynes and seeing first-hand the blanket of self-flagellation she was living under.

'Has Pen told you that we both think this is a major waste of time.' Freya smiled at Molly when she spoke, but she could see she meant was she was saying.

'This really is just a courtesy call.'

'Look, ignore me,' Freya said. 'I need to finish off in the kitchen. You two enjoy your coffee and chat.'

When they were alone, Penny said, 'She's trying to pretend everything's OK, but I can tell she's worried about me.' She narrowed her eyes. 'You really do think someone is determined to kill us? And by us, I mean everyone who was involved in what happened with Noah Daniel.'

'Of course, it's possible this is about something else entirely, but so far the only people who have been targeted are the staff that were on duty that day,' Molly said quietly. 'And Euan Livingstone, although as head teacher at the time he could be argued was ultimately to blame for authorising the trip in the first place.'

'The trip,' she echoed, rubbing her hand over her face. 'It wasn't even that...' Molly thought she was going to say something more, but her words trailed off into silence.

'Nobody did anything wrong,' Molly said. 'It was an accident, a terrible accident.' She'd seen so many people punishing themselves over that day. And now someone else was punishing them too. As if the guilt and pain they already felt wasn't punishment enough.

'The park was literally less than ten minutes from the school,' Penny said, a faraway look on her face. 'We'd been there many times with them in the past and there was never a problem…' She shook her head. Like Marion Haynes, it must have been painful having the whole sorry story raked over again.

'I couldn't cope with the guilt. I left the job the following year. Freya had been made redundant from her job as a chef in a hotel, so we thought we'd open our own restaurant. It was something we'd always talked about and we had a bit of money put away, helped by a small inheritance from Freya's late gran.' She gave a tinkly little laugh. 'When we'd said "our own restaurant", I'd imagined somewhere in the South West… Devon or Cornwall. But we didn't get any further south than West Norwood.'

'Any particular reason?'

'It's virtually on our doorstep. We live in Dulwich. This is pretty close. Plus this whole area's on the up. It seemed like the sensible option at the time. Maybe if we had gone for Devon or Cornwall, we wouldn't be in the situation we're in now.'

'It might be our killer's achieved their goal now,' Molly said, though she knew Penny Garnett was too smart to believe her.

'Sue, Kieran, me and Laura were the staff on duty in the park that day. Euan was head. Three of them are dead. That just leaves Laura Grieve and me.'

Molly didn't want to alarm Penny any further by mentioning what Denning had just told her about Laura Grieve having very likely been the first victim, but clearly Penny could read something in her face that gave the game away.

'Laura…? Has something happened to her?'

Molly stared at her latte, hoping Penny would let the matter drop, but knowing she wouldn't.

'Is Laura dead?'

'Yes.'

'Murdered?'

'No. We haven't had her cause of death confirmed yet, but we know she wasn't murdered.' They were checking through coroner's reports. 'Until we've had it confirmed, we have to assume her death could be suspicious.'

One momentary lapse of concentration on Laura's part had resulted in so much hurt for so many people. 'We need to confirm it and we need to establish the exact cause of death.'

A pale look washed over Penny Garnett's face. 'Poor Laura. I think, of all of us, she took it the worst.' She shook her head. 'I always felt bad about Laura. We'd been friends. She was my TA and worked with my pupils. I know she wanted to be a teacher, but she lacked the confidence to go for it. And then there was the nightmare situation of her personal life. We were friends, but Laura's life fell apart after her divorce and she began drinking.' She rubbed her hands over her face. 'I could see she was in a mess. I could see it and I did nothing about it.'

'When you say she was drinking…'

'She would turn up for work with a hangover, which wasn't exactly the crime of the century. I mean, we've all done it.' She looked at Molly. 'Then things started to get out of hand. She was turning up for work late, dishevelled, and I could smell the booze on her. I tried my best to cover for her – I mean, she'd split up from her husband and was living with a friend, not the easiest of times for her. Prior to the divorce she'd lived the perfect life: nice big house, good money coming in. Then it all went pear-shaped for her. You just had to feel sorry for her.'

'And nobody at work was concerned about this? What about school management and senior staff, surely someone must have realised she needed help?'

'We tried to cover for her. She'd received a written warning about a month before this happened and she seemed to be sorting herself out. Then Rachel Atherton started pushing to have her fired, saying she wasn't up to the job. But Euan over-ruled her. He felt sorry for her, I suppose. The school holidays were coming up. The plan had been to suggest to Laura that she took some time off to sort herself out. Maybe come back for the start of the new school year in September.'

'But she should never have been on the school trip that day. If she was struggling to cope, she should never have been allowed to supervise children.'

'Don't you think I don't know that? Hindsight is a wonderful thing. It was the end of term. Everyone's nerves were frazzled. We'd just had an Ofsted report that had flagged up various failings in management. Nothing serious, but enough to put Euan and Rachel at each other's throats for the umpteenth time that term. We just wanted something nice for the kids, and OK, yes, for us too. Laura had seemed OK that morning. I would have asked another TA to cover for her if I'd suspected she wasn't fit.'

Molly couldn't think of what to say. Penny was right: these situations were always a lot more clear-cut in hindsight, especially for anyone who wasn't directly involved.

'Ultimately,' Penny continued, 'Laura was blamed for what happened and she accepted that blame like a lamb to the slaughter.'

What she was saying resonated with Molly. She worried that she was heading down a similar route. She tried to chase the thought from her mind. 'Are you saying she was made a scapegoat?' The coroner's report had stated that there was no one individual to blame.

Penny looked uncomfortable. 'She was the obvious choice. You have to realise, we were desperate to cover our backsides. If the coroner's report had found the school had been in any way negligent then there would have been significant consequences, both for the school, and very likely for the staff members in charge that day. We all agreed we wouldn't mention Laura's state of mind and make it clear that no one member of staff was responsible. In return, Laura would resign. Then if there was any kind of backlash, the school would lay the blame at Laura's door and make it clear she no longer worked there.'

'And none of this came out during the inquiry?' There had been no mention in the official report of Laura Grieve's state of mind.

'We all agreed we'd keep quiet about Laura.' She looked at Molly and shook her head. 'Yes, I know we should have been more honest, but what good would it have done? Laura already blamed herself. Having her condemned by an official inquiry would have destroyed her. And there was the chance she might have ended up facing a manslaughter charge if it had been agreed she was unfit to supervise the children that day.'

'So you kept quiet to protect Laura?' The tone in Molly's voice made it clear she didn't believe that, at least not entirely.

Penny Garnett looked embarrassed. 'I wish I could say that was true. In reality we all had our own reasons for keeping Laura's name out of it. In my case it was guilt. I was the one who should have taken the blame for letting her work that day.'

'But Laura would have been asked to give evidence at the inquiry?'

'We persuaded her to stick to the agreed story: it was an accident and no one was to blame.'

'Was that fair?' Molly was thinking about Peta and Adam Daniel. They had been denied justice by being denied the truth about their son's death.

'I'm not sure any of it was fair,' Penny said. 'We all felt guilty, but Laura more than most. Technically, Noah was under her care. It wasn't difficult to persuade her to say what we'd agreed, just as it wasn't difficult to persuade her to resign. I think, considering the state poor Laura was in, it wouldn't have been difficult to persuade her to ride round Coventry naked like Lady Godiva.' She looked apologetically at Molly. 'I'm sorry, I know that sounds flippant. I didn't behave well at the time. None of us did. I admit I went along with it all because it seemed the easiest way of bringing the whole sorry saga to an end. But it sat badly with me for a long time.'

'What did you mean when you said you were the one who should have taken the blame for letting her work that day? Surely that decision should have been down to either Euan Livingstone or Rachel Atherton?'

'Laura was my TA, but I was Noah's teacher. Ultimately, he was in my care. If anyone should have taken responsibility and resigned over it, then it was me. If anyone is coming after us for what happened that day, then I can't say I entirely blame them for feeling the way they do.'

Molly glanced over in the direction of the kitchen, but Freya was either too busy or she was determined to let Molly and Penny chat uninterrupted. 'You've got police protection. You work in a public place. That's going to make it difficult for anyone to get to you.'

'But not impossible,' Penny said. 'If they're determined enough, they'll get to me.'

'Not if we catch them first,' Molly said, though she knew with such little to go on at the moment, that didn't look like it would be happening any time soon.

Chapter Forty-Three

'It's DI Denning, isn't it?' Denning spun round and saw Tony Hallam walking towards him. He quickly hid his alarm and pretended he was more confident than he felt.

'Is there something I can do for you?' Denning asked. He wasn't sure what kind of plausible explanation he could give for being outside Hallam's wife's flat, especially now it had been established that Hallam was in no way involved in the murder investigation.

'Can I ask what you're doing outside my wife's flat?'

Thinking on his feet, Denning decided attack was going to be the best form of defence. 'It's police business, Mr Hallam.'

Hallam stood there, legs slightly apart, arms folded across his chest. 'How does your investigation into multiple stabbings involve my wife, exactly?' His tone wasn't aggressive, but there was a clear hint that he was prepared to turn nasty if he wasn't happy with the answers Denning offered.

'This is a murder investigation,' Denning said. 'If we suspect someone has knowledge that might be of interest, then we are entitled to speak to them. We don't need the permission of their partners. Especially if they're separated.' He hoped he sounded convincing.

'She's got nothing to do with those murders. It must be clear to you bunch of clowns that I was never a target.

I don't know why that bloke who lived downstairs from me got stabbed, but that's not my concern. So, I'll ask you again: what are you doing outside my wife's flat?'

Denning could feel the car key in his pocket. He should just unlock the car, get in and drive away. He didn't have to explain himself to a criminal such as Tony Hallam. But there was something about this he just didn't like. Men who abused their partners were beneath contempt in Denning's book.

'I asked you a question.' Hallam was now standing so close, Denning could smell the cigarettes on his breath.

They stood there eyeballing each other, like a pair of rutting stags each waiting for the other to make the first move. 'If you have a problem with me being here, I suggest you take it up with my superior officer. I'm sure she'd be very happy to explain to you how a police investigation works.'

Hallam opened his mouth. He was on the point of saying something when he spotted Maria on the landing outside her flat. She was looking down at him. He looked up and was clearly going to say something, but then shook his head and walked away. Denning got back into his car, locked the doors and watched Hallam cross the road and get back into his own car before driving off.

Denning was gripping the steering wheel a little more tightly than felt comfortable. He felt his hands trembling slightly from either adrenaline or fear. If Hallam had tried something, he would have arrested him on the spot. But what if it had turned nasty? It would have been too late to have called for back-up. He guessed the residents of the estate had insufficient love for the police to intervene. It would have been him and Tony Hallam.

What had Hallam wanted? Why was he even here? Whatever the connection between Tony and Maria Hallam, Denning wasn't sure he wanted to get dragged into it. But there was something about Tony Hallam that worried him. He was up to something and Denning knew he had to find out what. A part of him didn't want to get involved, but another knew he couldn't simply walk away. It wasn't enough to say it wasn't his job: arresting criminals and looking after the vulnerable was his job. But he knew his options were limited.

Chapter Forty-Four

Josh Grieve shared a flat in Brixton with another lad in his twenties.

'Excuse the mess,' he said, clearing some papers off a chair in the living room. 'There is a rota for cleaning, but nobody pays it the slightest bit of notice.' The flat was above a launderette and the cloying smell of fabric softener filled the air.

Josh was a bright lad, slim-to-athletic build, wearing a Mr Men T-shirt and a pair of baggy tracksuit bottoms. His sandy-blond hair had been recently washed as it bounced off his head when he spoke. He worked in a bar in Northumberland Street, he told Molly, although it was more of a private drinking club, popular with footballers and celebrities. He said the name, but naturally she'd never heard of it.

She made herself comfortable on the rickety sofa. The flat was – like Cassie Bane's – small, but cosy. It smelled clean, but that was very likely down to the aroma of fabric softener that permeated up from downstairs.

There were framed prints of music gigs on the wall; one of which – Glastonbury from three years ago – Molly had been at with Jon. It felt like a lifetime ago now.

There was an open can of lager on the floor. He noticed her looking at it. 'Would you like something to drink? I'm never sure if you guys are really not allowed to drink on duty, or if that's just something they put on TV cop shows?'

It was hard to tell if he was joking. 'I'll pass, but thanks for the offer.' Molly wasn't sure what to make of Josh Grieve. He seemed chatty, friendly even, but that could be hiding how he really felt. 'Firstly, I'd like to say that I'm very sorry about your mother, and I appreciate this must be difficult to talk about. I understand your mother's death was recent.'

'Yes,' he replied flatly. 'And, no, I don't mind talking about it.' He looked pained, staring at the floor, then his face turned towards Molly's and he offered a weak smile. 'But I don't know why you're asking about her now? She died over a month ago.'

Another young man, Molly assumed to be the flatmate, stuck his head round the door. He was dressed in a T-shirt and a pair of boxer shorts, and looked like he'd just got up. 'Soz. Didn't realise you had company.' He offered Molly a cheeky grin. 'I'll give you guys a bit of space.'

'She's police,' Josh said, giving the DS an apologetic look.

'Cool,' came the reply. 'Whatever floats your boat.' With that comment he ambled out of the living room.

'Sorry,' Josh said. 'That's Steve. He was clubbing last night – a mate's twenty-first. It's a miracle he's up before lunchtime.'

Molly briefly wondered if this was what the future held for her: sharing a flat with someone who had barely experienced puberty. She turned her attention back to Josh. 'Like I said, Josh, I'm so sorry to have to bring this all up again, but I need to know what happened.' She paused, inwardly taking a deep breath before moving in with the killer question. 'How did your mum die?'

He stared at the can of lager still sitting on the floor. 'She killed herself.' He looked over at Molly. 'I thought you knew that. I assumed that was why you were here. Following up on it.' She could sense his bravado was starting to falter. There was what looked like the prickling of a tear in his eye.

'I'm sorry, Josh. I'm here in connection with something else.' She tried to relax, part of her wishing she'd accepted his cheeky offer of a can. On duty or not, today was not one she'd look back on with a cheery smile: dredging up painful memories from people who would prefer to put the past behind them and move on. 'I need to ask you how it happened?'

'She jumped to her death from the top floor of a multi-storey car park in Hammersmith,' he said. 'About two months ago.' He was very matter of fact about it, as though it was an everyday occurrence and not something the police should be concerning themselves with. 'At least it was quick,' he added. 'Or so the paramedics said at the time. But who knows, maybe they always say that.'

'I'm so sorry,' she said, meaning it. She had to frame her next question carefully: it was difficult to ask, but they had to be certain of their facts. 'It was definitely suicide, Josh? There was nothing suspicious about your mum's death?'

He shot her a look that mixed confusion with shock. 'Yes. Of course it was. Mum...' His voice cracked, but he quickly composed himself. 'Looking back, there was something almost inevitable about what happened to Mum. She'd always suffered from depression and it got worse after what happened to her. She'd been depressed for a while. But things had gotten worse for her in recent weeks. She was struggling to cope. She wasn't able to get out of bed some days. Other days she would just cry. It was obvious she was suffering from depression, but none of us realised just how bad things had got.'

'Did she ask for help?'

'It turned out her GP had prescribed sleeping pills. But I suspect what she really needed was antidepressants.' He shook his head, as if he was trying to rid himself of the unhappy thoughts. 'But no, to answer your question, there was nothing suspicious about her death.'

Molly wondered though. If their murderer had wanted to make the first murder look unsuspicious, faking a suicide would be a clever way of doing it. 'Again, I'm very sorry. It must have been difficult for you.'

'It was. For both of us. Obviously, you're aware of what happened: my parents splitting up and my mum going off the rails? That child being run over and killed.'

'Yes, that's really why I'm here.'

'Her whole life fell apart when my dad told her he was leaving her for another woman. Well, a girl really. She was in her mid-twenties when they got together. My dad was forty-five.'

'Mid-life crisis?' Molly said, knowing Jon had constantly been on the verge of one.

'Maybe…' He smiled again. 'Predictably, it didn't last. My dad and his new girlfriend split up after a year and a half. If anything, that made things worse for my mum. She realised her marriage had ended for nothing.'

'This led to her having problems at work?'

'Not just that. My parents had always been drinkers. Not alcoholics, or at least if they were, they were functioning ones. Or perhaps, to be more accurate, they functioned up to a point. Mum began drinking more after the divorce. It was her way of coping. She was never very good at drinking, though. She'd pretend that she wasn't drinking too much, or convince herself that wine wasn't really alcohol. All the usual excuses someone with a drink problem comes up with.'

'I realise things must have been difficult for your mum. And what happened that day was terrible. But there have been a number of fatal stabbings in London recently and we believe it might have something to do with the death of Noah Daniel.' She didn't want to give too much away, or to alarm him unnecessarily.

'How?' he asked.

'We don't know exactly at the moment. We just think there's a connection with the little boy's death.'

'But that was an accident.' He gazed at Molly, his eyes wide with shock. 'Are you saying you don't think my mum's death was suicide? You think it could have been suspicious?'

'No. At least there's nothing to suggest your mum's death was anything other than a tragic suicide.'

'Nothing to suggest... But you would have investigated it at the time, wouldn't you? You'd know for sure if there *was* anything suspicious about her death?'

'Her death wouldn't have been investigated by us, we're another department. However, I've spoken to the team that dealt with your mum's suicide and they've assured me there was nothing suspicious. There were two witnesses who saw her jump to her death that day.' Molly had double-checked the post-mortem report that morning, as well as having spoken to Hammersmith CID: they said they'd look into it again if Molly was aware of any new evidence that could potentially cast doubt on Laura Grieve's suicide, but as far as they were concerned both witnesses were reliable and CCTV from the multi-storey car park supported this.

'I suppose that should be some reassurance,' he said, doleful eyes fixed on the floor. 'At least she wasn't murdered.'

'What about the rest of your family?' Molly asked. 'Is your dad still in the States?'

'As far as I know. We haven't had much contact with him. Naturally I told him about mum's death. He sent flowers for her funeral...'

Molly could sense this was still a raw wound. This was one part of the job she hated: forcing people to revisit dark places in order to find that one piece of information that could turn a murder investigation on its head. But right now, Josh Grieve needed some words of comfort. 'It's difficult when parents split,' she said. 'Sometimes one of them just wants to move on and forget about the past.'

'Maybe...'

'You said "we". I take it there was more than just you?'

'My sister. Daisy. If anything, she took it worse than I did. She's always been slightly flaky. And she and Mum were always very close.'

Molly could only feel sympathy for him and his plight. 'How's she coping now?'

He shrugged. 'Dais? I wish I knew. I haven't seen her for a while. Last I heard, she was travelling around Europe. Probably trying to put things behind her and sort her life out. Sometimes she just likes to cut herself off from the world. She was the same when we were kids. There were times when she'd shut herself away in her bedroom for days on end just listening to music. Mum would leave her meals outside her door. Sometimes she'd eat them and sometimes she wouldn't. That was Dais. She likes her space.'

Molly smiled. 'We all like a bit of "me time" on when we want to shut the world out.' But even as she said it, the words felt meaningless. She had a terrible feeling things were very far from alright for the Grieve family.

Chapter Forty-Five

Denning knew he had to tell McKenna about his encounter with Tony Hallam. He would have to explain why he'd been talking to her in the first place when he had been told to pass the whole matter over. It smacked of unprofessionalism and if Denning prided himself on anything, it was his professionalism.

'Tony Hallam?' McKenna looked at him from across her desk. Her face told him she wasn't happy. If he was expecting anything else, he would have been disappointed. 'The husband of Maria Hallam?' She exhaled loudly. 'This is despite you knowing Tony Hallam is no longer involved in our ongoing murder investigation?'

'I know how this seems, but...'

'Do you, Matt? Because I'm not entirely sure you do.'

McKenna had fixed him with one of her stares. She was sitting at her desk, an exasperated look on her face. He knew he was going to have to explain himself.

'She contacted me. She's concerned about her ex-husband and she's certain he's planning something with her brother.'

'But she didn't say what it was?'

'She doesn't seem to know.'

'And none of this is relevant to the case we're currently working...'

He was uncomfortable, but determined to stand his ground. 'I've explained to her that we have to pass this over, but she says I'm the only person she trusts. She's nervous of the police, understandably after what happened with her husband.

'I don't feel like I can just pass her over to another department without it feeling like she's being fobbed off,' he argued. 'It would feel like we were letting her down.'

'That's not how it would be,' McKenna said coldly. 'She would get the support from the people who are best placed to deliver it. And that isn't from a detective inspector with the Major Investigation Team who is engaged in trying to catch a dangerous killer.'

It was a dressing down, but not as brutal as he'd expected. That was the thing with McKenna: you could never truly predict what kind of response you would get with her. But he knew she was right. He just didn't know what he could do about it.

'If I'm honest, I feel sorry for her. She's vulnerable and she's frightened. I don't want to throw her to the wolves.'

There was a silence that began to fill the room, creeping into the corners and then gradually filling the void. It was like an impasse: she was behind her desk, arms folded defiantly, fully prepared to pull rank and discipline him if necessary; he was equally determined to do what he thought was right by a woman who was in need of help from the very police force of which he was a member. Ultimately, however, McKenna was his DCI and she called the shots.

'You have to walk away from this, Matt,' she said. 'Rip off the plaster and hand this over. The more you dance to Maria Hallam's tune, the more demands she's going to place on you. For your own sake, and for that of your team, you need to draw a line in the sand here.'

He nodded his agreement. She was right, and, even if she wasn't, she had the final say here. He just wasn't sure how he was going to break the news to Maria.

Chapter Forty-Six

'Right, everyone, time is now of the essence, so let's not waste it.' It was part of Denning's job to galvanise his team. That meant keeping spirits up whenever his team were showing signs of flagging – such as now, but also to kick backsides, as McKenna would have put it, when he felt progress was too slow. Motivation was always difficult when the investigation had started to plateau, and that was exactly what it was doing now.

'We now have a credible motive,' Denning said. 'I've spoken to Hammersmith CID, and they confirmed that there were no suspicious circumstances. Obviously they'll need to wait for the official say-so from the coroner, but Laura Grieve is believed to have committed suicide shortly before these murders began. Without jumping to any immediate conclusions...'

'No pun intended,' Kinsella interrupted with his usual inimitable lack of tact.

Denning waited for the inevitable groans to pass and continued as though Kinsella had never spoken. 'Without jumping to any immediate conclusions, we can't ignore the fact that this gives her family an obvious motive.'

'Why didn't we know about the suicide?' Trudi asked. 'It should have been flagged up on the system somewhere.'

'We weren't looking for a suicide, Trudi,' Denning said. 'The databases only give us the information we ask them for.'

'Are we saying this Josh Grieve is now our most likely suspect?' Neeraj asked.

Denning looked at Molly. 'Molly, you've spoken to him. What are your thoughts?'

There was a moment before Molly spoke, probably thinking over what she was going to say. 'I don't know.' She looked round the room at her fellow officers. 'He came across as a decent enough bloke. Obviously upset at what happened to his mother, but upset enough to stab three people to death…?' She shook her head and then shrugged. 'I can't see it somehow.'

'Based on what?' Kinsella asked dryly. 'Female intuition?'

Molly shot him a filthy look. 'Based on psychology, Dave. It's the direction of travel in modern policing.' She looked at Denning when she said it, knowing he had a degree in psychology and criminology. These were the very kind of qualities the Met were looking for in new recruits to MITs. Old-fashioned coppers like Dave Kinsella were on their way out, and Kinsella knew it. 'However, I admit,' she added, somewhat reluctantly, 'I could be wrong about Josh Grieve.'

'Do we bring him in for questioning?' Neeraj asked.

'See if he has alibis for the days and times of the murders,' Denning said. 'If not, then we need to formally interview him. But remember, he's recently lost his mother in tragic circumstances and we don't, as yet, have anything concrete to connect him with these murders.'

'So are we now conclusively ruling out Noah Daniel's family?' Kinsella asked. 'Whichever way we look at it, they still have the strongest motive.'

'We've checked them out, Dave. Both Adam and Peta Daniel have alibis: Peta Daniel was in hospital the evening Kieran Judd was murdered and Adam Daniel was working late. There are witnesses who can confirm this in both cases. They also have alibis for the other murders.'

'What about extended family?' Kinsella asked.

'Uniform have spoken to them, Obviously we still need to confirm all their alibis, but at this stage in the investigation it's looking unlikely that our killer is a relation of Noah Daniel's.'

'A dead end,' Kinsella said, arms folded across his chest. 'Shame. If it had been one of them they might have got on a sympathy vote.'

Denning ignored his tactless comment and continued. 'I'm certain Laura Grieve is the connection here. I think this is about revenge for what happened to her rather than Noah.'

'Her suicide?' Neeraj asked.

'That, and the actions of Thomas Blake Primary School which led her to ultimately take her life.'

'We're accepting that the school definitely tried to cover up what happened that day?' Trudi Bell asked.

'By the looks of it, the school knew Laura Grieve was struggling with the job due to her personal circumstances. If it had come out at the inquiry that she shouldn't have been allowed to supervise those children that day, the school would have had some serious questions to answer.'

'In a way, they were doing her a favour,' Trudi said. 'If the truth had got out about how her mind hadn't been fully on the job the day of the accident, she could potentially have faced a manslaughter charge.'

'Perhaps that would have been better in the long run,' Molly said. 'It was the guilt of blaming herself that drove her to do what she did. Maybe if she'd served time for manslaughter she might have felt that was penance enough?'

'For killing a child?' Kinsella said. 'Some people might argue that was getting off lightly.'

'She clearly suffered for her role in Noah's death, Dave,' Molly fought back. 'She had to live with the guilt.'

Denning felt he had to intervene. 'Let's not get too hung up on what happened and who was or wasn't to blame. At the end of the day, it was an accident. Would it really have made a difference if Laura Grieve had her wits about her that day or not? She was momentarily distracted and a child ran out onto the road and was knocked down and killed. It was horrific and it shouldn't have happened, but it did and no one can change that. We need to focus on the here and now. Someone has decided to punish the people they see as being responsible for Laura Grieve's suicide, and the obvious suspects are her family.'

Denning headed to the whiteboard. He wrote the name Josh Grieve on the board and underlined it. 'Let's check out his alibis. And look into his life some more. Find out all we can about him.'

'He mentioned a sister,' Molly said.

'Name?'

She thought for a moment. 'Daisy.'

'OK,' Denning replied. 'Daisy Grieve: let's check her out too. Do we have an address for her yet?'

'Not yet,' Molly said, 'but I'll try and find one. Her brother seems to think she's travelling round Europe right now, but she may well have a base in the UK somewhere.'

'Good. In the meantime I think we need to focus on Rachel Atherton and Penny Garnett. Atherton was only deputy head at time, and claims she was against the school trip from the start. If I had to take a punt, I'd say our killer is going to go after Penny Garnett.'

'She and her partner have been given police protection,' Molly said. 'They've also moved in with a friend for now, but they're reluctant to close the restaurant as it will impact on business. You can see their point: it is their livelihood after all.'

'They might not have a choice,' Denning said. But he considered the odds: it was unlikely the killer would strike while the restaurant was open as there would be too many people around, and there would be someone with them on the journey between the restaurant and wherever they were staying, but it was still risky. He had to make a judgement call. 'OK, let's keep things as they are for now. We can't force them to close the restaurant, but I can't say I'm entirely happy about the situation.'

'I can pop round and check on them this evening,' Molly offered. 'Just make sure everything's alright.'

'It's a bit out of your way,' Denning said, but he appreciated the offer.

Molly shrugged. 'It's not like I've got anything else to do.'

He looked at the clock on the wall near the whiteboard. 'It's getting late. We'll call it a day and start again tomorrow, eight a.m. sharp.' He ended the briefing. As his team returned to their keyboards, he noticed there was a message on his phone from Anna Klein: *call me*. He headed out into the corridor and phoned her back. 'Anna, how's things?'

'The hearing's tomorrow.' A pause, but he could guess what was coming. 'Have you come to a decision about my reference?'

In all honesty it had gone right out of his head. 'I'm sorry, Anna. I just haven't had time.' It wasn't a lie, but it wasn't entirely truthful either.

'I've been doing some digging about Tony Hallam.' There was another pause, making sure Denning was getting the message: a favour for a favour.

'What did you find out?'

'I've got a friend who used to work in the Community Safety Unit, specifically dealing with domestic abuse... she's still talking to me, which is something. She told me there was a domestic assault case against Hallam over his wife,' she said. 'Maria Hallam. The case was dropped.'

This much Denning already knew courtesy of the PNC. 'Yes, Maria Hallam withdrew the charges. I'd heard something along those lines...' The law had recently changed where even if the accuser changed their mind about pressing charges, the police could still make a case if they felt there was sufficient evidence.

'There's more to it than that,' Klein said, leaving another pause, emphasising the fact this was a favour that needed repaying. 'The person I spoke to told me they'd heard a rumour the real reason the case was dropped was because Tony Hallam was a police informer. I mean this is before he was sent down, obviously.'

'So you're saying Maria Hallam was pressurised into dropping the domestic assault charges to protect her husband?' Denning couldn't quite believe what he was hearing.

'Well, that's the rumour. I can't confirm it. The person I spoke to insists it has to be strictly off the record, so you can't make this official.'

It didn't make sense. Yet, in a way, it explained so much. 'But if Hallam was a police informer, how come he was sent down?'

'He was caught red-handed at the scene of a crime. There was no way of dodging that particular bullet.'

Was it possible Meech could have framed Hallam? 'Did Meech suspect Hallam might be an informer?'

'I don't know. It's possible, I suppose. There's a line of thinking that believes Meech framed Hallam, but there's no evidence to back that up.'

'Thanks, Anna. That's very helpful.'

'You won't forget my reference? I'll text you a reminder of who to send it to…' But Denning had already ended the call.

Chapter Forty-Seven

It had only just gone seven o'clock when Molly called round at the Laughing Parrot. She tapped on the door, which already had the closed sign turned to face the street. Penny Garnett saw her, waved and then opened the door.

'I was about to tell you to get lost,' she said. 'Before I recognised who it was, of course.' She smiled at Molly. 'We've decided to close early tonight. It's always quiet on a Thursday and, to be honest, we've both spent most of the day looking over our shoulders.' She gave a nervous laugh that suggested she was trying to come across as more confident than she felt. 'Can I offer you a coffee. Or something stronger? Freya and I were going to have a brandy,' she said. 'We don't usually, but, under the circumstances, we felt we've earned it today.'

'I shouldn't, though I am technically off duty.' She looked round but couldn't see the officer. 'Where is he?'

'Freya sent him home. He was putting off our customers.'

From somewhere in the kitchen, Molly heard Freya say, 'He might as well have had a neon sign over his head saying "police officer".'

Molly sat down at one of the tables. 'Hopefully it won't be too much longer. We have a lead we're pursuing at the moment. Obviously I can't say too much, but with a bit of luck this nightmare will be over soon.'

'Just as well,' Penny said, pouring out a large glass of brandy. 'Every time a customer walked through the door my heart was in my mouth thinking, "have they come to kill me?".'

Molly tried not to laugh, but did so despite herself. There was something refreshing about Penny Garnett. Even under stress she managed to keep smiling.

'I just wanted to try to reassure you that we're doing everything we can.' It was true she wanted to call round and offer words of encouragement, but also she was delaying having to head back to Trudi and Charys's. Calling their place home just didn't sit right with her.

'It still haunts me,' Penny said. 'If it's any consolation, we all felt guilty, both about what happened to Noah and how we treated Laura.' She began toying with the brandy glass. 'But there's nothing we can do about that now. What's done, cannot be undone.'

Molly wanted to offer her more in the way of reassurance. But until they'd caught the person responsible, all she could offer were empty words.

They were suddenly distracted by a crash coming from the kitchen area. Penny shouted for Freya, but there was no reply. Immediately she jumped from her seat and made to head for the kitchen. Molly told her to wait where she was. She ran into the kitchen; the back door, leading to a small alley, was open. She shouted for Freya but there was still no reply. She spotted her lying beside a bin, unconscious. Penny had ignored Molly's request to remain in the restaurant area and joined her at the back door. She knelt beside her, taking Freya's hand. 'Phone for an ambulance,' Molly shouted. 'And the police.' There was only confused panic on Penny's face, so Molly repeated her instructions. Penny fished her phone from her jacket pocket.

Molly checked the alley at the back of the restaurant, edging her way along the wall and past some industrial bins with caution. She jumped when she heard a noise and saw a shadow moving behind the bins. A fox popped its head out from behind one and then ran off, something indescribable in its mouth. She waited until her heartbeat returned to something close to normal, then exhaled slowly. There was nobody there. Whoever had attacked Freya had probably run off too.

Then she heard a shout coming from the kitchen area. She darted back along the alley and in through the kitchen door. A figure, wearing a hoodie and dressed in black, was standing over Penny Garnett, holding a knife. Penny had her arm raised to protect herself; a look of horror on her face. Molly reached into her pocket for her pepper spray. But the momentary distraction of her bursting through the door was enough. The figure dropped the knife and ran into the deserted restaurant. Molly chased after them but tripped over a chair that the assailant had thrown into her path. By the time she'd got back on her feet, the assailant had reached the restaurant door, unlocked it, opened it and ran onto the street. Molly followed onto the pavement, but the road was deserted. She heard the noise of a motorbike and watched as the assailant sped past on a scooter. Molly ran onto the road to note the number plate, but they were already disappearing at speed round a corner. She could hear the sound of a siren in the distance meaning either the police or ambulance were on their way.

She went to the restaurant. Freya was sitting up now, looking slightly dazed with a cut to her forehead. She was trying to sit up. Penny was still kneeling next to her; her face looked deathly pale in the dim light.

'Are you both OK?' Molly asked. 'The ambulance is on its way.'

'I'm fine,' Freya insisted. 'It's just a cut.'

'You might have concussion,' Penny argued.

'What happened?' Molly asked, kneeling down next to Freya to make sure there were no other injuries.

'I don't know. It all happened so fast. I opened the door to put the rubbish out and I saw this figure standing by the bins. There's a security light that should come on automatically, but it's broken. I asked them what they were doing and they rushed at me, knocking me over. That's when I screamed.'

Molly looked round the kitchen. They must have hidden there and waited until she'd gone out the back to look for them, then tried to stab Penny when she'd come through to check on Freya.

'Whoever it was planned this. They must have been watching us,' Penny said, her voice a pitch higher than normal. 'They were waiting for an opportunity to do this.'

Molly wondered. Had the assailant been waiting for the right time, or was this opportunistic? Had their plans changed when she had arrived unexpectedly this evening?

If the attacker had been watching them, why would they have waited until she arrived? Wouldn't it have been better to do it when they first locked up? Were they now getting desperate? They must know that the police were on to them. If they were upping their game then there was a real danger they would become unpredictable. Were they now flaky?

Flaky. Why did that word jar...?

She heard the restaurant door open and a voice call out. She glanced through the door into the kitchen and saw a couple of paramedics entering the restaurant, looking around. The swirling blue light of their ambulance reflected on the shiny table tops.

'In here,' she shouted.

Freya was struggling to sit up again, resting on her elbows, but blinking as though she was going to pass out. The paramedics pushed their way into the kitchen: a man and a woman. They knelt down next to Freya, who was still insisting she was fine. Molly headed back out onto the street just as a police car was pulling up outside the restaurant. As the two uniformed officers got out, she explained what had happened, then phoned Denning to tell him.

Molly's gut was right: Penny was their killer's main target. Thank god she'd been there, otherwise there might have been two more victim pictures up on the board. Had the attacker known she was there? Or had they panicked and tried to kill Penny irrespective of that? It told her one thing: the killer was getting desperate.

Chapter Forty-Eight

Denning arrived at the restaurant twenty minutes after receiving Molly's call. By the time he arrived at the scene, the paramedics were packing up and Freya was sitting in the restaurant nursing her brandy.

As soon as Molly saw him, she hurried over. 'Whoever did it was quick and they knew what they were doing. The only question is, did they know I was here?'

Denning sat at the table next to Freya. 'Are you sure you don't want to go to A&E?'

'I keep telling everyone: I just want to go home,' Freya said through slightly clenched teeth. 'It's been a long day.'

He turned to Penny. 'Are you all right?'

She nodded. 'A bit shaken up, but otherwise OK. Lucky Molly was here.'

'What about the uniformed officer who was supposed to be with you at all times?'

'He was wasting his time here,' Freya said quickly. 'Besides, I doubt there's much he could have done. The whole thing happened so fast.'

One of the two uniformed officers who had arrived after the 999 call came over to speak to Denning. 'We've searched the immediate area, sir. There's no sign of anyone. Whoever did this has long gone.' He nodded at a CCTV camera above the counter. 'Hopefully there'll be something there worth looking at.'

Penny got to her feet. 'Yes, I forgot about CCTV. Mind you, it will only show us what we already know.'

'What about out the back by the bins?' Denning asked. 'Is there any out there?'

A shake of the head. 'We rarely use that door, except for deliveries sometimes and to put the rubbish out.'

'But if someone had been watching the place, there's a good chance they'd know you put the rubbish out after you shut the restaurant?' Denning asked.

Penny Garnett rubbed a hand over tired eyes. 'I suppose. I can't think straight at the moment. This is a bit of a shock.'

'Great, isn't it,' Freya said. 'You're the one he's after and I'm the one with the bleeding head.'

Penny gave a weak laugh, but it looked like she was struggling to see the funny side.

Denning gestured for Molly to join him at another table. 'How much of a look did you get at the assailant?'

She shrugged. 'Like Freya and Penny said, it all happened so quickly. CCTV might help throw up a decent description, but his face was covered. Otherwise all I could say is: slim build, average height. Fast on their feet.'

'The description fits Josh Grieve better than it does either Peta or Adam Daniel.'

'It also fits a lot of people.'

'But Josh Grieve is a likely candidate?'

She sighed. 'It could have been him. But...' She was thinking about it. 'I don't know.'

'OK, we'll speak to him. If he can't verify where he was this evening, we'll take him in for formal questioning.'

Molly nodded.

'In the meantime, I think you should get home. I'll make sure someone takes Penny and Freya back and stays with them tonight. But there's not much more you can do here. You look shattered.'

'Thanks.' But she smiled, agreeing with him. 'Actually, it has been a long day. I'm surprised Trudi hasn't rung to see where I've got to.'

Denning watched her head out the restaurant then flag down a taxi. Penny and Freya were being helped towards a waiting police car. Forensics would go over the place in the morning looking for fingerprints, they would ask to have the CCTV sent over and then it would be checked. But, in the meantime, there wasn't much anyone could do.

He'd phone Neeraj and ask him to meet at Josh Grieve's flat.

–

Neeraj was already waiting for him when he arrived at the address they had for Josh Grieve. He tipped his chin at Denning as he approached.

'Have you checked if he's in?' Denning asked.

'I've literally just got here, boss. Thought it better to wait for you before we go in all guns blazing.'

Denning hoped that wouldn't be necessary. He walked up the short path to the front door, Neeraj following. He rang the bell for flat B and waited. There was no answer, so Denning rang the bell again. A few moments later a light came on and a figure could be seen behind the frosted glass descending the stairs. The door opened a crack and they found themselves looking at the face of an unshaven man in his early twenties.

'We're looking for Josh Grieve,' Denning said, showing his ID.

'That's me,' the man said. 'What do you want?'

'Can we come in?' Denning asked. 'We'd rather not do this in the street.'

Grieve opened the door and let them in. They followed him upstairs to the flat on the first floor. He showed them in to the living room. 'What's this about?' he asked. 'Has something happened?'

'Where were you earlier this evening?' Neeraj asked.

'I was here,' Grieve replied. 'Watching telly.'

'Can anyone verify that?' Neeraj asked.

'My flatmate got back about half an hour ago,' Grieve said, looking from one detective to the other.

They were disturbed by the sight of a man of a similar age ambling into the living room. He looked at the three men sitting there, quickly taking in the situation. 'What is this? A drugs raid?' He grinned.

'It's the Old Bill, Steve,' Grieve said in a weary tone. 'They're here to speak to me.'

'Just a moment,' Denning said. 'You're Josh Grieve's flatmate?'

'Steve Barley,' the flatmate said. He smiled at them. 'What's he gone and done now?'

'Can you confirm whether Mr Grieve was here all evening?'

'Josh. Yes. I mean I only got back here half an hour ago, but he'd been here all night. We had a couple of cans, then I was just about to have a bath when you guys rang the bell loud enough to wake the dead.'

Denning looked at Grieve. 'So you've definitely been here all evening?'

'Yes,' Grieve said, a note of annoyance in his voice. 'Are you going to tell me what this is about?'

Denning was trying to work it out in his head. It was possible the flatmate was covering for Grieve. Relaying an alibi they'd concocted between them. Could Josh Grieve have got from his flat to south London and back this evening? It was just about possible, especially if he had his own transport? But Denning wasn't convinced. 'Do you own a scooter?' he asked Grieve.

'A scooter? No. Why? What exactly am I being accused of here? Look, if this has got anything to do with what happened to my mum, then I spoke to one of your people earlier today and answered a load of daft questions.'

'So, just to confirm, you don't own a scooter?' Denning asked.

'No. I've just said.'

'And you weren't anywhere near Gipsy Hill this evening?' Neeraj asked.

Josh looked at both detectives, then at his flatmate, who gave an indifferent shrug as though to indicate that he didn't have a clue what was going on. 'No. I was nowhere near Gipsy Hill this evening. I was watching telly until you two rang the bell.'

Denning wasn't entirely satisfied, but felt there was no point pushing matters further right now. It was late and bed seemed the obvious option. 'OK, Mr Grieve. Thank you for your help. We might need to ask you some more questions, but that's all for now.'

Once they were back on the pavement, Denning turned to Neeraj. 'Apologies for dragging you out, Deep, but I thought it was important that we spoke to Josh Grieve as soon as possible.'

'No probs, boss.' Neeraj glanced up at the flat. 'What do you reckon? Think they've invented that story about watching telly together?'

Denning followed his gaze and looked up at the flat. It was entirely possible Josh Grieve had been in Gipsy Hill that evening and it would be convenient to assume his guilt. But Denning wasn't sure. 'Either he's a first-rate actor, or he's telling the truth. And I can't help thinking it's the latter. In which case, we've got a problem, Deep. Three dead bodies, one attempted and we're still no closer to finding out the truth.'

'You think they'll try again with Penny Garnett, boss?'

Denning was still staring up at the living room window of the flat they'd just been inside moments ago. He was sure he could see a silhouette behind the curtain.

'I think it's almost certain, Deep.'

Chapter Forty-Nine

Charys and Trudi were enjoying a glass of wine when Molly returned home, tired but still buzzing with the last vestiges of adrenaline. They were watching *Bridgerton* on Netflix, something Molly had never been able to get into.

'Alright, Moll?' Trudi asked. She waved the wine bottle in Molly's direction. 'Grab a glass from the kitchen and join us for one?'

'I won't, if you don't mind. I might just get some water and head to my room.'

Trudi pulled a face and poured some more wine into her glass, then the remaining trickle into Charys's.

Molly headed into the kitchen to get a glass of water, then headed into her tiny bedroom and relived the events of that evening in her head. She was still too wired to switch off. Everything had happened so quickly that her brain had struggled to process all the details at the time. She'd mostly acted on impulse, her training kicking in and taking over.

The attack had obviously been planned rather than being something the assailant had done on the spur of the moment; the intention had clearly been to kill Penny Garnett. Only luck and her quick-thinking had prevented that. She guessed the attacker hadn't known she'd be there. But there should have been some kind of police presence.

Or had the attacker known this and pressed ahead with their plan anyway? A desperate move.

And then there was the other mystery gnawing away at her... Denning seemed certain their killer was Josh Grieve: he had an obvious motive, but Molly had her doubts. Somehow it didn't *feel* like it had been Josh Grieve who had been in the restaurant that evening. She'd met him, she'd chatted to him and she was almost certain the person in the restaurant that evening hadn't been the same man...

But she was sure there was something he wasn't telling her.

Her head was throbbing and her brain was too tired to think clearly. She'd placed her phone on the coffee table, aware it had to be charged before tomorrow. The icon indicated a message. She checked it, thinking it would be from Denning thanking her for saving Penny Garnett's life. Instead, Cassie Bane's name flashed up. She felt guilty that she hadn't updated Cassie with what they now knew. Cassie's FLO would keep her up to speed with the case's progress, but she felt she owed it to Cassie to speak to her face to face.

She read the message with a heavy heart: Cassie had decided to move out and take up her friend's offer of a room. It wasn't ideal and was hopefully only temporary. It meant her flat would be available for rent. Molly's head was swirling with too many thoughts. It was a nice flat: the location was OK and it was large enough for one person. And then there was the murder... She might get it cheap if she played up the fact a murder had taken place there. But then she reminded herself this was London; very few people would be bothered by a property's grisly history. Ironically, she thought it would actually bother

her. The memory of Kieran Judd's blood on the walls and the carpet. The thought of his body lying there...

Cassie... that phone call... *a woman's voice*... not Kieran's ex... Scarlett had insisted it hadn't been her. Molly hadn't entirely believed her at the time.

She'd dismissed that as not being relevant. But *why* wasn't it relevant...?

While Scarlett Rennie was never really in the running for Kieran Judd's murder, she hadn't entirely believed her when she'd claimed not to have phoned the flat. But what if she'd been telling the truth? What if it hadn't been Scarlett Rennie but someone else? Another woman...

She heard a noise and looked up. There was a tap on the bedroom door. She shouted to come in and Trudi appeared from behind the door. 'Everything alright, Molly?'

She sat on the edge of the bed while Molly filled her in on what had happened. She would hear all the details at work the next day, and they had a golden rule in the flat not to talk shop, but Molly had to get the events of the evening out of her system.

She touched Molly on the shoulder. 'At least you're OK,' Trudi said. 'We could have been looking at more fatalities if things had gone the other way.'

'I know. Just lucky I guess.' She smiled at Trudi. 'Look, I really am so grateful to you and Charys for letting me crash here. I'm sure I'm in your way.'

'You know you can stay here for as long as you need to. We love having you here.'

'Thanks,' Molly said. 'I appreciate your kindness. Both of you. I don't know what I would have done if I couldn't have stayed here. It's given me the time and space to get my head clear.'

'Stay as long as you need to.' Charys was shouting something from the living room. Trudi got off the bed and headed back to Charys. Molly thought some more about Josh Grieve. The more she thought about it, the more certain she was that the person in the restaurant this evening wasn't him. Which raised the question: if it wasn't Josh Grieve, who was it?

She had a feeling she knew the answer already.

Chapter Fifty

Denning closed the door to the flat as quietly as he could. He didn't want to disturb Sarah. He was shattered. They had been enjoying dinner when Molly had phoned to tell him about the attack at the restaurant. Luckily it hadn't taken him long to drive to south London.

It was the last thing they needed right now. The case was progressing too slowly for his liking and he knew McKenna would be breathing down his neck the next day. He glanced at the large vintage-style clock in the living room and realised another couple of hours and it would be the next day. He was tempted to pad into the kitchen and grab a beer from the fridge, but he knew he would need to keep a clear head for the morning.

He sat on one of the two large linen sofas that dominated the living area. Sarah was in the office, emailing New York probably.

He found himself thinking about Noah Daniel. Then he thought about Jake. In fact, every time he thought about Noah Daniel it was Jake who came to mind. Rachel Atherton's words echoed in his head: *Noah was a difficult boy...* Had Jake's teachers said the same thing about him before he changed schools?

Noah Daniel... running out into the road because he wanted an ice cream. It was the sort of thing Jake might easily have done when he was Noah's age. Jake had little concept of danger or risk, and they'd both had to drum it into him that he had to be careful around roads, rivers, lakes. And as for warning him about strangers... Jake thought very literally and anyone he didn't know was a stranger. He'd once ignored a supply teacher for several weeks simply because he didn't know her and therefore she fell into the 'stranger' category. It had taken them a long time to explain the difference between strangers he could trust and strangers he couldn't. Even then, there were so many grey areas...

He sat there, staring out of the oriel window at the far end of the room. The lights of London twinkled back at him. Then he thought about Claire. Until recently, she'd worked as a teaching assistant in a primary school. The same job as Kieran Judd and Laura Grieve. What would she have done in the circumstances? How would she have behaved and how much guilt would he have felt?

So many things about this case didn't make sense. The biggest detail of all was Rachel Atherton; she was clearly holding something back, but was it relevant? He'd checked her out: nothing. She had a good reputation and – with the exception of Noah Daniel's death – an exemplary work history. He couldn't put his finger on it and he was too tired to fully focus. The attack on Penny Garnett demonstrated how their killer was upping their game. He knew if they didn't do something soon, they would try again.

Then his thoughts turned to Maria Hallam. She and her children were afraid of her husband, and he felt help-less to do anything about it. Tony Hallam's very clear and specific threat had told him all he needed to know: Hallam was dangerous and he was planning something. Maria and her children were probably in danger. But he could hear McKenna's voice in his head reminding him that this wasn't their case, wasn't their problem. Someone else's problem... But was that enough to persuade him to walk away...?

Chapter Fifty-One

First thing next morning, as soon as the team were in and seated at their desks, Denning held another briefing. The events of the previous evening were now common knowledge and they were under even greater pressure to catch the killer.

There was something still niggling away at Molly. Something that didn't quite fit about the attack on Penny and Freya last night. She waited for the right moment to voice her concerns.

Denning was at the front of the room. He looked tired. As did the whole team. It was always the same story during a lengthy investigation: nobody slept until it was over.

'Penny Garnett and her partner were attacked at their restaurant yesterday evening,' Denning said. 'Both women are all right now, thanks to the quick-thinking of DS Fisher.' She blushed slightly as the team gave her a round of applause. 'Luckily, Freya White only needed minor stitches and head wound dressed. Penny Garnett is shocked, but physically unharmed. We'll send a couple of uniformed officers round later this morning to take a formal statement. Despite our best attempts, the attacker got away. We have to assume it's our killer.'

'I'd say that's a fairly safe bet,' Kinsella offered dryly.

'Fortunately, the CCTV at the restaurant captured the incident,' Denning said, ignoring Kinsella, 'and we now have access to it. Trudi, I believe you've already had a brief look over it this morning.'

'Yup. Bear in mind I've only glanced at it first thing this morning, but it confirms what Molly said about the assailant having their face covered. I can send it over to the tech team after I've studied it in more detail to see if they can improve the image resolution, but it doesn't look like there's much to work with. I think our killer knows what they're doing.'

'What's Josh Grieve's story?' Kinsella asked. He looked like he was wearing the same shirt as yesterday. There was still an egg stain down the front. 'Why haven't we brought him in? At least to ask him a few awkward questions.'

'We spoke with Mr Grieve last night,' Denning said, looking over at Neeraj. 'He has an alibi. Obviously, we'll confirm that, and we'll check CCTV from both the streets around the restaurant and the area around his flat. But it's beginning to look like he isn't our killer.'

'Which brings us back to Noah Daniel's parents,' Kinsella said. 'It has to be them.'

'We'll speak to them again, Dave. But I'm still not convinced they're the murdering type. OK, I know, I know, there isn't exactly a type, but you know what I mean. I just don't think it's them.'

'But we'll question them again, but I think we need to start exploring other options.'

'Except there aren't any,' Kinsella insisted. 'At least not credible ones. To all intents and purposes, we're back at square one.'

Molly felt now was the time to voice her theory. As soon as Kinsella was sitting back on his chair, arms folded, she raised a Biro to attract Denning's attention.

'Molly?'

'There is something we haven't considered.' She wanted to frame the words in her mind before she spoke them out loud, in case she was completely barking up the wrong tree and about to make a fool of herself.

'Go on,' Denning prompted after it became obvious she'd let the pause grow too large.

'Have we taken the Grieve family into consideration enough?'

'She's got an ex-husband,' Denning said. 'But we've ruled him out.'

'How come?' Trudi Bell asked.

'He's in the States. He's been working in Denver,' Denning said. 'The hotel he's staying at confirmed he's been there for the past fortnight. There's no record of him entering or leaving the UK during that timeframe.'

'Besides,' Kinsella added, 'he and Laura Grieve divorced years ago. Would he really still have feelings for his ex-wife that are strong enough to want to kill for?'

'OK,' Denning replied. 'What else?'

They were all looking through their notes. Molly had already googled Josh Grieve, but there was nothing about his family that could prove there was anything in her theory. At the moment all she had was a niggling doubt and some very circumstantial evidence. 'What about Josh Grieve's sister?' she said. 'Daisy.'

It was Denning who spoke first. 'OK. Explain...'

She told them about the mystery phone call to Kieran Judd shortly before he was murdered – the female voice. 'It was when I spoke to Josh the other day. He mentioned he's got a sister; I'm still trying to find an address for her. He said she was "slightly flaky" after their mother's death. I didn't think it was significant at the time. Grieve wasn't even a suspect at that point. But taking that into

account alongside this woman who called the house…'
She looked around the team. 'OK, I might be putting
two and two together here and coming up with fifty-six,
but it's something to consider, especially if we're talking
about ruling Josh Grieve out of our enquiries.'

'A woman?' Kinsella said, as though the idea seemed
preposterous.

'The description we have from the neighbour about
the person seen running away *could* be that of a young
woman,' Neeraj said. He looked over his notes, 'Slim
build, wearing a hoodie. It's possible…'

'The CCTV certainly supports the possibility,' Bell
said. 'The figure seen fighting with Molly and Freya
White is slight, fast. Nimble on their pins.' She scratched
her head. 'It could be a woman.'

Molly quickly tapped away on her keyboard, then
emailed the CCTV footage that she had round the team.
They all clicked on the videos.

'It's too dark to tell,' Kinsella said.

'But it certainly could be a woman,' Neeraj argued. 'At
least, we couldn't say for certain that it isn't.'

Denning was looking closely at the footage. After a
minute he looked up. 'What exactly did Josh Grieve say,
Molly?'

'Just that – "we were knocked for six by Mum's death".'

'We need to speak to him again,' Neeraj said. 'Find out
where the hell she is.'

'The big question,' Kinsella said, 'is was she working
alone? Or was Josh Grieve in on it too?'

Chapter Fifty-Two

Denning knocked cautiously on McKenna's door and waited for the call to enter. She was seated behind her desk as usual, pen in hand, staring at the paperwork on her desk. She looked bored. *No*, not bored. Fed up.

'I hope you're bringing me good news,' she said. 'We've got three dead bodies and one near-miss. Our killer is getting bolder and we don't seem any closer to catching him.'

'I might have something positive there,' Denning replied. 'For a start, we're now very much of the opinion that "him" is a "her".'

She tossed her pen onto the desk. 'Oh, yes? Enlighten me.'

He told her about Daisy Grieve, and how she now seemed to be the obvious suspect. 'We're still trying to trace her. We've checked she's not at the addresses we had for her. Seems she and her last boyfriend split up about two months ago, around the time of her mother's suicide. She moved out and Josh reckons she could be travelling. However, it's possible she's back in the UK. And if she is, then we need to find her. Josh has given us a list of her friends, and we're still working through that list. Molly's has no luck trying to find a current address. Nobody at any of her previous known addresses knows where she could be living, assuming she is back. In fact, nobody seems to have seen her since her mum died. We get the impression she's a bit of a loner.'

'Right, let's get a description of her circulated. There's a chance she'll try and kill again, so we need to get to her before she does. And let's have another word with her brother. There's a good chance Josh Grieve knows more than he's letting on.' Her dark eyes flashed at Denning. 'In fact, it's entirely possible he knows his sister's responsible and is trying to protect her.'

'We don't know for certain Daisy Grieve *is* our killer,' Denning said, 'but it looks like she's the most obvious suspect. This is definitely about Laura Grieve's suicide. It makes sense.'

McKenna nodded, steepling her fingers under her chin, something she did when she was chewing things over in her brain. 'I hope you're right, Matt. The press are giving us grief over this. They've worked out the murders are linked. Luckily, they haven't yet traced it back to the incident in the park two years ago, but it won't take them long to join the dots. And then there's the DCS, buzzing in my ear, demanding to know why we haven't got a result yet. I can only fob her off for so long. We need a result.'

'Agreed. And we're hopeful of a breakthrough.' He knew that sounded like he was trying to fob her off with the kind of excuses they offered to the media when a case was stalling. But there was something else he had to say. Something that had bugged him for a while.

'Tony Hallam.' He sat back on the chair and waited for her response.

'Not this again, Matt. I thought we'd exhausted this conversation last time we chatted.' She sighed and tugged at her hair, something else she did subconsciously when her mind was agitated. 'Tony Hallam – or, to be more precise, Maria Hallam – is not your concern. Do I have to make it official? Because the message doesn't seem to be getting across.'

He could feel that gimlet stare burrow into him. 'Look, I know. And I appreciate the timing could be better. I'm just concerned that nothing's happening on that front.' He paused, hoping what he had to say next would sound neither paranoid nor over-dramatic. 'He threatened me the other night.' He looked at the pile of papers on her desk, sliding his gaze right to where a coffee mug sat on a square coaster; looking anywhere except at McKenna. 'Well, OK, not threatened exactly. But he made it clear he wants me to keep away from Maria.'

He could still feel McKenna's coal-black eyes on him. 'Good. Well, with a bit of luck he'll succeed where I seem to have failed, and you'll get the message this time.'

He ignored the barbed comment and the withering sentiment behind it. 'And what if something happens? We know Hallam's dangerous. He's got form.'

'We also know CID are keeping an eye on him. If he as much as puts a foot out of line, they'll have him.' She continued looking at Denning. 'But you're still not happy?'

He couldn't articulate what it was he was concerned about. Sympathy for Maria? Dislike of Hallam? Or was he just irked by the sense that a criminal was getting away with it? It wouldn't be the first time, and he knew he shouldn't let this get to him, but there was something about Hallam that spelt trouble, and until he got to the bottom of it, he couldn't let it go.

'I know you're right. And I know I'm probably blowing this out of proportion, or even on the wrong track entirely, but I've just got this gut feeling. I wish

I could simply walk away from the whole thing with Hallam and switch off what I'm feeling.'

'Well, you're going to have to,' McKenna said coldly. 'And I'm really going to have to insist.'

Denning knew she was right. His focus had been wrong throughout the whole case. He'd allowed Maria Hallam to become a distraction from what mattered here. Three murders and so far Denning had failed to make any significant breakthroughs. Molly had been doing most of the legwork; something he was all too aware of. They had to find a killer, and time wasn't on their side.

Chapter Fifty-Three

Molly phoned Josh Grieve, but there was no answer. She left a message urging him to contact her immediately. She tried to keep any sense of urgency from her voice in case she panicked him, but she was keen to stress the importance of the situation. This could still turn out to be nothing, she thought to herself. She'd also contacted the local police and asked them to send someone round to the flat, both to confirm whether or not he was actually there, and if he wasn't, then ask either neighbours or his flatmate to contact them the moment he appeared. His flatmate had insisted Josh had left for work as usual that morning, despite his rude awakening the night before. Neeraj was checking out the bar where Josh worked.

In the meantime she was desperately trying to track down Daisy Grieve. There was little to go on. She'd tried the number Josh had given her, but the line was dead. She could contact the service provider, but that would take time she didn't have. She googled her name, but Daisy Grieve was a surprisingly common name. There were at least a dozen Twitter and Facebook accounts with that name, all with profile photos varying from anonymous-looking young women to family pets. She quickly scanned them hoping to see if Josh Grieve's name popped up as a friend or a follower, but there was nothing. She could do a more detailed search, go through each account one to see if she could find the right Daisy Grieve, but again it would take time. Similarly, she'd googled Laura Grieve. There was mention on various news sites about the accident. There was a whole section on *London Echo*'s website about her subsequent resignation. However it was light on detail. The article gave her age, mentioned she was divorced with two grown-up children, but gave little else away. The children weren't named and there were certainly no photos of them.

She scrolled through some more websites looking for a name, but there was nothing. She tried Josh Grieve's mobile again: still no answer. She could feel time was beginning to run out here. Word had leaked out to the local media about the attack on Freya White in the restaurant last night. Luckily there was no mention of the murders, and no suggestion that the attack was linked to them. But it would only take a dedicated journalist to do a bit of background research on Freya to find the link with Penny Garnett, and from there it was just a question of time until someone found the connection between the names. Jon would have done without even breaking sweat. Jon... She found herself thinking about him even when she was trying hard not to. Relations were still civil between them, but for how much longer...?

She sat back in her chair and thought things through carefully. It was times like this she wished she still smoked. She'd only recently given up after months of trying. She used to enjoy sharing a fag break with Trudi in the car park; swapping gossip and having a good natter. She glanced over at Trudi's desk: she was still searching through the CCTV footage from the restaurant last night. They'd now received what limited CCTV footage there was from the streets around the murder sites to see if anyone matched the figure who had attacked Freya, but it would take time.

Then she had a thought. While she'd had no luck tracing Daisy Grieve through social media, Josh Grieve might yield a more productive response. She checked: he had accounts with Twitter, Facebook and Instagram. Starting with Instagram, she clicked on his profile. There were over 480 posts. Although he'd only been on the site for about three years, he seemed to be the kind of person who liked to post photos of everything from his dinner to his nights out, and there looked to be plenty of those.

There were photos of him and his mates on wild nights out, and some work related. In some he was pictured alongside various young women, some of whom had their arms draped round him, or he around them. But judging by the expressions on their faces, most seemed to be either friends or girlfriends. There was no one who looked like they might be family. Molly glanced at the clock on the screen. She wasn't sure how much time she could justify on this, especially if it failed to yield any kind of productive response. However, until she heard back from Josh Grieve, or received confirmation that he was back in the flat, there wasn't much else she could do.

She kept going until she found a photo of the woman she recognised from the *Echo*'s article as being Laura Grieve. Josh was pictured alongside her and a younger woman. The photo was dated from three years ago, just before the accident that would change their lives for ever. Laura Grieve, already divorced, is trying to smile and pretend her life hasn't just fallen apart at the seams. Josh is pulling a silly face. The girl next to him is smiling but still managing to look serious. The caption under the photo says:

Mum, me and Dais in Regent's Park.

It had over a hundred likes, and about a dozen comments.

Molly tried to enlarge the pic. There was something familiar about the photo of his sister, but she couldn't quite say what it was. Nothing about the hair, or the face too much, but the eyes...

She copied and saved the photo, then emailed it to the technical support team asking them to enlarge and clarify it. Not that she expected that to do much good if she couldn't place the sister. As soon as the email was sent, she felt she'd made a mistake. Why would she recognise Daisy Grieve? And until they had a name, they hadn't a hope in hell of finding her. She could reverse image it and do a Google search. That would take time, admittedly, but they were running out of options here.

She checked an incoming message on her phone: it was Neeraj, confirming that Josh Grieve's work said he hadn't turned up and no one could get hold of him. She realised they really needed to speak to him.

Then she remembered where she knew Josh's sister from. She clicked on the image again and stared at it for a few seconds. Yes, the hair was a different style and different colour and if you added a pair of glasses, then that was definitely her...

She picked up her phone and searched for Denning's number.

Chapter Fifty-Four

Denning arrived at Thomas Blake Primary School shortly after the school day had just started. He pressed the intercom by the main door, announced who he was and waited to be buzzed in. It was difficult to figure out what was happening as the school office seemed to be awash with chaos when he arrived. The acting deputy head, Caroline Vaughan, was occupying the desk where Alice usually greeted them. She was on the phone and signalled for Denning to take a seat.

From the gist of what Denning could gather from the phone conversation, he'd pitched up in the middle of a staffing crisis.

'Both Mrs Atherton and Alice have failed to turn up for work,' Caroline Vaughn said as she came off the phone. Her face was reddened; panicked. 'It's not like either of them.'

'Both of them?' It seemed strange, but possibly just a coincidence. Rachel Atherton might have heard about what had happened at Penny Garnett's restaurant last night and decided it was safer at home. But why hadn't she phoned in to let them know? And why would the school secretary take the day off too? There was nothing to suggest her life was in any danger; she hadn't even been working in the school at the time. Bad luck, he wondered? Or was this something he should be worried about?

'You've tried phoning them?' he asked. From some-where outside the office a bell rang, signalling either the start of a lesson, or the end of something.

'Both of them. Rachel's husband says she left for work as usual this morning and everything seemed to be normal. There was no answer from Alice's phone. We rang the agency. They've said it's not like Alice and they'll try to arrange for someone else to cover until she gets back.' They were hurrying towards the head teacher's office now, passing a crocodile line of children in red pullovers, some of whom shot curious glances in their direction.

'The agency?' Denning asked, confused. 'What agency?'

'She's here through a temp agency until we can find someone to take on the job permanently. She came highly recommended. In fact, until today, she's been an excellent employee.'

'She's a temp?'

'Yes. Apparently, she specifically asked to work here. Like I say, she's usually very good. Very reliable. This is the first time she's not turned up for work. It's unfortunate she chose the same day as Rachel to not come in.' She was unlocking the head teacher's office door now, flicking on the lights although sunlight streamed through the wide window.

'Did Mrs Atherton say anything about not coming in to work today? Is there, perhaps, an appointment she could have forgotten to mention? A meeting outside of the school?' His brain was whirling. If Rachel Atherton was sitting in a school governors' meeting, or speaking to the school authorities, then all their problems would be over. But if she wasn't...

The deputy head was sitting at Rachel Atherton's desk now, accessing her computer. She scrolled through a list of diary entries. 'No. There's nothing down for today. I don't know what could have happened to her.' She glanced at the clock on the screen. 'Of course, she might just be running late and hasn't been able to contact us.'

Denning tried calling her. There was no answer. 'When did her husband say she left home?'

'I don't know...' She was stammering now, realising something was very wrong. 'She's usually here from about half seven, so she must leave the house around seven, or thereabouts.'

'So it only takes her half an hour to get here?'

'If the traffic's not too bad then yes.'

Denning wasn't aware of any major problem with the traffic around Chiswick that morning, so that probably wasn't a reason she should be late. Certainly not this late. 'Keep trying her mobile. If it's switched off, leave a message to contact us immediately. Also, phone round anywhere you think she might be. Let me know the moment you hear of her whereabouts. You should already have my contact details, but, just in case you don't...' He took his card from his pocket and handed it to her. 'Phone me straight away, and on the mobile number.'

'Has something happened?' she asked. 'If there's a problem, I need to know...'

But Denning had already left the room.

Chapter Fifty-Five

Molly was still at her desk when Denning returned her call.

'Alice Hennicke,' she said before he had a chance to speak. 'I've checked online. She's Daisy Grieve. Alice is her middle name and Hennicke was Laura's maiden name. She's Josh's sister.'

'Neither of them has turned up for work this morning.' Denning's voice sounded strangely calm, as though he was trying too hard to keep a lid on the situation. He sounded like he was on hands-free, so probably driving.

'Coincidence…?' Molly knew that was ridiculous, but said it out of hope rather than expectation.

'I've notified Uniform to keep an eye out for either or both of them. We need to put in a request for any CCTV from Rachel Atherton's home address. I'm heading there now to speak to her husband. It's just possible Rachel might have said something to him. If we are assuming they're together, then where would they go? Any ideas?'

Molly tried to force her brain to work. 'I don't know. I presume the school has an address for Daisy Grieve?'

'Neeraj is already heading there now. But assuming she's given them the right address, it's unlikely they'll be there. Have you heard from Josh Grieve yet?'

She explained that she'd left messages, but he hadn't got back to her.

'Keep trying to get hold of him, Molly. He's our best bet for finding these two.' He ended the call.

Molly sighed. It was almost impossible: assuming Daisy Grieve and Rachel Atherton were together, they could be anywhere. But if Daisy really was their killer, why would she change her MO? The other victims had been stabbed in their own homes, so why was Rachel different? Unless she was already dead and they were about to find another body… That was something she didn't want to consider until they had to. She had to assume Rachel Atherton was still alive.

She was on the point of leaving another message for Josh Grieve when she didn't have to: her phone pinged with a text. He wanted to meet.

—

Molly suggested they met in a nearby police station. This had to be done officially, she'd argued; worried about her own safety if nothing else, but he'd suggested meeting at an outdoor cafe in a park not far from where he lived. If they were going to meet, he'd insisted, then it had to be on his terms or not at all. She texted Denning to let him know what she was doing, but insisted she didn't want this made official. Josh Grieve was their best chance of finding Daisy, and therefore their best chance of finding out what had happened to Rachel Atherton.

With time against them, she knew there was no point in arguing with him.

She reached the cafe twenty minutes later. He was already there, sitting in a corner, looking out on a boating lake. He gave a half-smile when he saw her approach, but the furrow in his brow and the lines around his lips told her he was worried. Molly looked around, sensing this might be a trap. There were dense shrubs and bushes beside the cafe, from which Daisy Grieve could easily leap, knife in hand, nothing left to lose. But there was a couple and their young children here; a man and a woman who looked like they were on a date. An older man reading a copy of the *Echo*. Nothing sinister.

'Thanks for coming,' he said. 'Do you want something to drink?' The remains of a latte sat at his elbow.

She sat opposite and shook her head. 'What's going on, Josh? Why did you want to meet here?'

'It's Daisy,' he said, like he was reading her thoughts. 'My sister, Daisy. I expect by now you've probably sussed that she's been working at the school.' He said *the* school as though it explained everything, which Molly supposed in many ways it did.

'The school secretary?'

'Yes.' He gazed at his coffee. 'I suppose I should explain. Though I expect you've guessed most of it already.'

'Wait, you knew about this plan?'

He picked at his fingernails. 'She told me she wanted to get back at the staff responsible for what happened to Mum. I didn't realise she planned to go this far. I didn't think she was serious when she said she wanted to kill them.'

'Why didn't you come forward when Kieran Judd was stabbed? You must have heard about it on the news?'

'The news said the police believed he'd been targeted in a case of mistaken identity. It was only after the others that I sussed what was going on. I didn't want to believe it really was Daisy at first. When I finally managed to get hold of her, she confessed; about getting the job at the school and about going after everyone she felt had made Mum suffer. I tried to stop her. I tried to persuade her to stop.'

'And you still didn't think at this stage to go to the police? To let us know what she was doing?'

'I panicked. She promised she would stop. Daisy's always been a bit unpredictable. If I told her I was going to go to the police then there was no saying what she might do. She's not thinking straight. The combination of grief and anger... She's not herself. It was only when I heard about the two women in that restaurant that I knew this wouldn't end. When they came knocking on my door that night my first thought was that you'd caught her and she'd told you it was me.'

'Is that why you've been keeping a low profile?'

'I needed time to think. I couldn't sleep last night. I tried contacting Daisy but without any luck. I went for a walk first thing, then my flatmate said the police had been round asking where I was and then you kept phoning. I didn't know what to do.'

She could see he was genuinely scared. He'd contacted her more out of desperation than any sense of doing the right thing, but that had to count for something.

'When our mum died, it hit Daisy hard. It hit both of us hard, but it was worse for Daisy. She and Mum had always been close. More like sisters than mother and daughter. When Daisy was young, she was ill. She had peritonitis after suffering a burst appendix and she nearly died. Mum stayed with her in hospital until she recovered. Even then, it took months for her to fully recover. The experience stayed with Daisy. She trained as a nurse when she left school, and everything was great. Until it stopped being great.'

A nurse, Molly thought... That would explain how she knew exactly where to aim a knife to ensure the killings were quick and fatal.

'Daisy's marriage ended about a year after our parents divorced,' Josh continued. 'Their split exacerbated Daisy's downward spiral. Her mental health had never been great. She struggled with her job and her marriage. Looking back, I think she had a breakdown.' He looked at Molly. 'Mental health issues seem to run through the female side in our family.' She wasn't sure if he said this as a means of trying to diffuse a tense situation, or if he was trying to bring uncomfortable home truths out into the open. 'The men are boozers and the women are depressives. But, either way, Daisy was in a bad place. She gave up her job and her marriage ended, within six months of each other. Mum did everything she could for Daisy, even though her own life was shit at the time. Eventually, she pulled Daisy through it. She got her life back together, left nursing altogether and retrained as an administrator. She seemed settled. Even tried her hand at a new relationship, though that didn't work out. When our mum killed herself last month, it set Daisy back. She blamed herself for Mum's death, insisting she could have done more to support her as Mum had supported *her*. Actually, she said we both should have done more for Mum, and maybe she had a point. Anyway, she completely dropped off the radar. I didn't hear from her: she never answered her phone. She told me she got rid of it. She stayed with a friend. To be honest with you, I hardly knew her friends. I had no idea where she was.'

He drew a finger round the rim of the coffee cup. Molly didn't want to hurry him, but they needed to find Daisy Grieve as a matter of urgency. 'Go on,' she prompted.

'Mum always blamed herself for what happened to that little boy, even though it wasn't entirely her fault. But the school made things worse by making her leave the job and admit full responsibility. They had to take their share of responsibility too. But it was easier to blame Mum.' His eyes met Molly's. 'As you can probably understand, she took it badly. She was never given the support she needed or deserved. They just threw her under a bus so they could get off the hook themselves.'

'I understand all this, and I do understand that your mum was treated unfairly at the time. What I don't get is why someone now feels they have to murder the people involved.'

'Our mum's death set Daisy back. Her new relationship had come to an end and she began to think she'd made a mistake giving up nursing. At the time Mum took her life, Daisy was struggling to cope anyway. Suddenly she didn't have our mum to rely on any more. She and Dad were never close, and he has little or nothing to do with either of us now: he's got a new wife and a new kid. It's easier for him to pretend that part of his life is over. He didn't even come to Mum's funeral.' He shrugged. 'But then again, why would he?'

'Daisy?' Molly prompted, aware that the clock was ticking and every second that passed was placing Rachel Atherton's life in greater danger.

'She blamed everything on what happened to Mum. Mum's death was the final straw for her. She snapped. She blamed the school for Mum's death, said they were responsible. So she must have planned to get her revenge. She got the temp job at the school… it wouldn't have been too difficult. The turnover of staff was always high she said when I eventually found her. Apparently the head teacher is a nightmare to work for. That was how she'd got the addresses of the staff involved.'

'We need to find Daisy,' she said. She told him about Rachel Atherton going missing, emphasising the urgency of the situation.

'Rachel Atherton? The head teacher. She was deputy head when Mum worked there.'

'Do you have any idea why Daisy would kidnap Rachel rather than kill her at home like the others?'

A look of panic spread over his face. 'She's the one person Daisy blamed most for our mum's death.' He looked at Molly. 'It was her idea. Mum said it was Rachel Atherton who persuaded the other members of staff to make Mum wholly responsible for what happened. Daisy hates her more than anyone. If Daisy's got her...'

He didn't need to say anything else. Molly already knew how much trouble Rachel Atherton was in. It made it even more important that they found her before it was too late. But she did have one very good hunch as to where to look first.

Chapter Fifty-Six

Denning reached Rachel Atherton's house fewer than twenty minutes after they'd left the school. Her husband, David, was an architect and was working from home. He opened the door and checked the ID of the two detectives standing on his doorstep. The moment he'd come off the phone from Molly, Denning had phoned to explain the situation. If there was a note of panic in David Atherton's voice at the possibility his wife had been abducted by a dangerous killer, he didn't let it show.

'I've tried phoning Rachel, but there's no answer,' he said, ushering Denning into his house. 'Obviously I've left messages asking her to get in touch. But I don't understand this. Rachel mentioned something about those people who were stabbed in their homes having worked at the school, but she didn't go into detail.' David Atherton was a broad-shouldered man in his late forties, slightly greying at the temples. He looked like he was a sporty type, despite the sedentary nature of his job.

'Can we just go over everything that happened this morning,' Denning said calmly. 'How did she seem?'

'There was nothing unusual,' he said. 'She left for work at her normal time. She seemed OK, didn't mention anything strange. I mean, I'm sure this stuff about these people being killed must have played on her mind, but she told me it was all to do with something that happened at the school years ago and she wasn't involved.'

'But she told you about the death threats against her?' Denning asked.

He looked shocked. 'What death threats? What are you talking about? What death threats?'

'She didn't tell you?' Denning told him how in light of the recent murders they'd advised Rachel to take some precautions, especially after she refused police protection.

'This is absurd,' he said. 'Are you really telling me that Rachel's life was in danger and you did nothing?'

'No, Mr Atherton, we did everything we could. Your wife refused to take the matter seriously, despite our insistence that she did.'

'But what happened that day had nothing to do with Rachel. If it had been down to her then those children would never have been anywhere near that bloody park in the first place. If you want to blame anyone, blame Euan Livingstone. Rachel had to do his job for him half the time because he was so bloody useless.'

'If he hadn't been murdered, then perhaps we could,' Denning said.

'I'm sorry. I didn't mean to sound insensitive. I just don't see how any of this is Rachel's fault. She's damned good at her job. That school was a joke before she took over.'

Denning sat him down on a padded armchair. 'Mr Atherton, it's not so much that these murders are about what happened in the park that day but everything to do with what happened afterwards.'

'I don't understand... Somebody resigned over the incident. They took full responsibility.'

'That's the problem. They were made to, and I'm afraid your wife was part of that decision-making process. Now, I understand your anger and frustration, but none of this is going to help us find Rachel. Can you think of anything that has happened recently, anything unusual or out of the ordinary?'

'No. Except…' He thought about it. 'She received a phone call last night that seemed to disturb her. Well not exactly upset her, just annoyed her slightly. I wasn't listening in so I only overheard bits of it, but she said something like she wasn't sure if she had time, but would try and fit it in if she could. Something like that.'

'And you've got no idea what she was referring to?'

'Like I said, I wasn't really listening.'

'OK, I understand that. It's just from what we know so far, we believe Rachel knows the person who we suspect might have taken her. And, initially at least, she wouldn't have suspected she was in any danger.'

'Taken? Someone has… what… kidnapped my wife? Why?'

'We don't know why, Mr Atherton, and that's the worrying thing.' All the others had been stabbed. So why would Rachel Atherton have been kidnapped? It didn't make sense.

'If she's been kidnapped then you need to get out there and look for her.'

Chapter Fifty-Seven

A small crowd had already gathered on the pavement outside the multi-story car park by the time Molly arrived at the scene. A uniformed police officer was ushering people back from the hastily erected perimeter cordon. He raised his arm when he saw her approach.

'Sorry, madam, the car park's off limits for the time being, due to an ongoing situation.'

Molly looked up. The building was at least eight storeys high and surrounded by concrete. Anyone falling from that height didn't stand a chance.

She'd already fished her warrant card out of her bag and was showing it to the officer. 'Where are they?' she asked, trying to keep any hint of panic out of her voice.

The young officer looked at her ID, his face wrinkling in puzzlement. 'They're on the top level. There's an officer with them now. A middle-aged woman and a younger woman. I've called for back-up and a trained negotiator. Best wait until they get here.'

Molly ducked under the barrier. 'We haven't got time,' she said. 'I can talk to them. I know what all this is about.'

'Just a minute,' she heard the officer say, 'you can't just...'

But the remainder of the sentence went unheard as she headed in the side entrance to the car park. There was a lift next to a kiosk, but Molly decided to take the stairs;

she wanted the adrenaline rush to give her some focus. Plus the extra time would give her the chance to work out how she was going to play this. Of course she really *should* have waited for Denning to get there, but if Daisy Grieve was planning what Molly thought she was planning, time really was of the essence.

It had been an educated guess on Molly's part: this was where Laura Grieve had died, and that was what had started this whole thing. It seemed like the most obvious place to finish it. And by now, Daisy Grieve had nothing left to lose.

By the time she reached the eighth level, she was slightly out of breath and shaking just a little bit more than she'd have liked.

She pushed open the heavy door to the car park. The area immediately in front of her was deserted and there was a strange echoing silence. She walked towards the far end, legs still slightly wobbly from both the climb and the apprehension of what she might discover; her brain powered by the sheer adrenaline of the situation.

She turned a corner and was immediately aware of a commotion coming from the far end of the car park. A uniformed police officer was talking to two women who were standing against the barrier. She recognised them as Rachel Atherton and Daisy Grieve. Grieve had a knife against Rachel's throat and had her pressed against the low wall. The uniformed officer was talking to them, his arms outstretched, he was standing about six feet away. They all turned to face Molly when she approached.

'Help me!' Rachel Atherton shouted as soon as DS Fisher was in earshot. 'She's gone mad. She keeps saying I killed her mother.'

The officer turned to face Molly, who already had her ID in her hand. 'We already have this under control,' he said, though his face suggested otherwise.

'Daisy,' Molly said, ignoring the officer. 'You need to stay calm.'

Molly turned to the uniformed officer who was still talking at her. 'Leave this to me. I know both parties. I know what this is about.'

There was a crackle of static from his radio and a voice telling him something Molly couldn't quite hear. 'I don't know,' he said. 'We should really wait for a trained negotiator.'

'I've been trained in hostage negotiation,' Molly said. It was yet another lie. She'd watched a documentary about hostage negotiation on Channel 5 a couple of years ago, and had always intended to apply for one of the Met's official courses, but had never got round to it. Now could be the chance to prove she had what it took, assuming she didn't mess up and the situation culminated in two further deaths...

She could see the look of blind fear in Rachel's face; Daisy was eerily calm. She remembered the organised, together secretary she'd met at the school just a couple of days earlier. Perhaps that demeanour wasn't down to efficiency but the fact she was now so cut off from her emotions that there was only a chilling and efficient clarity of thought – a task to complete. The knife was pressed against Rachel's throat, a red line where it had bit into her flesh. Molly edged closer, ignoring the mutterings of protestation from the uniformed officer. 'We should do nothing until the official hostage negotiator gets here,' he muttered.

She ignored him again and approached the two women, not so close that she was in danger of panicking Grieve – not that she looked like she was going to be easily panicked – but close enough to speak to them both without having to shout. Molly glanced over the edge of the wall. Far below she saw the pavement teeming with people. She wasn't particularly frightened of heights, but looking down at the drop made her feel unsteady. She was taking a massive risk. Technically she shouldn't be there. There were rules for these kinds of situations and they were there for good reasons.

She could hear Denning's voice in her head, warning her about overstepping the mark, again. She could hear Betty Taggart's voice too; berating her and threatening her with demotion and god knows what else.

She tried to hide her nerves, all too aware that if anything were to go wrong, it would be her head being squeezed through the mangle.

'What's your plan, Daisy?' Molly asked, as much to keep her talking if nothing else.

But it was Rachel who answered. 'She phoned me last night. Said she'd forgotten to tell me about a meeting this morning with the educational support team. She said she'd pick me up and drive me there. My car had been playing up over the past couple of days, so I was glad of the lift. Instead, she brought me here, bundled me out of the car at knifepoint and threatened to push me off. She's mad.'

Molly ignored her. She was focusing on Daisy, trying to get inside her head. 'This is about your mum,' she said. 'And I understand that. You blame everyone for what happened to her and you're trying to make amends. But you've made your point and you need to let Rachel go.'

'I want her to admit what she did. I want her to tell the truth about how she was responsible for my mum killing herself.'

'I don't understand any of this,' Rachel said. 'She told me her mum committed suicide, but that wasn't to do with me. I'm very sorry about what happened to her, but I don't see how I can be to blame. The others, yes – they were all directly involved, but I was only deputy head of the school at the time. This has nothing to do with me.'

'It was your decision,' Daisy said. 'You forced my mum into resigning. You told her there was a chance she would be charged with manslaughter if it got out about her state at the time. You then persuaded everyone else involved to make my mum the scapegoat, because you were ambitious; you wanted the top job. You saw this as a way of getting it! It wasn't difficult to persuade the others to blame my mum, was it? It suited them, but nobody thought about the effect it would have on her. It destroyed her. She already blamed herself, the added guilt just made things worse.'

'Your mother *was* to blame! We'd all turned a blind eye to her turning up for work hungover or still smelling of drink. We'd run round after her and covered for her. I told Euan we should have asked her to leave long before the day trip to the park. If he'd had the guts to do what I suggested, this whole shitstorm would never have happened. But he was weak… weak and indecisive!'

'But it wasn't difficult to persuade him to resign either, was it? Whispering in his ear, dropping your poison, saying he was as much to blame as my mum.' She was looking at Rachel, but still glancing back at Molly who was working out if she could be quick enough to grab the knife. She didn't want to risk it. 'Working at that school gave me an insight into what really went on. The staff all like to gossip, especially when you're not around. None of them like you: "pushy, arrogant, rude". And those are just the nice comments. In fact, I'd probably be doing everyone a favour if I pushed you off.'

'I told you: she's mad!' Rachel struggled to try and free herself of Daisy's grip, but Daisy just pulled her closer to her and pushed the knife against her throat. Blood began to drip onto the floor of the car park.

'Daisy, this isn't going to help anyone,' Molly said calmly. 'You've made your point.' She tried not to grimace at the unfortunate pun. 'But you have to let her go. It's the only way this will end well.'

'She's not going anywhere until she admits it was all her fault. I want to hear her say it. I want to hear her admit this was all down to her.'

Rachel Atherton struggled again. Molly wanted to tell her to stop it as she was clearly antagonising Daisy, whose calm demeanour was either fake or in danger of breaking down completely. Either way, Molly knew it wouldn't take much to crack.

'Daisy, we know what happened. We know Rachel persuaded the rest of the staff to go along with her plan. We know it was all her idea. But killing her isn't going to change anything. It won't bring your mother back.'

Molly wondered how long it would be before Grieve either plucked up the confidence to kill Rachel, or Thomas Blake Primary School's rather undiplomatic head teacher said something clumsy and her assailant snapped. She suspected the latter was most likely. Time was already starting to run out.

'What difference does it make?' Grieve said. 'What difference will any of it make? I'm already going down for the other murders. One more isn't going to change anything, is it? I just want to hear her say the words before I either rip her throat out or chuck her over the edge. Or maybe I'll do both. Either way, she's fucked. And so am I. So what have I got to lose by taking her with me?'

Chapter Fifty-Eight

'Daisy, if you drop the knife and let Rachel go, you'll be treated favourably by the courts. There are clearly mitigating circumstances here. People would be sympathetic. A jury would be sympathetic. But if you kill Rachel in cold blood, in front of me and all those people down there, then it's a very different story.'

Molly hoped she sounded more confident than she felt. In truth, she had a very different idea about how the courts would treat a woman who had already murdered three people and attempted to murder another. Daisy Grieve would be going to prison for a very long time. Even if they could make a case for saying her mind was unbalanced, the absolute least she'd be looking at would be a lengthy stay at Broadmoor.

'Let's hear her admit it! Then I'll think about letting her go.'

Molly down at the street eight storeys below. She saw what looked like Denning, Neeraj and several uniformed officers. As well as the trained negotiator, there was a good chance an armed response team would be on its way, which, if the situation got out of control, would only end in disaster for all involved. Molly had to think fast – there was one grenade left in her armoury that might work, but if it didn't then she was in danger of making the situation worse.

'Daisy, do you really think your mum would have wanted this? When she came here, she was desperate. She probably felt she had no other choice. If she'd thought her actions would have led to you doing what you did, it would have destroyed her.'

'She still did it though,' Daisy said. 'She still jumped. She didn't think what effect it would have on us.' It was the only time so far Molly had detected any vulnerability from their killer. It meant she was getting through to her, but was that a good thing…?

'She wasn't thinking straight, Daisy. When people have depression, it clouds their thinking. They're driven by desperation and despair rather than logic.' She was thinking about Jon, trying to remember what she'd learned when she'd lived through his dark clouds and been through the joint therapy sessions they'd taken together after the last serious bout a couple of years ago. 'Your mum was ill. Her decision to kill herself wasn't anything to do with you, or with Josh. I suspect it wasn't anything to do with what happened at the school, not really. In her head it had all got jumbled up together. What happened was terrible, but killing Rachel isn't going to redress any of that.'

There was the briefest glimmer of something in Daisy's eyes, as though at some level Molly was making contact.

'She wouldn't have felt like that if it hadn't been for what *they* did to her.'

'I know. And now everyone knows the role Rachel Atherton played in what happened to your mum. Everyone will see that your mum wasn't to blame for Noah Daniel's death.'

She could see that Rachel Atherton wasn't happy about the direction the conversation was taking, but was also savvy enough to know that her only chance of getting out of this situation alive was to keep her mouth shut. 'If you kill Rachel now, all you get is a brief moment of satisfaction. Then what? The remainder of your life in prison? Is she really worth it?'

Molly looked down to see another couple of squad cars had pulled up at the entrance to the car park. It was only a matter of time before an armed response team would pitch up. If Daisy didn't let Rachel go, it wasn't going to end well for her.

Rachel Atherton struggled, but Daisy had her in a tight hold. She looked down to the street below. A news crew had arrived now, a camera aimed in their direction. Soon Daisy would panic and do something stupid… or the armed response team would aim a rifle at her…

Molly edged closer. She was now close enough to reach out and grab the knife, but she would have to be quick. She could probably manage to grab Rachel if Daisy were to push her, but it would take split-second timing to stop her from stabbing her or cutting her throat. But she could sense that she was getting through. She was nearly there; just another little push…

'Give me the knife, Daisy.' She held her hand out and then stood there, waiting for a reaction. She could see Daisy's hand shaking, the look of terror in Rachel Atherton's eyes. She edged slightly closer. Her hand was underneath the knife now. She could just reach up and grab it, pull it away from Rachel Atherton's throat. She reckoned she was stronger than Daisy, strong enough to wrestle the knife out of her hand.

Then Daisy pulled Rachel closer to her, gripped the knife so tightly Molly could see her knuckles turning white. The look of terror in the head teacher's eyes had been amplified now. Molly thought she was too late. She thought this was it: Daisy was going to stab her boss and then jump, just like her mother had. There was a pause that seemed to last an eternity.

'Daisy. Give me the knife.'

She looked at Molly, then looked at Rachel, the woman she hated; the one person she blamed more than all the others for her mother's death. In a split second, Daisy threw the knife on the ground, shoved the terrified Rachel at Molly and climbed on to the parapet. She stood there for a second and closed her eyes, not wanting to look at the ground so far below.

Rachel Atherton was screaming, clinging on to Molly for all she was worth. The DS pushed her aside towards the uniformed officer and leaped towards Daisy just as she leaned forward to jump. Molly ran, arms outstretched, and grabbed her just as she fell forward. The two of them landed in a tangled mess of arms and legs on the cold, hard floor of the car park. Daisy was crying. Molly, who was certain she'd broken her arm, was trying to calm her; telling her over and over that she was going to be OK, though she knew that was very unlikely.

She looked up to see Denning running towards them, the armed response team behind him.

Daisy was sobbing uncontrollably now, asking for her mum – saying she was sorry. Molly didn't know who she was sorry for: her mum or the people she'd killed. In the end she settled for both. But, mainly, she was just glad it was finally at an end.

Chapter Fifty-Nine

Molly Fisher was trying hard not to wallow too much in the adoration that was coming her way. She was enjoying a coffee at her desk, typing up her report on the events on the car park rooftop, and, so far, both Denning and Kinsella had told her what a brilliant job she'd done.

Denning had naturally offered up the usual lecture on personal safety and the importance of waiting for back-up in such situations. But he'd acknowledged her bravery and quick-thinking had almost certainly saved Rachel Atherton's life, and probably that of Daisy Grieve too, which would now mainly be spent facing justice.

Not that Molly felt particularly heroic. By the time Daisy Grieve had been formally arrested and subsequently charged with murder, and Rachel Atherton had been put into an ambulance and taken to A&E to be checked over, all the time insisting she hadn't done anything wrong, Molly was aware that she couldn't stop shaking. Denning had called her reckless – and not for the first time in their working career – and asked if she wanted to go to hospital as a precaution. She'd said she was fine. He'd placed an awkward hand on her shoulder as a clumsy gesture of reassurance, thrown her a faint smile and then he and Neeraj had spoken to Daisy Grieve to reassure themselves that she had been working alone. It appeared that Josh Grieve was in the clear.

She'd watched Daisy being led away in a police car and felt a strange mix of emotions: pity at the poor girl who was obviously not in the right frame of mind, but also anger at the damage her actions had caused. Three people dead and two attacked. A child left without a father... a sorry mess.

There was no victory here. Everybody came out of this worse off than when they went in. Her mind kept turning over all the possibilities of how things could have been avoided: if Rachel Atherton hadn't insisted on a cover-up. If Marion Haynes had chosen a different route home from the supermarket. If Laura Grieve hadn't been near catatonic with depression and booze. If someone hadn't decided to take the kids to the park that day...

But these permutations were all irrelevant now. It *had* happened. As a consequence, so many people had either died or were living with the pain of knowing what had happened that day.

Denning left McKenna's office and headed towards Molly at her desk.

'Daisy Grieve has admitted everything,' he said when he got there. 'She's confirmed that she worked alone and Josh had nothing to do with it.'

He still knew she was planning it, Molly thought. But his mother was dead and his sister was about to go to prison for a very long time. What was the point in making him suffer even more? It was very likely he thought his own life might have been in danger if he did, and panicked? Molly was willing to give him the benefit of the doubt.

'What will happen to Daisy?' Molly asked.

Denning didn't answer straight away. Eventually he said: 'This was planned, Molly.' She thought about it and then went to extraordinary lengths to kill those people.

It would take a lot to persuade a jury that she wasn't of sound mind at the time.'

Molly nodded. These hadn't been random spur-of-the-moment type killings. 'But still... The grief of her mother's death would have counted towards something. There is a case for arguing that her mind wasn't sound?'

'That isn't really up to us. We'll pass what we have over to the CPS and let them argue over the finer points. But, to be honest, Molly, I wouldn't feel *too* sorry for Daisy. Her brother had to live with what happened with their mother... he managed to avoid becoming a cold-blooded killer.'

She didn't know why she felt sorry for Daisy Grieve. She was a killer and her actions had destroyed so many other lives. Yet she *did* feel a pang of sympathy for what had happened.

'All true, but...' She let the rest of the sentence hang in the air. She wasn't sure how to finish it without backing herself into a corner.

'And before I forget,' Denning added. 'DCI McKenna wants a word. I imagine she'll want to offer up some official reprimand for going into a dangerous situation and not waiting for armed back-up, but off the record I think she believes you did the right thing.'

Molly threw a glance in the direction of McKenna's office. The thought of having to sit through one of Betty Taggart's patronising lectures on responsible policing was something she could do without right now. Especially as the whole thing would be laced with hypocrisy; she knew for a fact that back in the day McKenna wasn't averse to taking risks if it meant getting the job done.

'Actually, I've arranged to meet someone.' She smiled at Denning. 'It's nothing urgent, just a loose end that needs to be tidied up.'

'Can't it wait?'

'Not really.' She made a show of looking at her watch. 'In fact, I'm already running late.' She grabbed her jacket from the back of her chair and stood to leave. 'I'll speak to McKenna the moment I get back, I promise.'

He looked like he was about to say something, but changed his mind. 'OK,' he said. 'I'm sure DCI McKenna can wait.'

Chapter Sixty

Denning watched as Molly Fisher headed out the MIT suite. He should have asked her where she was going; they still had a final briefing to formally conclude the investigation, though he reluctantly supposed that could wait until tomorrow. A glance in the direction of McKenna's office told him she was on the phone, probably to the DCS reassuring her that the case had now reached a comfortable conclusion.

He could never understand Molly and her impetuous attitude. She put herself at risk more often than was good for her and he was certain one day she'd push her luck too far…

Right now, he should have been focusing on taking the team and the support staff out for a drink. They needed to unwind and this was his job as team leader to ensure it happened. As he headed over to his desk, he was suddenly aware of McKenna standing by her office door, the phone call to the DCS clearly having been concluded.

'DS Fisher not around…?' she asked, making a point of looking round the office but clearly aware that who she wanted wasn't there.

'Tying up a few lose ends,' he replied. He could tell from the sardonic look on her face that she didn't buy it, but there wasn't much she could do, even if she wanted to. Molly had got them a good result. If things had turned out differently it could have been very messy for everyone involved.

'OK. You'll do.'

'Sorry?'

'A word, Matt. It won't take five minutes.'

She turned on her heels and went back into her office. He followed her in and sat in front of her desk.

'We're still waiting for a psychiatrist to assess Daisy Grieve,' she said. 'I doubt it'll make much difference. She's looking at a life stretch irrespective.' She paused. 'Rachel Atherton may have some questions to answer about her handling of the Noah Daniel situation. Yes, I know she wasn't head teacher at the time, but it's clear from what we've discovered she was the one driving the decision to dump the whole sorry shitshow on to Laura Grieve. A matter for the local authority, however, and not us.'

'I expect she'll find some way of wriggling out of it,' Denning said. 'Her sort always do.'

Denning smiled despite himself. If Rachel Atherton hadn't put her personal ambition ahead of her protecting the staff at her school, none of this would have happened. But ultimately, he supposed, she'd paid a massive price for her decision, almost losing her life in a very public way.

'Is there anything else?'

McKenna sat back on her chair, a sure sign that she was about to say something uncomfortable. 'Declan Meech has been arrested.'

'Right' he nodded. 'Well, that's good. What happened?'

'He was arrested inside a bookie, armed with an imitation gun. The finer details are sketchy and this is purely on a need-to-know basis. But he's going down for a long time based on this.'

'And Tony Hallam…?'

She looked at him for a moment. 'That's the tricky bit.' She paused. 'The intel came from Hallam.'

'Hallam grassed on Meech?' Denning was waiting for the punchline.

'It seems, from what I can gather from my contact, that this had been Hallam's plan all along. Don't ask me why, but my money would be on revenge. He's always blamed Meech for being sent down last time, maybe this is his way of getting his own back. I don't know. I don't care. This was never our bag, Matt. Meech is going down. Let's leave it at that.'

'That doesn't let Hallam off the hook. What about the threats he made against Maria?'

'We've only got her word for it that he made any threats. And what threats? From what I can gather, it was *you* he threatened: to keep away from his ex-wife? Well, to be honest here, Matt, I think that was sensible advice. It's a shame you chose not to take it.'

'I now know Maria was pressurised to drop the claim of domestic assault. She told me she was worried. She thought Hallam might harm the children, just to get at her.' He could tell by the stony expression on McKenna's face that she wasn't buying any of it. He was fighting a losing battle. 'I'm not happy about this situation, Liz. Not by a long way.' He wanted to say more. It was OK for McKenna to be objective about this: she hadn't met Maria. He'd made promises to Maria Hallam that it now looked like he was going to be unable to keep. Yes, McKenna was right this wasn't their call. At the end of the day, policing was all about priorities. They were SCD1, part of the Homicide and Serious Crime Command. Domestic violence wasn't part of their remit.

'You've done well, Matt. You got a good result here. If Tony Hallam steps out of line, he'll be back inside faster than he can belch. But until that time, we don't go looking for trouble. Not unless we have good reason to. And I'm afraid your concern for the wellbeing of Maria Hallam isn't good enough reason. Leave it, Matt. End of.'

Denning thanked her and left her office.

Back at his desk he thought over the significance of what she'd told him.

On his way home that evening, he found himself driving along the street where Maria Hallam lived. As though on autopilot he stopped outside their block of flats, parked the car and looked up at the flat. The lights were on, but that didn't necessarily mean they would be at home. He got out the car and climbed the stairs to the second floor. He knocked on the front door, still not sure why he was there. McKenna was right, *this was never our bag...* But he couldn't just let this lie.

He knocked on the door. Maria answered. If she was surprised to see him, she didn't let it show. 'What do you want?' She wasn't unfriendly, just matter of fact. He wasn't sure what to say.

'I wanted to make sure you're OK. I heard about Declan getting arrested. I just wanted to reassure you that had nothing to do with me.'

'I know.' She glanced over her shoulder. He could hear her children playing in the living room. 'It doesn't matter. About Declan, I mean. He was always going to get caught out eventually.'

'OK. I just wanted to reassure you that it had nothing to do with me.'

He was suddenly aware of a shadow in the hallway behind her. A figure, then a voice. 'It was down to me, Denning.'

Tony Hallam ambled into view. He was wearing a cardigan and a pair of jeans, and looked like he'd made himself at home.

'What are you doing here?' Denning tried to find a bravado he didn't feel.

'We're going to give things another go,' Maria said. Her face was impassive and her eyes refused to meet his. 'Tony and me,' she added. 'It's for the children's sake.'

Tony Hallam was standing behind her now, his hand on her shoulder – not threatening, but with a look that warned Denning to back off.

Denning nodded, taking in the sight and instantly getting the message.

'Go back, sweetie,' Tony Hallam said to his ex-wife, kissing her lightly on the top of the head. 'I think the kids want you.'

She gave Denning a final look, then her eyes dropped to the floor and she turned back into the flat, disappearing in the direction of the living room.

'It was me,' Hallam said. 'I grassed up Dec. I was never in this for the long haul. Prison... the last time, I vowed it would be my last time. I shared a cell with a young lad for six months. I came back from the showers one morning and he's cut his wrists. Some homemade shiv, basic but effective. He was twenty-three. On drugs and convinced life had nothing left to offer him.' He looked Denning in the eye. 'It makes you reassess life. I don't want my kids growing up without an absent father. Kids need their dads around. Maria understands that. Declan didn't. You don't need to come round here again, Mr Denning. We're going to be all right. I'll make sure we are.' He smiled, not a sinister smile but one that said he was serious about what he was saying. 'I wish you all the best, but I don't want to see you again. I hope you get the message.' He closed the door. Denning headed back downstairs and into his car. He wasn't sure he believed him. The look on Maria's face suggested she wasn't happy with the situation. Was she being threatened by Hallam? If she wasn't, why had she agreed to let him back in to her life?

People's lives were complicated, he had to admit that. His own personal life wasn't exactly like *Little House on the Prairie* but at least everyone knew where they stood. Maria and Tony Hallam, however; there was clearly something highly dysfunctional going on there.

He glanced back up at the flat for one last time, started the engine and headed for home.

Chapter Sixty-One

Molly waited by the bench that overlooked the lake. It had turned suddenly chilly; an autumnal breeze blowing in from the east.

She didn't have long to wait until she saw the figure approach, pushing a pram.

'Thanks for meeting,' Cassie said. 'I appreciate this. And I appreciate all you've done for me.' She lifted Arthur out of his pushchair and placed him on her knee. He smiled at Molly, though he could just have been happy to be out of his pushchair.

'I wanted to make sure you were OK. I know it's a lot to deal with.' It was Arthur she was thinking about the most. Growing up without a father. She'd seen first-hand what losing a mother had done to Daisy Grieve.

'What will happen to the woman who killed Kieran and the others?' she asked.

'In all honesty? I don't know. She's been charged with murder. It's possible she might be sent to a secure unit somewhere, but that depends on whether or not there's any evidence to suggest she was suffering mental health issues at the time.'

'I won't be expected to give evidence or anything, will I?'

Molly shook her head. 'I don't think so. I imagine this case is going to be fairly cut and dried. She as good as admitted she killed them.'

Cassie stares into space for a moment. 'I had no idea. About any of it. I knew Kieran had the odd nightmare and there were things he didn't like talking about, but I had no idea about the accident.' She pulled Arthur closer to her, kissing him on the head. 'Awful. To lose a child like that. I couldn't bear to imagine it.' She shuddered. 'And Kieran was part of that...'

Molly tried to console her. 'It's better not to think about it. It's in the past and we can't change it. The really sad thing is that no one person is really to blame. A young child wanted an ice cream. That's all it boils down to.'

Cassie attempted a smile. 'Once Kieran's funeral is over, I'll be able to think more clearly. Moving out the flat is the first step. I know I can't go on living there and I don't just mean because of the money. Not after what happened: spend all my days thinking about Kieran lying there, bleeding to death. And it's not fair on Arthur having to live in the place where his father was killed.' She looked at Molly. 'Why don't you move in? You said you were looking for somewhere to live, and it's a lovely little place.'

Molly didn't like to admit that she'd been thinking about that herself. The flat was far from perfect, but she imagined the rent would be within her price range and the location was convenient for work.

Cassie kissed Arthur again, hugging him, knowing that the journey ahead for both of them would be fraught with difficulties and challenges. A desire for ice cream would be the least of their worries.

Chapter Sixty-Two

As Denning headed into Shoreditch and towards the flat, he thought about how badly he had handled the investigation.

Molly Fisher had been more on the ball than he had been initially. He liked her; she took risks and, in his experience, that was always dangerous. One day she'd take one risk too far and her luck would run out.

But, for now, he had to acknowledge she'd done a good job.

A call came in just as he turned off Commercial Street. It was Anna Klein. He answered the call hands-free.

'Anna. How did it go?' Luckily he'd remembered to write her a reference. It hadn't been glowing, but he'd said she was a good officer who had made a silly mistake rather than a corrupt one. He'd kept it deliberately vague and light on detail.

'I've heard back from Professional Standards. I'm being knocked down from a DS to a DC. Could have been worse.' A demotion would have had a knock-on effect on her pension, naturally, as well the inevitable loss of face. However, it meant she could keep her job. 'It was decided, on balance, that my actions hadn't jeopardised the investigation into the burglary gang, though my lack of transparency had compromised me.'

'So that's an end to it?'

'Hopefully. And, Matt… thank you. I appreciate your reference. Let me buy you a drink sometime.'

Denning had reached the car park in the basement of the warehouse where he lived. He pulled into his parking space and turned off the engine. There was one further favour he needed to ask Klein, and now seemed like the best time to do it.

'Anna, there is just one thing. Can you have a word with your friend from the CSU, the one who deals with domestic abuse? Ask them to keep an eye on Maria Hallam. I know Tony Hallam is probably flavour of the month right now after offering up Declan Meech's head on a plate, but someone needs to keep an eye on him.'

There was a pause from the other end, then: 'OK. I'll put the word out.'

Denning ended the call. Tony Hallam thought he'd got away with it. But he wasn't Teflon. He had to trip himself up at some point. Perhaps if Denning could persuade Maria to make a formal complaint against him…

–

When he got home, Sarah was in the kitchen preparing something on the stove. He'd lost track of whose turn it was to cook that evening; after a big investigation, he had other things on his mind. He popped his head into the kitchen and gave her a kiss.

'Smells nice,' he said.

'Won't be long. And, by the way, I've decided I won't be taking the job in New York after all.'

'Really? Why the change of heart?'

She turned to face him, lowering the heat on the hob as she did so. 'I've thought about it, over and over. In fact, I've thought of little else over the past few weeks. It wouldn't be fair on you, and it wouldn't fair on Jake. And, what's more, I've just heard that one of the directors in the London office is leaving at the end of the year. There's a good chance I could get his job.' She shot him a winning smile. 'It would mean more money. We could move out of this place and find somewhere bigger.'

'But I thought you had your heart set on New York?'

Sarah gave an indifferent shrug and headed back to the dinner prep. 'I think I was more in love with the idea. You know, living somewhere exciting, fresh challenges… that kind of thing. You know what I mean?'

Matthew Denning wasn't sure he did know what she meant, but he couldn't deny her decision was going to make life a lot easier for him. He sat on the sofa and breathed a sigh of relief. A difficult decision had just been made for him.

A Letter from Graeme

Firstly, many thanks for reading *Shame the Devil*. I hope you enjoyed the book – the fourth outing for detectives DI Matt Denning and DS Molly Fisher, as well as the rest of the team.

If you did enjoy reading *Shame the Devil*, please let the world know! A review on Amazon, Kobo, Goodreads, etc can make all the difference. And please share your thoughts on social media. Spreading the word helps to get the book noticed, and that in turn helps bring new readers to the series.

I always believed writing would get easier with each book, however, that has never been the case. *Shame the Devil* was no exception – despite starting with a strong idea (and despite the fact I always plot my books in advance), the story seemed determined to head in its own direction, which wasn't necessarily the direction I'd initially intended it to go in. And this time the writing process wasn't helped by my moving house in the middle of it all!

But it was the subject matter that proved to be the most challenging. When writing the book, I found myself thinking about my primary school, and although my years there were mostly very happy, the school would later face its own tragedy. While there are no comparisons between what happened there and the events in this book, I was aware of how it must feel to send your child off to school in the morning and then having to deal with the aftermath of what happens if they don't come back. Something which I hope no parent ever has to experience.

Thank you again for reading the book. I love hearing from readers, so please do get in touch, either via social media or the contacts page on my website – details below.

Very best wishes,

Graeme

Website: www.graemehampton.com
Twitter: @Ghamo01
Instagram: graeme_hampton

Acknowledgments

A huge thank you to Keshini Naidoo and Dan O'Brien at Hera Books for their hard work, dedication and continued support, and to Andrew Brassleay and Nicky Lovick for their editorial and proofreading input. A hearty shout out to my fellow Hera/Canelo authors whose generosity and encouragement is always appreciated, especially my 'Twitter writer chums' Marion Todd and Jason (JA) Andrews, who always seem to know when to send the right tweet to spur me on or lift my spirits.

I'd also like to thank Graham Bartlett at www.policeadvisor.co.uk, who – as always – provided me with much-needed information regarding the workings of the Met Police and the technicalities involved in a major police investigation, as well as making some wise suggestions to make certain scenes more credible. Any errors are mine alone. Incidentally, Graham is himself an author, and well worth checking out.

A massive thank you goes to Christine Warrington for looking over the manuscript and spotting the (the occasional!) typo and missing word, and to Barry Kemp for offering valuable feedback on the book. Thanks too to James Bacon for providing information about how primary school trips are organised; luckily events such as those referred to in the book are mercifully rare.

And as always, thanks go to Gary Metalle, Jessica Dyson, Dave Longbottom, Jean Sinclair and Tracey Caswell for their constant encouragement and enthusiasm for my writing.